CONTENTS

THE IDOL

A Casey Elkins Investigation

Charles Cloninger
Candis Elkins

Kindle Direct Publishing

This work of art is dedicated to the friends, classmates, and family in my life that most of, if not all of, these characters are based on.

But most importantly, this book wouldn't even exist without Candis Elkins pressing for the character of Casey Elkins to lead her own book.

ISBN 9798331404772

Cover design by: Art Painter
Library of Congress Control Number: 2018675309
Printed in the United States of America

INTRODUCTION

This book series will take place in the some connected universe as Hometown Justice, my first book series. The character of Casey Elkins first appears in Hometown Justice: Aftermath.

Casey's side of the world will focus more on the supernatural. Things like Lycans, Elementals, The Undead, etc etc. The first outing into her side of the world, introduces you, the readers, to lycans. This outing also deals with Casey setting up her shop in Blacksburg, SC, a vastly different setting from Polkville, in the Hometown Justice series.

There will be returning characters from the HTJ series, I wont reveal those characters here, but Casey will also be joined by some original characters created just for this series. I hope you all enjoy this portion of the world.

PROLOGUE

The Blacksburg History Museum stood silent, its halls empty and echoing in the late-night hours. The grand building, once bustling with curious visitors and eager historians, now lay dormant, the secrets of the past hidden within its walls. Among the countless artifacts and exhibits, one, in particular, drew the attention of those in the know: the Idol of Lycoan.

Nestled in a carefully guarded room, the Idol rested on a pedestal, encased in a state-of-the-art protective display. The ancient relic, carved from an otherworldly stone, seemed to pulse omnisciently with an unseen energy. Its surface was adorned with intricate symbols and markings, hinting at its mysterious origins and the power it held over lycans and humans alike.

Unbeknownst to the museum's security, a shadowy figure moved through the corridors with the fluid grace of a predator. The Were-Panther, a creature of legend, had infiltrated the building with a singular purpose: to claim the Idol of Lycoan. With feline agility, they bypassed the sophisticated alarms and sensors, their keen senses guiding them towards their prize.

As the Were-Panther approached the exhibit, the air grew heavy with anticipation. The thief's eyes, a striking amalgamation of human and feline, glinted in the darkness, fixed upon the Idol. With clawed hands that belied immense strength, they deftly dismantled the protective case, their movements precise and calculated.

The moment the Were-Panther's fingers grasped the Idol, a surge of energy coursed through their body. The relic's power pulsed like a living thing, ancient and untamed. The thief's breath caught in their throat, a mixture of reverence and fear washing over them. They knew the legends surrounding the

Idol, the whispers of its ability to transform lycans into feral beasts and humans into lycans. And now, it was theirs.

But the Were-Panther's moment of triumph was short-lived. The museum's alarms pierced the silence, triggered by the disturbance in the exhibit. The thief's reflexes kicked into overdrive as they swiftly pocketed the Idol and made their escape. With supernatural speed and agility, they navigated the winding corridors, evading the security guards who rushed to investigate the commotion. Shadows formed around their body, granting them a unique camouflage within the confines of the darkness.

As the Were-Panther vanished into the night, the weight of their actions began to sink in. The Idol of Lycoan, a relic of immense power, was now in the hands of an unknown entity with unknown intentions. The balance of the supernatural world hung precariously on this item, and the consequences of this theft would soon be felt by all.

Miles away from the chaos of the Blacksburg History Museum, the Were-Panther came to a stop in a secluded alleyway. With a shimmering blur, their feline features melted away, revealing the human form beneath. The thief, a man with a reputation that preceded him in the supernatural underworld, stood tall and proud, the Idol of Lycoan clutched tightly in his grasp.

The man's eyes gleamed with a mixture of triumph and malice as he examined the ancient relic. He had spent years searching for the Idol, following whispers and legends, and now, it was finally his. With this artifact in his possession, he could reshape the world to his liking, bending both lycans and humans to his will.

A wicked smile played across the man's lips as he tucked the Idol into the folds of his jacket. He knew that his actions would not go unnoticed, that the authorities would soon be on his trail. But he was prepared for the challenge, eager to test his wits and power against those who would try to stop him.

As the thief melted into the shadows of the alleyway, his mind raced with plans and possibilities. The Idol of Lycoan was only the beginning, a key to unlocking a future where he reigned supreme. And heaven help anyone who dared to stand in his way.

In the aftermath of the heist, the Blacksburg History Museum descended into chaos. The authorities, baffled by the audacity of the crime and the lack of evidence, scrambled to make sense of the situation. Little did they know, the theft of the Idol was far more than a simple crime; it was the first move in a dangerous game that threatened to upend the delicate balance between the human and supernatural worlds.

As news of the stolen artifact spread, whispers began to circulate among those in the know. The Idol of Lycoan, long thought to be a myth, was now in play, and its power would surely attract the attention of those who sought to wield it for their own gain. The stage was set for a battle that would determine the fate of both lycans and humans alike, and only time would tell who would emerge victorious in this shadowy war.

CHAPTER 1

The harsh, icy winds of the Arctic whipped across the stark landscape, battering against the walls of the Regional Investigation of Preternatural Crimes Department (RIPD) Headquarters. Inside the fortified structure, two agents navigated the winding corridors, their footsteps echoing off the metal floors.

Special Agent Mick Parker, a seasoned veteran of the RIPD, walked alongside his partner, Special Agent Casey Elkins. Despite the chill that seemed to permeate the building, both agents maintained a composed demeanor, their minds focused on the summons that had brought them to this remote location.

As they approached the office of Sargent Leon Hawkins, Mick glanced at Casey, a hint of concern in his eyes. "What do you think this is about?" he asked, his voice low.

Casey shrugged, her gaze fixed ahead. "No idea. But if Hawkins called us all the way out here, it must be important."

Mick nodded, his jaw clenching slightly. He had a feeling that whatever awaited them behind that door would change the course of their careers, and perhaps their lives.

They entered Sargent Hawkins' office, the room spartan and efficient, much like the man himself. Hawkins, a grizzled officer with a no-nonsense air, looked up from the files spread across his desk. "Agents Parker and Elkins," he greeted, his voice gruff. "Take a seat."

As they settled into the chairs opposite Hawkins, Casey couldn't help but notice the tension in the room. Something was different, a shift in the usual dynamic.

Hawkins leaned forward, his eyes locking with each agent in turn. "I'll cut to the chase. We have a situation. The Idol of Lycoan has been stolen from the Blacksburg History Museum."

Mick's eyebrows shot up in surprise, while Casey's expression remained neutral, her mind already racing with the implications.

"The Idol of Lycoan?" Mick repeated, disbelief coloring his tone. "I thought that was just a myth."

Hawkins shook his head. "It's very real, and now it's in the hands of an unknown thief. The local authorities are out of their depth, and we need to act fast."

He turned his attention to Casey. "Agent Elkins, you'll be taking point on this investigation. We need your unique skills and experience to track down the Idol and bring it back into secure hands."

Casey nodded, a flicker of excitement mingling with the weight of responsibility. "I understand, sir. I'll leave for Blacksburg immediately."

Hawkins then shifted his gaze to Mick. "Agent Parker, I have a different assignment for you. Effective immediately, you're being transferred to Field Support Operations. You'll be coordinating resources and providing backup for Agent Elkins and other field agents as needed."

Mick's face registered shock, then confusion. "But sir, I—"

Hawkins held up a hand, silencing any protest. "This isn't

a request, Parker. We need your expertise in a different capacity. Agent Elkins is more than capable of handling the investigation on her own."

A heavy silence fell over the room as the agents absorbed the news. Casey glanced at Mick, seeing the conflicting emotions playing out on his face. She knew how much he valued their partnership, but she also understood the importance of following orders.

Hawkins stood, signaling the end of the meeting. "Agent Elkins, you have your orders. Report to Blacksburg and begin your investigation. Agent Parker, report to FSO for your new assignment. Dismissed."

As they left the office, Casey's mind was already racing with the implications of her new assignment. Blacksburg. The name alone sent a chill down her spine, stirring up memories she had long tried to bury.

Mick, ever attuned to his partner's emotional state, placed a comforting hand on her shoulder. "Casey, I know going back to Blacksburg won't be easy for you. But you're not alone in this."

Casey managed a weak smile, appreciating his brotherly concern. "I know, Mick. It's just... there are a lot of ghosts in that town. Ghosts I thought I'd left behind."

Mick nodded, understanding the weight of her past. "I remember the stories you told me about your time in Polkville. The adventures you had with Alex, the bonds you forged. Maybe... maybe reaching out to him could help. He knows the area, and he knows you. He could be a valuable ally in this investigation."

Casey considered his words, a flicker of warmth igniting in her chest. Alex. The name brought a rush of memories, their recent exchanges over the phone, the laughter and shared stories. It had only been weeks since their last conversation, but the thought of seeing him in person, of having a familiar face in the midst of the chaos...

"You're right," she admitted, a genuine smile tugging at her lips. "Alex has always been there for me, even from a distance. And his knowledge of the local supernatural scene could be invaluable."

Mick grinned, pleased to see a spark of the old Casey shining through. "There you go. Don't forget, you've got a whole team behind you, even if we're not all on the front lines. You're not facing this alone."

Casey's smile widened, a newfound determination settling in her bones. "Thanks, Mick. I needed that reminder."

As they parted ways, Casey's mind was already racing with the possibilities. Blacksburg, with its dark secrets and haunted memories, still loomed on the horizon, but now she had a glimmer of hope to cling to. The prospect of reuniting with Alex, of facing the challenges ahead with a trusted friend by her side...

She knew the path forward wouldn't be easy. The Idol of Lycoan was still out there, waiting to be found, and the shadows of her past still lurked in every corner of Blacksburg. But with the support of her team and the promise of a familiar face, Casey felt ready to face whatever lay ahead.

****

Casey stepped onto the sleek, private jet, her mind still reeling from the briefing with Sargent Hawkins and the weight of her new assignment. As she settled into her seat, the luxurious interior of the plane a stark contrast to the icy landscape outside, she couldn't help but feel a mix of anticipation and trepidation.

The plane took off smoothly, leaving the Arctic behind and setting course for Blacksburg, South Carolina. Casey gazed out the window, watching the endless expanse of white give way to a patchwork of green and brown as they flew over the continent.

Once they reached cruising altitude, Casey pulled out her secure RIPD-issued tablet and initiated a video call. After a few moments, Alex's familiar face filled the screen, his warm smile instantly easing some of the tension in her shoulders.

"Well, well, well, if it isn't my favorite Shortstack," Alex greeted, his voice playful yet laced with concern. "I've been worried about you, Case. It's been weeks since we last talked."

Casey couldn't help but grin at the sound of his pet name for her. "I know, Tigger. I'm sorry for keeping you in the dark. Things have been crazy with this new assignment."

Alex leaned closer to the screen, his eyes scanning her face. "I heard about Blacksburg. Are you sure you're ready to go back there?"

Casey sighed, running a hand through her hair. "Honestly, I'm a little overwhelmed. But I don't have a choice. This case is too important."

"I get it, Case. But promise me you'll be careful. I don't know what I'd do if anything happened to you."

The sincerity in his voice sent a warm flutter through Casey's chest. "I promise, Tigger. Besides, I know I've got you watching my back."

Alex's smile turned mischievous. "Always, Shortstack. Someone's got to keep you out of trouble."

Casey laughed, the sound feeling foreign after the intensity of the last few days. "You're one to talk, Mr. Adventure."

They fell into a comfortable banter, catching up on the little things they'd missed in each other's lives over the past few weeks. It was a welcome respite from the looming challenges of the investigation.

Eventually, Casey steered the conversation back to the case. "So, about the Idol of Lycoan..."

Alex's brow furrowed. "I've heard the name mentioned in passing, but I don't know much about it. My hands are a bit tied up with a case of my own at the moment."

Casey's shoulders slumped slightly, hoping for more insight. "I understand, Tigger. I know you've got your own responsibilities."

Alex's expression softened. "Hey, just because I can't be there in person doesn't mean I can't help. I might not have the details on the Idol, but I know someone who can assist you on the ground."

Casey's interest piqued. "Oh? Who did you have in mind?"

A knowing grin spread across Alex's face. "A certain tech whiz who you've always been fond of. Aidan Kenta."

Casey's heart skipped a beat at the mention of Aidan's name. "Aidan? You think he'd be willing to help?"

"Are you kidding? For you, Shortstack, he'd drop everything. Besides, I seem to recall you two always had a special connection. He'll be more than happy to lend his expertise."

A faint blush crept onto Casey's cheeks. "We just worked well together, that's all."

Alex chuckled. "Sure, Case. Whatever you say. But in all seriousness, Aidan's the best. With him by your side, you'll have a major advantage in this investigation."

Casey smiled, feeling a surge of gratitude and excitement. "Thank you, Alex. Having Aidan's support will make a world of difference."

"I'll let him know to expect your call. And Case? Don't hesitate to reach out if you need anything else. I might be busy, but I'm always here for you."

"I know, Tigger. That means more than you know."

With a final exchange of smiles and a promise to stay in touch, Casey ended the call, her heart buoyed by the prospect of working with Aidan once again.

As the plane began its descent, Casey's mind raced with the possibilities. Having Aidan's technical skills and their undeniable chemistry on her side could be the key to unraveling the mystery of the Idol of Lycoan.

She made a mental note to call Aidan as soon as she landed, eager to reconnect and dive into the investigation together. With his support and the strength of her RIPD team, Casey felt ready to face whatever challenges Blacksburg had in store.

****

As the plane touched down at the Blacksburg Airport, Casey felt a mix of nostalgia and apprehension wash over her. It had been years since she'd set foot in this town, and the weight of her past seemed to linger in the air like a heavy fog.

She made her way through the familiar airport, her mind already racing with the details of the case. After picking up her rental car, a non-descript sedan that would blend in with the local traffic, Casey set out towards the heart of Blacksburg.

The drive along Highway 198, also known as North Mountain Street, brought back a flood of memories. She passed the Pilot Truck Stop, a beacon for weary travelers and a regular haunt for the town's residents. The golden arches of McDonald's loomed in the distance, a reminder of countless late-night meals and impromptu meetings with informants.

But as Casey approached the spot where the local Waffle House once stood, her heart sank. In its place, a shiny new strip mall had sprung up, all glass and steel and generic storefronts. The sight of it felt like a punch to the gut, a stark reminder of how much had changed since she'd last been in Blacksburg.

She pulled into the parking lot of the strip mall, needing a moment to gather her thoughts. The Waffle House had been more than just a restaurant to her; it had been a sanctuary, a place where she'd forged connections and found solace during her darkest days in Blacksburg. Seeing it gone felt like losing a piece of herself, a tangible link to her past.

Casey took a deep breath, pushing down the wave of emotions that threatened to overwhelm her. She couldn't afford to get lost in memories, not when the Idol of Lycoan was out there, waiting to be found. She had a job to do, and she needed to stay focused.

With a renewed sense of determination, Casey put the car in gear and pulled out of the parking lot. She had a meeting with the local police chief scheduled, and she couldn't afford to be late. The investigation was just beginning, and every minute counted.

As she navigated the familiar streets of Blacksburg, Casey couldn't shake the feeling that this case would be unlike any other she'd faced before. The Idol of Lycoan held secrets and dangers that she could only begin to imagine, and she knew that she'd need every ounce of her skill and resolve to unravel its mysteries.

But with Alex's support, Aidan's technical expertise, and the backing of the RIPD, Casey felt ready to take on whatever challenges lay ahead. Blacksburg may have changed, but her dedication to protecting both the human and supernatural communities remained as strong as ever.

****

Alex ended the video call with Casey, a mixture of concern and relief washing over him. He knew she was more than capable of handling the investigation, but the thought of her facing the dangers of Blacksburg alone left an uneasy feeling in his gut.

Without hesitation, he scrolled through his contacts and hit the call button next to Aidan Kenta's name. The line rang a few times before a familiar voice answered.

"Alex! Long time no talk, my friend. What's the occasion?" Aidan's cheerful tone rang through the speaker.

"Hey, Aidan. I wish I could say this was just a social call, but I've got a favor to ask."

"Shoot. You know I'm always ready to lend a hand."

Alex took a deep breath. "It's about Casey. She's been assigned to a case in Blacksburg, and I have a feeling she's going to need some backup."

There was a brief pause on the other end of the line. "Casey's heading to Blacksburg? That's some serious business. What's the case?"

"The Idol of Lycoan has been stolen from the Blacksburg

History Museum. Casey's tasked with tracking it down and bringing it back into RIPD custody."

Aidan let out a low whistle. "The Idol of Lycoan? I've heard stories about that artifact. If it falls into the wrong hands, it could spell disaster for both humans and lycans."

"Exactly. Which is why I need you to be ready to assist Casey when she calls. She's going to need your technical expertise and your knowledge of Rei manipulation."

"Consider it done. I'll start packing my gear right away. Anything specific I should bring?"

Alex hesitated for a moment. "Make sure you pack the Rei Dampening Equipment. We don't know what kind of supernatural threats Casey might face out there, and it's better to be prepared."

"Got it. I'll make sure to have everything ready to go at a moment's notice."

"Thanks, Aidan. I knew I could count on you. And one more thing..."

"What's that?"

"Keep an eye on Casey for me, will you? I know she's tough, but even the strongest agents need support sometimes."

Aidan's voice softened. "You don't have to worry, Alex. I'll make sure Casey has everything she needs, both in terms of tech and moral support. We'll get to the bottom of this case together."

Alex felt a weight lift from his shoulders. "I appreciate it, Aidan. Casey will be calling you soon to fill you in on the details and coordinate your assistance."

"Got it. I'll be ready and waiting for her call. And Alex?

Don't be a stranger, okay? We should catch up properly once this case is wrapped up."

A smile tugged at Alex's lips. "Definitely. I'll hold you to that. Take care, Aidan."

"You too, Alex. Talk to you soon."

As the call ended, Alex leaned back in his chair, a sense of relief washing over him. Knowing that Aidan would be there to support Casey eased his concerns, even if he couldn't be by her side himself.

He glanced at the files scattered across his desk, a reminder of his own pressing case. With a sigh, he dove back into his work, trusting that Casey and Aidan would unravel the mystery of the Idol of Lycoan and keep each other safe in the process.

****

With a heavy heart, Casey pulled out of the strip mall parking lot and continued her journey into the heart of Blacksburg. The familiar streets and landmarks stirred up a mixture of memories, both good and bad, as she navigated the town she once called home.

As she drove, a sudden realization hit her. If there was one place that could provide her with the pulse of the town and any potential leads, it was Danny's Cafe. The local watering hole had always been a hub of gossip and information, and Casey knew that her best friend Amber Collins still worked there as a waitress.

Casey made a sharp turn, heading towards the cafe. Within minutes, she found herself pulling into the parking lot, the neon sign casting a warm glow over the asphalt. She stepped out of the car, the scent of coffee and greasy diner food hitting her nostrils, instantly transporting her back to countless late-night conversations and laughter-filled gatherings with Amber.

As she pushed open the door, the jingling bell announced her arrival. The cafe looked just as she remembered it - the worn vinyl booths, the flickering fluorescent lights, and the constant chatter of patrons. Casey scanned the room, her eyes searching for the familiar face of her best friend.

"Casey? Is that really you?"

The voice rang out across the cafe, and Casey turned to see Amber emerging from behind the counter, a look of surprise and joy on her face. Amber rushed over, enveloping Casey in a tight hug.

"I can't believe it! What are you doing back in Blacksburg?" Amber asked, her eyes wide with excitement.

Casey returned the hug, feeling a wave of comfort wash over her. "It's a long story, Amber. I'm here on official RIPD business."

Amber's expression shifted, a mix of concern and intrigue. "RIPD business? In Blacksburg? This must be serious."

Casey nodded, her voice lowering. "It is. I could really use your help, Amber. You've always had your finger on the pulse of this town. Have you heard anything about the Idol of Lycoan or any unusual supernatural activity lately?"

Amber's brow furrowed as she considered the question. "The Idol of Lycoan? Can't say I've heard that name before. But there have been whispers, Casey. Strange things happening in the shadows. I'll ask around, see what I can find out."

Casey smiled, grateful for her friend's willingness to help.

"Thanks, Amber. I knew I could count on you."

Amber grinned, her infectious energy lighting up the room. "Of course, Casey. You know I've always got your back. Now, sit down and let me get you a cup of coffee. You look like you could use it."

As Casey settled into a booth, watching Amber bustle around the cafe, she felt a sense of warmth and familiarity wash over her. Despite the weight of the case on her shoulders, knowing that she had Amber's support and the resources of Danny's Cafe at her disposal gave her a renewed sense of hope.

The investigation was still in its early stages, but with each passing moment, Casey felt more determined than ever to unravel the mystery of the Idol of Lycoan and protect the town she once called home.

As Amber returned with a steaming cup of coffee, she slid into the booth opposite Casey, a mischievous glint in her eye. "So, Casey, tell me. How's your love life? Any special someone I should know about?"

Casey laughed, shaking her head. "You know me, Amber. Married to the job. Between RIPD cases and trying to keep the supernatural world in check, there hasn't been much time for romance."

Amber leaned back, a knowing smile on her face. "I get it, Casey. But you know what they say about all work and no play."

Casey raised an eyebrow. "Oh? And what about you, Amber? Any juicy gossip from the dating scene?"

Amber's expression softened, a hint of vulnerability in her eyes. "Actually, Casey, there's something I've been meaning to tell you. I've realized that I'm bisexual."

Casey's eyes widened, but a warm smile quickly spread

across her face. She reached across the table, taking Amber's hand in her own. "Amber, I'm so proud of you for sharing this with me. You know that I love and support you, no matter what."

Amber squeezed Casey's hand, a look of relief and gratitude on her face. "Thank you, Casey. I knew you'd understand. It's been a journey of self-discovery, but I'm finally feeling comfortable in my own skin."

Casey nodded, her voice gentle. "I'm happy for you, Amber. Love is love, and you deserve to be with someone who makes you feel cherished and accepted, regardless of gender."

Amber grinned, the tension in her shoulders easing. "Thanks, Casey. You're the best friend a girl could ask for."

The two women fell into comfortable conversation, catching up on the years they'd spent apart. They laughed over shared memories, swapped stories about their respective adventures, and marveled at how far they'd come since their early days in Blacksburg.

As the hours ticked by, Casey found herself feeling more and more at home in Amber's presence. The weight of the investigation still loomed large, but having her best friend by her side made everything feel a little more manageable.

Eventually, the conversation circled back to the case at hand. Amber leaned in, her voice low. "Casey, I promise I'll keep my ears open. If I hear anything about the Idol of Lycoan or any strange supernatural occurrences, you'll be the first to know."

Casey smiled, grateful for her friend's unwavering support. "Thank you, Amber. I have a feeling I'm going to need all the help I can get on this one.

As the conversation wound down, Amber fixed Casey with a thoughtful look. "Hey, Casey, I just realized. Do you have a place to stay while you're in Blacksburg?"

Casey paused, the realization hitting her. With everything that had happened since her arrival, she hadn't even thought about accommodations. "Actually, no. I was so focused on getting here and starting the investigation that it completely slipped my mind."

Amber's face lit up. "Well, you're in luck. I have a spare room in my apartment, and you're more than welcome to stay with me. It'll be just like old times, except with less studying and more supernatural crime-solving."

Casey felt a wave of gratitude wash over her. "Amber, are you sure? I don't want to impose."

Amber waved off her concerns. "Nonsense, Casey. You're my best friend, and I'd love to have you stay with me. Plus, it'll give us more time to catch up and strategize about the case."

A smile spread across Casey's face. "In that case, I'd love to take you up on that offer. Thank you, Amber. You're a lifesaver."

Amber grinned. "That's what best friends are for. Now, let's get you settled in. We've got a lot of work ahead of us, but at least we'll be facing it together."

With that, Amber led Casey out of the cafe and towards her apartment, the promise of a comfortable bed and the support of her closest friend making the challenges ahead seem a little less daunting.

As they walked, Casey couldn't help but feel a sense of warmth and belonging. Blacksburg may have changed over the years, but the strength of her friendship with Amber remained a constant. With her best friend by her side and the resources of the RIPD at her disposal, Casey felt ready to take on whatever the investigation might throw her way.

Little did she know, the mystery of the Idol of Lycoan would test her in ways she never could have imagined. But for now, she allowed herself a moment of respite, grateful for the small comforts and unwavering support that Amber provided

****

Casey settled into Amber's spare room, feeling a sense of relief wash over her. Knowing that she had a safe place to stay and the support of her best friend made the daunting task ahead seem a little more manageable.

As she unpacked her bags, Casey's thoughts turned to Aidan. With his technical expertise and knowledge of Rei manipulation, he would be an invaluable asset to the investigation. She pulled out her phone and dialed his number, her heart racing with anticipation.

After a few rings, Aidan's voice came through the speaker. "Casey! I was just about to call you."

Casey smiled, the sound of his voice instantly putting her at ease. "Aidan, I'm so glad I caught you. I need your help with a case here in Blacksburg. It's about the Idol of Lycoan."

There was a brief pause on the other end of the line. "The Idol of Lycoan? Casey, you know how dangerous that artifact is. Of course, I'll help you. In fact, I'm already on my way to Blacksburg."

Casey's eyes widened in surprise. "You're coming to Blacksburg? But how did you know?"

Aidan chuckled. "Let's just say a little birdie named Alex filled me in. He knew you'd need my expertise, so I've been making preparations. I've already purchased a warehouse in town to use as our base of operations. It should be up and running by the time I arrive tomorrow afternoon."

Casey felt a surge of gratitude and excitement. "Aidan, you're amazing. I can't thank you enough for dropping everything to help me with this case."

"Casey, you know I'd do anything for you," Aidan replied, his voice softening. "We're a team, and we'll face this challenge together. I'll see you tomorrow, and we'll get to work on unraveling the mystery of the Idol."

As the call ended, Casey couldn't help but smile. With Aidan by her side, she felt a renewed sense of confidence and determination. They had faced countless supernatural threats together, and this case would be no different.

She glanced out the window, taking in the familiar sights of Blacksburg. The town may have held painful memories, but it was also the place where she had forged unbreakable bonds with her closest friends. With Amber's support, Aidan's technical prowess, and the backing of the RIPD, Casey knew that she could face whatever challenges lay ahead.

As the sun began to set over the horizon, Casey allowed herself a moment of peace. Tomorrow would bring new obstacles and dangers, but for now, she was exactly where she needed to be. The hunt for the Idol of Lycoan was just beginning, and Casey Elkins was ready to see it through to the end.

CHAPTER 2

The Blacksburg History Museum loomed before Casey as she stepped out of her car. The grand, neoclassical building stood in stark contrast to the modern structures surrounding it, a testament to the town's rich past. Casey took a deep breath, steeling herself for the investigation ahead.

As she climbed the steps to the museum entrance, Casey spotted a familiar figure waiting for her. Chief Dustin Blackwell stood rigid, his uniform crisp and his expression sour. He was chewing gum, his jaw working furiously as he watched Casey approach with barely concealed disdain.

"Special Agent Elkins," Chief Blackwell greeted her, his tone cold and unwelcoming. "I don't recall requesting the RIPD's involvement in this case."

Casey met his gaze, her own expression unflinching. "Chief Blackwell. The theft of the Idol of Lycoan is a matter of supernatural significance. The RIPD has jurisdiction, and I'm here to ensure a thorough investigation."

Blackwell's eyes flashed with annoyance, but he forced a tight smile. "Of course. We wouldn't want to step on any toes. Please, follow me."

As they entered the museum, Casey couldn't shake the feeling that the Chief was hiding something. His hostile attitude and reluctance to accept her presence suggested a desire to control the investigation and keep certain details under wraps.

The museum's interior was eerily quiet, the usual bustling crowds absent in the wake of the theft. Chief Blackwell led Casey through the grand foyer and into the exhibit hall where the Idol of Lycoan had been displayed.

The room was cordoned off with police tape, and a team of forensic experts were already at work, dusting for fingerprints and cataloguing evidence. Casey's gaze was immediately drawn to the empty pedestal at the center of the room, where the Idol had once stood.

"What can you tell me about the theft, Chief?" Casey asked, her eyes scanning the scene for any clues.

Blackwell shrugged, his expression nonchalant. "Not much to tell. Someone broke in, disabled the cameras and alarms, and made off with the Idol. We're still investigating, but so far, we don't have any solid leads."

Casey frowned, her instincts telling her that the Chief was being evasive. "And the Idol itself? What do we know about its history and significance?"

Blackwell waved a dismissive hand. "It's just some old artifact. Probably valuable to collectors, but I don't see what the big fuss is about."

Casey's suspicions grew. The Chief's dismissive attitude towards the Idol and his lack of transparency about the investigation were red flags. She knew she'd have to dig deeper to uncover the truth.

"I'll need access to all the evidence your team has collected, as well as any security footage from the night of the theft," Casey said, her tone leaving no room for argument.

Blackwell's jaw clenched, and for a moment, Casey

thought he might refuse. But finally, he nodded, his expression tight. "I'll have my officers provide you with what we have. But I expect to be kept in the loop on any developments in the case."

Casey met his gaze, her own expression cool and determined. "Of course, Chief. We're all working towards the same goal here."

As they exited the exhibit hall, Casey's mind was already racing with theories and possible leads. She knew that Chief Blackwell's uncooperative attitude and attempts to downplay the significance of the Idol were signs of a deeper conspiracy at play.

****

As Casey finished her initial examination of the crime scene, Chief Blackwell cleared his throat, drawing her attention. "Special Agent Elkins, this is Joshua Butler, the museum curator. He can answer any questions you have about the Idol."

Casey turned to face the curator, taking in his appearance. Joshua Butler was a man in his mid-fifties, with graying hair and a well-trimmed beard. He had a scholarly air about him, his eyes sharp and inquisitive behind wire-rimmed glasses.

"Mr. Butler, thank you for taking the time to speak with me," Casey said, extending her hand in greeting.

The curator shook her hand firmly, his grip warm and steady. "Please, call me Joshua. I'm happy to assist in any way I can. The theft of the Idol is a terrible loss for the museum and the community."

Casey noted the genuine concern in Joshua's voice, a stark contrast to Chief Blackwell's dismissive attitude. "Can you tell me more about the Idol's history and significance? Any information could be crucial to the investigation."

Joshua nodded, his expression turning thoughtful. "The Idol of Lycoan is an ancient artifact, dating back to the time of the ancient Greeks. It was created to honor the god Lycoan, who was believed to have the power to transform humans into lycans."

Chief Blackwell shifted uncomfortably beside them, his gum chewing growing more aggressive. "Surely, this is all just myth and legend. The Idol is valuable, but it's not some mystical object."

Joshua glanced at the Chief, a flicker of annoyance crossing his features. "With all due respect, Chief, the stories surrounding Lycoan and his Idol have been part of lycan lore for centuries. The Idol is said to hold a portion of Lycoan's power, giving it the ability to enhance or control the transformative abilities of lycans."

Casey interjected, sensing the tension between the two men. "Joshua, have there been any recent inquiries or interest in the Idol? Anyone who might have had a motive to steal it?"

The curator hesitated, his eyes darting briefly towards Chief Blackwell. "There have been some... whispers within the lycan community. Rumors of a faction that believes the Idol could be used to assert dominance over other lycan groups and even humans, much like Lycoan himself was said to do."

Chief Blackwell scoffed, rolling his eyes. "Rumors and hearsay. Nothing substantiated."

Casey's instincts were on high alert. Joshua's hesitation and the Chief's dismissive response only fueled her suspicions that there was more to the story than they were letting on.

"Joshua, I'd like to speak with you further about these rumors and any other information you may have about the Idol.

Would you be available to meet with me privately?"

The curator glanced at Chief Blackwell, who was frowning deeply, before nodding. "Of course, Special Agent Elkins. I'll make myself available whenever you need."

Casey smiled, grateful for Joshua's cooperation. "Thank you. I'll be in touch soon."

As they parted ways, Casey couldn't shake the feeling that Joshua Butler held key pieces of the puzzle. His knowledge of the Idol's connection to Lycoan and the whispers within the lycan community could be crucial to unraveling the mystery of its theft.

But with Chief Blackwell's obstructive presence and clear disdain for the investigation, Casey knew she would have to tread carefully. She would need to find a way to gain Joshua's trust and uncover the truth, all while navigating the treacherous waters of Blacksburg's supernatural underbelly.

The game was afoot, and Casey Elkins was ready to play.

****

The sleek, black helicopter cut through the sky, its blades whirring as it descended towards the outskirts of Blacksburg. Inside, Aidan Kenta sat back in his plush leather seat, his eyes fixed on the rapidly approaching cityscape.

As the helicopter touched down on the private helipad, Aidan couldn't help but feel a sense of anticipation. He knew that Casey was counting on him, and he was determined to do whatever it took to help her crack the case of the stolen Idol.

Aidan stepped out of the helicopter, his crisp suit impeccable despite the long flight. He nodded to the pilot, who began to power down the aircraft, before making his way towards the waiting car.

As he settled into the backseat, Aidan pulled out his phone and dialed a familiar number. After a few rings, Alex's voice came through the speaker.

"Aidan! I take it you've arrived in Blacksburg?"

Aidan smiled, the sound of his friend's voice a welcome comfort. "Just touched down, Alex. I'm heading to the warehouse now to set up shop."

"Good. Casey's going to need all the support she can get on this one. The Idol of Lycoan is no ordinary artifact."

Aidan's brow furrowed, his mind already racing with the possibilities. "I've been doing some research on my end. The Idol's history is steeped in mystery and power struggles. Whoever stole it must have had a compelling reason."

Alex sighed, the weight of the situation evident in his voice. "Just be careful, Aidan. The lycan community in Blacksburg is complex and dangerous. There are factions that would kill to get their hands on the Idol."

"I'll keep that in mind," Aidan replied, his tone turning serious. "But you know me, Alex. I'm not one to back down from a challenge."

"I know. That's what worries me."

Aidan chuckled softly, appreciating his friend's concern. "I'll be fine, Alex. And I'll make sure Casey is too. We'll get to the bottom of this, one way or another."

"I have no doubt. Keep me posted, and give Casey my best."

"Will do. Talk to you soon, Alex."

As the call ended, Aidan leaned back in his seat, his mind

already shifting into high gear. He knew that the warehouse would be the perfect base of operations, a secure location where he could utilize his cutting-edge technology and Rei manipulation skills to aid in the investigation.

But even with all his resources and expertise, Aidan knew that the case of the stolen Idol would be a formidable challenge. The lycan community of Blacksburg was a tangled web of secrets and agendas, and navigating those treacherous waters would require all of his wit and cunning.

As the car sped through the streets of Blacksburg, Aidan's resolve hardened. He would stand by Casey's side, no matter what dangers lay ahead. Together, they would unravel the mystery of the Idol of Lycoan and bring those responsible for its theft to justice.

As the car pulled up to the warehouse, Aidan took a moment to survey the building. It was nondescript, blending seamlessly into the industrial area, but Aidan knew that appearances could be deceiving. Inside, the warehouse was equipped with state-of-the-art technology and security measures, the perfect base of operations for their investigation.

Aidan stepped out of the car and made his way inside, his mind already buzzing with ideas and strategies. But first, he needed to touch base with Casey.

He pulled out his phone and dialed her number, waiting patiently as the call connected.

"Aidan," Casey's voice came through the speaker, a mix of relief and determination. "Please tell me you're in Blacksburg."

Aidan smiled, appreciating the urgency in her tone. "I am, and I come bearing gifts. I've secured a warehouse that will serve as our base of operations. It's fully equipped with everything we need to tackle this case."

"That's fantastic news," Casey replied, the tension in her voice easing slightly. "I've just finished up at the museum, and I've got some leads to follow up on."

"Perfect. Why don't you come meet me at the warehouse, and we can go over everything you've learned so far? I'll send you the address."

"Sounds like a plan. I'll see you soon, Aidan."

As the call ended, Aidan quickly typed out a message with the warehouse address and sent it to Casey. He knew that time was of the essence, and the sooner they could pool their resources and knowledge, the better their chances of cracking the case.

Aidan began setting up his equipment, his fingers flying over the keyboards as he configured the cutting-edge computers and monitoring systems. With his expertise in programming and technology, Aidan knew that he could create a formidable network to aid in their investigation, tracking leads and analyzing data with unparalleled efficiency.

As he worked, Aidan's thoughts drifted to the lycan community of Blacksburg and the secrets it held. He had a feeling that the theft of the Idol was just the tip of the iceberg, and that they were about to uncover a web of intrigue and danger that would test them to their limits.

But Aidan was ready for the challenge. With Casey's investigative skills and his own technological prowess, he knew that they could face whatever lay ahead. The warehouse would be their sanctuary, a place where they could plan, strategize, and stay one step ahead of those who sought to keep the truth hidden.

****

The bell above the door jingled as Tyler Keal strode into Danny's Cafe, his signature sunglasses perched on his nose and his backwards baseball cap slightly askew. He sauntered over to a booth in the corner, his eyes scanning the room with a mix of boredom and disdain.

Amber watched him from behind the counter, her instincts on high alert. She had seen Tyler around town before, always in the company of Braydon Mitchell, the notorious leader of the Panther Prowl. Amber knew that wherever Tyler went, trouble was sure to follow.

As Tyler settled into the booth, Amber approached him, her notepad and pen at the ready. "What can I get for you today?" she asked, her tone carefully neutral.

Tyler barely glanced at her, his attention focused on the menu. "Coffee. Black. And a bacon cheeseburger, extra fries."

Amber jotted down the order, trying to ignore the unease that Tyler's presence stirred in her gut. She was about to turn away when Tyler's phone rang, the harsh sound cutting through the din of the cafe.

Tyler pulled out his phone, his expression shifting from annoyed to alert as he saw the caller ID. He quickly answered, his voice low and urgent. "Boss. What's up?"

Amber busied herself with wiping down a nearby table, straining to hear the conversation without being too obvious.

"The Idol's been moved," Tyler said, his tone laced with frustration. "The RIPD is onto us. We need to act fast."

There was a pause as Tyler listened to Braydon's response, his brow furrowing. "Understood. I'll handle it. We can't let them get their hands on the Idol. It's too important."

Amber's heart raced as she processed what she had overheard. The Idol. The RIPD. Casey. It all connected in her mind, painting a picture of a dangerous game unfolding in the shadows of Blacksburg.

Tyler ended the call, his expression grim. He glanced around the cafe, his eyes landing on Amber for a moment before he looked away, his jaw clenched.

Amber hurried back behind the counter, her mind spinning. She knew that she had to get this information to Casey as soon as possible. If Tyler and Braydon were involved in the theft of the Idol, then Casey was walking into a hornet's nest of danger and deception.

As soon as Tyler's order was ready, Amber delivered it to his table, her hands shaking slightly. She couldn't shake the feeling that she had stumbled onto something big, something that could change the course of Casey's investigation and the fate of Blacksburg itself.

As Tyler dug into his meal, Amber slipped into the back room, pulling out her phone. She quickly dialed Casey's number, her heart pounding in her chest.

"Casey," she said, her voice urgent. "It's Amber. I've got something you need to hear. It's about the Idol, and Braydon Mitchell. You're not going to believe what I just overheard..."

****

Casey pulled up to the warehouse, her mind still reeling from her encounter with Chief Blackwell and the museum curator. She knew that she was on the right track, but the pieces of the puzzle were still frustratingly scattered.

As she stepped out of the car, her phone buzzed in her pocket. She pulled it out, her eyebrows raising as she saw

Amber's name on the caller ID. "Amber? Is everything okay?"

"Casey," Amber's voice came through the speaker, urgent and slightly breathless. "I've got something you need to hear. It's about the Idol, and Braydon Mitchell. You're not going to believe what I just overheard..."

Casey's heart skipped a beat at the mention of Braydon's name. She had a history with the man, a past that she had tried to bury deep. But if he was involved in the theft of the Idol, then all bets were off.

"Slow down, Amber," Casey said, trying to keep her voice calm. "What exactly did you hear?"

As Amber recounted the conversation between Tyler Keal and Braydon, Casey felt a chill run down her spine. The Idol had been moved, and the RIPD was closing in. Braydon and his crew were getting desperate, and that meant that the stakes were higher than ever.

"Amber, you did the right thing by calling me," Casey said, her mind already racing with the implications of this new information. "I need you to stay safe, okay? Don't let on that you overheard anything. I'll handle it from here."

"Be careful, Casey," Amber said, her voice laced with concern. "These guys are dangerous. They'll stop at nothing to get what they want."

"I know," Casey replied, her jaw set with determination. "But I've got backup. I'm meeting with Aidan now. We'll figure this out together."

As the call ended, Casey took a deep breath, her hand tightening around her phone. She knew that she was walking into a hornet's nest, but she wasn't about to back down. Not when the safety of Blacksburg and the fate of the lycan community hung in the balance.

She strode towards the warehouse door, her steps purposeful and her mind focused. Inside, she knew that Aidan was waiting, his technological prowess and strategic mind ready to be put to the test.

Casey pushed open the door to the warehouse, her phone still clutched in her hand as she ended the call with Amber. Her mind was spinning with the new information, the pieces of the puzzle finally starting to fall into place.

As she stepped inside, she found Aidan hunched over a bank of computer screens, his fingers flying over the keyboard. He looked up as she approached, his eyes immediately drawn to the phone in her hand and the troubled expression on her face.

"Casey? What's wrong?" he asked, his brow furrowed with concern. "Who was that on the phone?"

Casey took a deep breath, trying to organize her thoughts. "That was Amber, my friend from Danny's Cafe. She overheard something, Aidan. Something big."

Aidan straightened up, his full attention now on Casey. "What did she hear?"

"Tyler Keal, Braydon Mitchell's right-hand man, was at the cafe. He got a call from Braydon, and Amber overheard their conversation. The Idol has been moved, and the RIPD is closing in. They're getting desperate, Aidan."

Aidan's eyes widened, his mind already racing with the implications. "Braydon Mitchell? The leader of the Panther Prowl? I've heard rumors about him, Casey. He's bad news."

Casey nodded grimly, her jaw tight. "I know. Braydon and I have a history, Aidan. One that I thought I'd left behind. But if he's involved in the theft of the Idol, then we need to act fast."

Aidan moved closer to Casey, his hand coming to rest reassuringly on her shoulder. "We will, Casey. We'll stop him, and we'll recover the Idol. But you need to tell me everything. What exactly did Amber hear?"

As Casey recounted the details of the overheard conversation, Aidan's expression grew more and more serious. He could sense the weight of the situation, the danger that they were facing. But he also knew that they had the skills, the resources, and the determination to see this through.

"Okay," he said, his voice steady and focused. "This changes things, but it also gives us a lead. If Braydon and his crew are on the move, then we need to be one step ahead of them. Let me see what I can dig up on their recent activities, any patterns or clues that might point us in the right direction."

Casey nodded, feeling a surge of gratitude for Aidan's unwavering support. "Thank you, Aidan. I don't know what I'd do without you."

Aidan flashed her a smile, his eyes glinting with determination. "We're a team, Casey. We've got each other's backs, no matter what. Now, let's get to work. We've got an Idol to find and a bad guy to take down."

As they dove into their respective tasks, Casey felt a renewed sense of purpose and resolve. Yes, the stakes were higher than ever, and the dangers more acute. But with Aidan by her side, and the knowledge that they were fighting for something bigger than themselves, she knew that they could face whatever lay ahead.

****

As Tyler Keal stepped out of Danny's Cafe, his stomach full and his mind buzzing with the implications of his recent phone call with Braydon, he nearly collided with a tall, muscular man entering the restaurant. Tyler's eyes narrowed as he recognized Rigo Balderas, a notorious figure in Blacksburg's supernatural community.

Rigo, known to some as the Joker, was a wild card - a powerful lycan with a reputation for unpredictability and a penchant for chaos. Tyler had always been wary of him, unsure of where his loyalties lay.

"Well, well, if it isn't the Joker himself," Tyler sneered, his lips curling into a mocking smile. "Better watch yourself, Balderas. Wouldn't want to get wrecked, now would you?"

Rigo met Tyler's gaze, his eyes flashing with a dangerous glint. "Funny, I was about to say the same thing to you, Keal. You and your boss might think you're untouchable, but you're playing with fire. Sooner or later, you're going to get burned."

Tyler's jaw clenched, his hand twitching towards the concealed weapon at his waist. But he knew better than to start a fight in broad daylight, especially with someone as formidable as Rigo. "We'll see about that, Joker. Just stay out of our way, and maybe you'll live to see another day."

With that, Tyler brushed past Rigo, his shoulder slamming into the other man's chest as he stalked off down the street. Rigo watched him go, his expression unreadable, before shaking his head and entering the cafe.

Inside, Amber looked up from her work, her eyes widening as she recognized Rigo. She had heard stories about the Joker, whispers of his strength and his mercurial nature. But seeing him in person was a different experience altogether.

Rigo slid into a booth, his large frame dwarfing the small table. Amber approached him cautiously, her notepad and pen at the ready. "What can I get for you today, sir?"

Rigo looked up at her, his eyes softening slightly as he took in her nervous demeanor. "Just a coffee, please. Black. And maybe some information, if you're willing to share."

Amber's brow furrowed, unsure of what to make of the request. "Information? About what?"

Rigo leaned forward, his voice low and conspiratorial. "About the Idol of Lycoan. Word on the street is that it's been stolen, and that the RIPD is in town to investigate. I want to know what you've heard, and who else might be poking around."

Amber hesitated, torn between her loyalty to Casey and her instinct to help someone who might be an ally. Finally, she made a decision. "I might know someone who can help you, someone who's working the case. Her name is Casey Elkins, and she's with the RIPD. If anyone can find the Idol and stop the ones who took it, it's her."

Rigo sat back, his expression thoughtful. "Casey Elkins, huh? I've heard that name before. She's got quite the reputation in certain circles. You think she'd be willing to meet with me, to hear what I have to say?"

Amber nodded, feeling more confident in her decision. "I think she would. Casey's not like most RIPD agents. She's fair, and she's willing to listen. I can put in a good word for you, if you'd like."

Rigo smiled, his eyes crinkling at the corners. "I'd appreciate that, Amber. Thank you. And who knows? Maybe together, we can put an end to this madness and keep Blacksburg safe."

As Amber went to get Rigo's coffee, she felt a flicker of hope in her chest. With Casey on the case, and potential allies like Rigo emerging from the shadows, maybe they stood a chance against the forces that sought to use the Idol for their own nefarious purposes.

CHAPTER 3

Amber returned to Rigo's booth, a steaming cup of black coffee in her hand. She placed it on the table before him, her mind still churning with the implications of their previous conversation. She slid into the booth opposite him, her curiosity getting the better of her.

"So, Rigo, I have to ask - why did Keal call you Joker just now?" she questioned, her eyebrows raised in interest.

Rigo chuckled, a deep, rumbling sound that seemed to fill the space between them. "Ah, that. It's a bit of a long story, but the short version is this: I'm the only known Hyena Hybrid in existence. And as I'm sure you know, hyenas are known for their distinctive laughter."

Amber's eyes widened, surprise and fascination warring on her face. "A Hyena Hybrid? I didn't even know that was possible. How did that happen?"

Rigo shrugged, taking a sip of his coffee. "It's a mystery, even to me. All I know is that I've always been different, even among lycans. My abilities, my strengths, even my sense of humor - they all set me apart."

Amber leaned forward, her elbows resting on the table. "And is that why you're interested in the Idol of Lycoan? Because you're different?"

Rigo's expression turned serious, his eyes locking with Amber's. "In part, yes. But it's more than that. I have a vested interest in keeping Blacksburg safe, and in making sure that powerful artifacts like the Idol don't fall into the wrong hands. I've seen firsthand what can happen when lycans let their ambitions override their humanity."

Amber nodded, her respect for Rigo growing by the second. "I can understand that. But why come to Casey? Why not handle this on your own?"

Rigo sighed, his fingers drumming against the tabletop. "Because I know when I'm outmatched. Braydon has resources, allies, and a level of ruthlessness that I can't compete with on my own. But Casey Elkins? She's got the backing of the RIPD, and a reputation for getting things done. If anyone can take Braydon down and recover the Idol, it's her."

Amber sat back, her mind racing with the new information. She could see the sincerity in Rigo's eyes, the genuine desire to do what was right. And if he was willing to put aside his own pride and reach out for help, then maybe he really was someone that Casey could trust.

"Okay," she said finally, her decision made. "I'll talk to Casey, tell her what you've told me. But I need you to promise me something, Rigo."

Rigo raised an eyebrow, curious. "And what's that?"

"Promise me that you'll have her back, no matter what. That you'll do everything in your power to keep her safe and help her see this through. Because if anything happens to Casey, I'll hold you personally responsible."

Rigo met Amber's gaze, his expression solemn. "You have my word, Amber. I'll stand by Casey's side, and I'll do whatever it takes to make sure that she succeeds. That's a promise."

Amber nodded, satisfied. She glanced at the clock on the

wall, realizing that her break was almost over. "I should get back to work. But I'll talk to Casey, Rigo. And for what it's worth, I hope that you two can work together to stop Braydon and keep Blacksburg safe."

As Amber stood to leave, Rigo caught her hand, his eyes filled with gratitude. "Thank you, Amber. For listening, and for giving me a chance. It means more than you know."

Amber smiled, feeling a warmth spread through her chest. She had a feeling that Rigo Balderas was going to be an important ally in the days to come, and she was glad that she had taken the time to understand him better.

As she returned to her duties, Amber's mind was already racing with the possibilities. With Casey and Rigo working together, along with Aidan and the rest of the team, maybe they really did stand a chance against the forces that threatened to tear Blacksburg apart.

****

Casey paced the length of the warehouse, her mind racing with the new information Amber had provided. The involvement of Braydon Mitchell and his right-hand man, Tyler Keal, added a dangerous new dimension to the case. She glanced over at Aidan, who was hunched over his computer setup, his fingers flying over the keys.

Just then, the shrill ring of Casey's phone pierced the air. She glanced at the caller ID and frowned. "It's Joshua Butler, the museum curator," she said, answering the call. "Mr. Butler, what can I do for you?"

Aidan looked up from his work, his interest piqued, as Casey listened intently to the curator's words. After a few moments, she nodded. "Understood. We'll meet you there in an hour. And Mr. Butler? Thank you for reaching out. We appreciate your cooperation."

As Casey ended the call, Aidan raised an eyebrow. "What was that about?"

Casey sighed, running a hand through her hair. "Butler wants to meet with us privately, away from Blackwell. He says he has information about the Idol that he couldn't share at the museum. We're meeting him at the old clocktower in an hour."

Aidan nodded, his expression thoughtful. "Sounds like he doesn't trust Blackwell any more than we do. This could be the break we need."

Casey agreed, feeling a flicker of hope in her chest. "Let's hope so. But before we head out, there's something I want to show you."

Aidan followed Casey to the center of the warehouse, where a large, sleek computer system stood. "Casey, meet KIVO - the Kenta Intelligent Voice Operator. It's the AI system I've been developing for our base of operations."

Casey's eyes widened as a holographic interface sprang to life before them. "Good afternoon, Special Agent Elkins," a smooth, artificial voice greeted her. "It's a pleasure to make your acquaintance."

Aidan grinned, clearly proud of his creation. "KIVO, from now on, you'll be following orders from both myself and Agent Elkins. We're going to need your help to track down the Idol of Lycoan and stop those who stole it."

"Understood, Mr. Kenta," KIVO responded. "How may I assist you?"

Casey stepped forward, her mind already racing with the possibilities. "KIVO, we need you to gather all available information on the previous users of the Idol. Anything you can find - historical records, eyewitness accounts, even rumors and legends. We need to know who has had access to this artifact in the past, and what they might have used it for."

"Right away, Agent Elkins," KIVO said, the holographic interface shifting and changing as the AI began its search. "I'll compile a comprehensive report and have it ready for you upon your return."

Aidan nodded, satisfied. "Thanks, KIVO. Keep us updated on any new developments."

As they prepared to leave for the meeting with Joshua Butler, Casey couldn't help but feel a renewed sense of determination. With KIVO on their side, they were one step closer to unraveling the mystery of the Idol and stopping those who sought to use its power for evil.

The clocktower loomed in the distance, a silent sentinel watching over the city. And as Casey and Aidan made their way towards it, they knew that the answers they sought were waiting for them, just beyond the horizon.

****

The Open Air Trailer Park was a far cry from the bustling streets of Blacksburg. Nestled on the outskirts of town, the park had become a haven for Braydon Mitchell's clan of Were-Panthers, a tight-knit community bound by loyalty and a shared thirst for power.

As Chief Dustin Blackwell navigated the narrow lanes of the park, he couldn't help but feel a sense of unease. The eyes of the Were-Panthers followed his every move, their gazes a mix of suspicion and disdain. He knew he was an outsider here, tolerated only because of his uneasy alliance with Braydon.

Braydon's mobile home was easy to spot, a gleaming

testament to his status as the alpha of the clan. It was the newest and most luxurious in the park, a stark contrast to the weathered and worn trailers surrounding it.

Dustin climbed the steps to Braydon's door, his hand hovering over the knock. He took a deep breath, steeling himself for the encounter ahead. Braydon was not a man to be trifled with, and Dustin knew that he was walking a dangerous line by aligning himself with the Were-Panther leader.

The door swung open before Dustin could knock, revealing Braydon's imposing figure. He was tall and lean, with a coiled strength that seemed to radiate from every pore. His dark hair was slicked back, and his eyes glinted with a predatory intelligence.

"Chief Blackwell," Braydon drawled, his voice a low purr. "To what do I owe the pleasure?"

Dustin swallowed hard, fighting to keep his composure. "We need to talk, Braydon. The RIPD is getting closer, and I don't know how much longer I can keep them off your trail."

Braydon's eyes narrowed, and he stepped aside, gesturing for Dustin to enter. The interior of the mobile home was a study in luxury, with plush leather furniture and gleaming chrome accents. Braydon settled himself on a couch, his long legs stretched out before him.

"The RIPD is not your concern, Dustin," Braydon said, his tone deceptively casual. "You just focus on keeping your men in line and making sure no one connects me to the Idol's disappearance."

Dustin's jaw clenched, a flicker of anger sparking in his chest. "It's not that simple, Braydon. They've sent a special agent, and from what I hear, they're relentless. They won't stop until they get to the truth."

Braydon's lips curled into a smirk, and he leaned forward, his elbows resting on his knees. "A special agent, huh? Well, let them come. They have no idea what they're up against. The Idol is just the beginning, Dustin. With its power, I'll be able to control not just the lycans, but the entire town. And you'll be right there by my side, reaping the rewards."

Dustin's heart raced, a mix of fear and anticipation coursing through his veins. He knew he was making a deal with the devil, but the promise of power and wealth was too tempting to resist.

"Just keep the RIPD off my back," Braydon said, his voice hardening. "I'll take care of the rest. And Dustin? Don't disappoint me. You wouldn't like the consequences."

Dustin nodded, his throat dry. He stood, eager to be out of Braydon's presence. As he made his way back to his car, he couldn't shake the feeling that he was in over his head.

As Dustin's car disappeared down the winding lanes of the Open Air Trailer Park, Braydon stood at the window of his mobile home, his eyes narrowed in thought. The news of an RIPD special agent sniffing around was an unwelcome development, one that could potentially derail his carefully laid plans.

He turned as the door opened, revealing Tyler Keal, his right-hand man and most trusted enforcer. Tyler was a wiry man with a perpetual sneer etched onto his face, his eyes glinting with a cruel intelligence.

"Tyler," Braydon said, his voice low and urgent. "We have a problem."

Tyler stepped inside, his posture tense and alert. "What's going on, boss?"

Braydon moved to the couch, sinking down onto the plush leather. "Blackwell just informed me that the RIPD has sent a special agent to investigate the Idol's theft. We need to know who we're dealing with."

Tyler's brow furrowed, his mind already racing with possibilities. "Want me to do some digging? I've got contacts in the department, people who owe me favors."

Braydon nodded, a slow smile spreading across his face. "Do it. I want to know everything about this agent - their name, their background, their weaknesses. We need to be prepared for any eventuality."

Tyler grinned, a predatory glint in his eye. "Consider it done, boss. I'll have the information for you by nightfall."

Braydon leaned back, his fingers steepled in front of him. "Good. In the meantime, I want you to double the patrols around the park. Make sure no one gets in or out without our knowledge. We can't afford any surprises."

Tyler nodded, his posture straightening with purpose. "I'll get the boys on it right away. And what about the Idol? Is it secure?"

Braydon's eyes flashed with a fierce possessiveness. "The Idol is safe, hidden away where no one will ever find it. But we need to accelerate our plans. The RIPD's involvement could complicate matters."

Tyler's smile turned vicious, his teeth glinting in the low light. "Don't worry, boss. We'll handle anyone who gets in our way. The Idol's power will be ours, and Blacksburg will tremble at our feet."

Braydon chuckled, a low and menacing sound. "That's the spirit, Tyler. Now get to work. We have a town to conquer and a special agent to destroy."

Tyler nodded, his eyes alight with anticipation. He turned and strode out of the mobile home, his steps filled with purpose and determination.

Braydon watched him go, his mind already spinning with plans and contingencies. The RIPD agent was an unknown variable, a potential threat to his carefully crafted schemes. But he was confident in his own power and the loyalty of his clan.

He stood and moved to the window, his gaze sweeping over the Open Air Trailer Park. This was his kingdom, his domain, and he would let nothing and no one stand in his way. The Idol of Lycoan was the key to his ultimate triumph, and he would wield its power with a ruthless and unrelenting hand.

The RIPD agent, whoever they were, had no idea what they were up against. Braydon smiled, a cold and cruel twist of his lips. They would learn soon enough, and by then, it would be far too late.

CHAPTER 4

The old clocktower loomed above the city, its weathered face a testament to the passage of time. Casey and Aidan stood at its base, their eyes scanning the surrounding area for any sign of Joshua Butler.

Casey checked her watch, a frown creasing her brow. "He should be here by now. You don't think he got cold feet, do you?"

Aidan shook his head, his gaze still fixed on the clocktower's entrance. "Butler seemed pretty adamant about meeting us. I don't think he's the type to back out."

Just then, a figure emerged from the shadows, his movements furtive and cautious. As he drew closer, Casey recognized the museum curator's distinctive features, his face lined with worry and tension.

"Mr. Butler," Casey called out, her voice low and urgent. "Over here."

Joshua Butler hurried over to them, his eyes darting around as if expecting danger at any moment. "Thank you for coming," he said, his voice trembling slightly. "I didn't know who else to turn to."

Casey placed a reassuring hand on his arm, her expression serious. "You did the right thing, Mr. Butler. Now, tell us what you know about the Idol of Lycoan."

Butler took a deep breath, his hands clenching and unclenching at his sides. "The Idol is more than just a historical artifact. It's a source of immense power, one that has been sought after for centuries by those who would use it for their own gain."

Aidan leaned forward, his interest piqued. "What kind of power are we talking about here?"

Butler's eyes took on a distant look, as if recalling an ancient tale. "To understand the Idol's power, you must first know the story of Lycoan, the Greek king who dared to defy the gods."

Casey and Aidan exchanged a glance, their curiosity growing with each passing moment.

"According to the legend," Butler continued, "Lycoan was a king who sought to test the omniscience of Zeus. In a foolish attempt to trick the god, Lycoan served him a feast of human flesh, believing that Zeus would not know the difference."

Casey's stomach churned at the thought, her revulsion mirrored in Aidan's eyes.

"But Zeus, in his wisdom, saw through the deception. Enraged by Lycoan's hubris, he cursed the king to become a wolf, doomed to transform at each full moon. Lycoan, however, learned to harness his curse, using it to create other were-wolves and build an army of loyal followers."

Aidan's brow furrowed, his mind racing with the implications. "So, Lycoan was the first lycan?"

Butler nodded, his expression grave. "Yes, but his story did not end there. Over time, Lycoan's power grew, and his control over his lycans became legendary. Zeus, seeing the potential in Lycoan's abilities, granted him the Idol as a means to help control the urges of his followers, to keep them from descending into mindless beasts."

Casey leaned forward, her eyes intense. "But something went wrong, didn't it?"

Butler sighed, his shoulders sagging with the weight of the tale. "Yes. Lycoan, drunk on his own power, began to corrupt the Idol. He twisted its purpose, using it to exert his will over not just his own lycans, but all those who crossed his path. The Idol became a tool of domination, a weapon in the hands of a mad king."

Aidan's jaw clenched, his mind already racing with the possibilities. "And now, someone has stolen the Idol, hoping to use its power for their own ends."

Butler nodded, his face etched with worry. "Yes, but there's more. The Idol's power can only be wielded by a lycan. In the hands of a human, it is nothing more than a historical curiosity."

Casey's eyes widened, the pieces of the puzzle falling into place. "Braydon Mitchell. He's a lycan, isn't he?"

Butler's gaze met hers, his expression grim. "I believe so. And if he has the Idol, if he learns to control its power..."

He trailed off, the implications hanging heavy in the air. Casey and Aidan exchanged a look, their faces set with determination.

"We need to find that Idol," Casey said, her voice hard with resolve. "Before Braydon can use it to create his own army of lycans."

Aidan nodded, his hand reaching for his phone, but Casey stopped him with a gentle touch on his arm. "Wait, Aidan. Before we have KIVO start searching for lycan activity, I have a few more questions."

She turned to Butler, her gaze intense. "Mr. Butler, what are the ramifications of Braydon simply possessing the Idol? How much does it increase his strength and speed, his healing factor?"

Butler's brow furrowed, his mind delving into the depths of his knowledge. "The Idol's power is not to be underestimated. Even in the hands of a lycan who has not yet fully mastered its control, it can grant a significant boost to their physical abilities."

He paused, his eyes distant as if recalling an ancient text. "According to the legends, a lycan in possession of the Idol can experience a tenfold increase in strength and speed. Their agility and reflexes become superhuman, allowing them to perform feats that would be impossible for even the most skilled human athlete."

Casey's heart raced at the thought, her mind conjuring images of Braydon as an unstoppable force. "And his healing factor? How much does the Idol enhance that?"

Butler's expression grew grim, his voice low and somber. "The Idol's influence on a lycan's healing is perhaps its most frightening aspect. With the artifact in their possession, a lycan can recover from wounds that would be fatal to a human in a matter of moments. Broken bones knit back together, torn flesh mends itself, and even the most grievous injuries become little more than temporary inconveniences."

Aidan's eyes widened, the implications sinking in. "So, if Braydon has the Idol, he's not just stronger and faster, he's practically invincible."

Butler nodded, his face etched with worry. "Yes, and that's not all. The Idol's power grows with each passing day, as the lycan attunes themselves to its energy. The longer Braydon holds the Idol, the more formidable he becomes."

Casey's jaw clenched, her resolve hardening with each revelation. "Then we don't have a moment to lose. Every second that Idol remains in Braydon's hands, he grows more powerful, more dangerous."

She turned to Aidan, her eyes blazing with determination. "Aidan, have KIVO run that analysis on the recent lycan activity. We need to find a pattern, a lead, anything that can help us track down Braydon and the Idol."

Aidan nodded, his fingers already flying over his phone's screen. "On it, Casey. KIVO will scour every database, every report, until we find something we can use."

Casey turned back to Butler, her expression softening with gratitude. "Thank you, Mr. Butler, for all your help. We couldn't do this without you."

Butler managed a small smile, his eyes filled with a mixture of fear and hope. "I only pray that you can find the Idol in time. The fate of Blacksburg, perhaps even the world, rests on your shoulders."

As the clocktower chimed above them, Casey and Aidan exchanged a look of grim determination. The stakes had never been higher, the danger never more pressing. But they would not rest until the Idol was found and Braydon's reign of terror was brought to an end.

The streets of Blacksburg were quiet, the stillness of the night broken only by the occasional passing car and the distant barking of a dog. Joshua Butler walked briskly, his hands buried deep in his pockets and his head bowed against the chill of the evening air.

His mind raced with the events of the past few hours, the weight of the knowledge he had shared with Casey and Aidan sitting heavy on his shoulders. He knew he had done the right thing, but the fear of the unknown, of the dangers that lurked in the shadows, gnawed at his nerves.

As he turned the corner onto his street, a figure stepped out from the darkness, blocking his path. Butler's heart leapt into his throat, his body tensing with instinctive fear.

"Mr. Butler," a familiar voice drawled, the sound sending a shiver down the curator's spine. "Fancy meeting you here."

Chief Dustin Blackwell emerged from the shadows, his face cast in sharp relief by the glow of the streetlights. His expression was hard, his eyes glinting with a dangerous light.

Butler swallowed hard, his mouth suddenly dry. "Chief Blackwell. What are you doing here?"

Blackwell stepped closer, his movements slow and deliberate. "I could ask you the same question, Mr. Butler. Out for a late-night stroll, are we?"

Butler's mind raced, searching for an excuse, a way to deflect the chief's suspicions. "I was just... I needed some air. It's been a long day at the museum, what with the investigation and all."

Blackwell's lips curled into a humorless smile, his eyes boring into Butler's. "Is that so? And I suppose your little meeting with Agent Elkins and her partner was just a coincidence, then?"

Butler's blood ran cold, his heart pounding in his chest. "I... I don't know what you're talking about."

Blackwell's hand shot out, grabbing Butler by the lapel

of his coat and slamming him against the wall of the nearest building. The curator gasped, the air driven from his lungs by the force of the impact.

"Don't lie to me, Butler," Blackwell snarled, his face inches from the curator's. "I have eyes and ears everywhere in this town. I know you met with Elkins and that tech geek of hers. What did you tell them?"

Butler's mind spun, fear and adrenaline coursing through his veins. He knew he couldn't betray Casey and Aidan, couldn't reveal the secrets he had shared. But the look in Blackwell's eyes, the barely contained rage and menace, made his resolve waver.

"I... I didn't tell them anything," he stammered, his voice shaking. "I swear, I don't know anything about the Idol or who stole it."

Blackwell's grip tightened, his knuckles turning white with the force of his anger. "You're lying," he hissed, his breath hot against Butler's face. "And I don't like liars, Mr. Butler. They have a habit of ending up in very unpleasant situations."

Butler's heart raced, his mind desperately searching for a way out, an escape from the chief's wrath. But before he could form a coherent thought, a voice cut through the night, sharp and commanding.

"Let him go, Blackwell."

The chief's head snapped around, his eyes widening in surprise. There, at the end of the street, stood Casey Elkins, her gun leveled at Blackwell's head and her expression hard as stone.

Blackwell's grip on Butler loosened, his hands slowly raising in a gesture of surrender. "Agent Elkins," he said, his voice dripping with false cheer. "What a surprise to see you here."

Casey's eyes narrowed, her aim unwavering. "Step away from Mr. Butler, Chief. Slowly."

Blackwell complied, his movements stiff and cautious. He glanced at Butler, his eyes filled with a promise of retribution. "This isn't over, Butler," he muttered, his voice low and menacing. "You'll regret crossing me."

With that, the chief turned and stalked away, his form quickly swallowed by the darkness. Butler sagged against the wall, his legs suddenly weak and his heart racing.

Casey holstered her gun, her expression softening as she approached the curator. "Mr. Butler, are you all right?"

Butler nodded, his voice shaking as he spoke. "I... I think so. Thank you, Agent Elkins. If you hadn't shown up when you did..."

Casey placed a comforting hand on his shoulder, her eyes filled with understanding. "It's okay, Mr. Butler. You're safe now. But I think it's best if you come with me. We need to get you somewhere secure, somewhere Blackwell and his men can't reach you."

Butler nodded, his mind still reeling from the encounter. As he followed Casey down the street, he couldn't shake the feeling that this was only the beginning, that the dangers lurking in the shadows of Blacksburg were far from over.

Butler's hands trembled as he followed Casey down the street, his mind still reeling from the encounter with Chief Blackwell. Despite the agent's reassuring presence, he couldn't shake the feeling of impending doom, the sense that nowhere in Blacksburg was truly safe.

"Agent Elkins," he said, his voice barely above a whisper. "I appreciate your offer of protection, but I fear that nowhere in this town is beyond the reach of Blackwell and his friends. They have eyes and ears everywhere, and they won't stop until they get what they want."

Casey glanced at the curator, her expression serious but determined. "I understand your concerns, Mr. Butler. But I can assure you, we have a place that even Blackwell can't touch."

Butler's brow furrowed, a flicker of hope springing to life in his chest. "What do you mean?"

Casey smiled, a hint of pride in her eyes. "Aidan and I have set up a base of operations, a secure location that's completely off the grid. It's equipped with state-of-the-art security systems and shielded from any form of surveillance. You'll be safe there while we continue our investigation."

Butler's shoulders sagged with relief, a weight lifting from his heart. "I... I don't know what to say, Agent Elkins. Thank you. Thank you for everything you're doing."

Casey placed a comforting hand on his arm, her touch warm and reassuring. "It's our job, Mr. Butler. And more than that, it's the right thing to do. We won't let Blackwell or anyone else hurt you or those you care about."

As they walked, Casey pulled out her phone, her fingers flying over the screen. "I'm letting Aidan know to expect us. He'll make sure everything is ready for your arrival."

Butler nodded, a sense of gratitude and awe washing over him. He had always known that the RIPD was dedicated to protecting the innocent and upholding justice, but to see it in action, to be on the receiving end of that commitment... it was humbling and inspiring in equal measure.

The streets of Blacksburg passed by in a blur, the familiar landmarks taking on a new and ominous character in the wake of his encounter with Blackwell. But with each step, Butler felt a growing sense of hope, a belief that maybe, just maybe, they could overcome the darkness that had taken root in his beloved town.

As they approached the outskirts of the city, a nondescript warehouse came into view, its exterior belying the secrets that lay within. Casey led Butler to a side entrance, her hand resting on the handle of her gun as she scanned the area for any signs of trouble.

Satisfied that they were alone, she pushed open the door, revealing a cavernous space filled with high-tech equipment and the low hum of powerful computers. Aidan looked up from his workstation, a smile of welcome on his face.

"Mr. Butler," he said, rising to greet them. "I'm glad you're safe. Welcome to our base of operations."

Butler looked around, his eyes wide with wonder. "This is incredible," he breathed, taking in the gleaming screens and the rows of servers. "I've never seen anything like it."

Casey grinned, a hint of mischief in her eyes. "And that's just the beginning. With Aidan's expertise and KIVO's capabilities, we have resources at our disposal that Blackwell can only dream of."

As if on cue, the holographic interface of KIVO sprang to life, the AI's soothing voice filling the air. "Welcome, Mr. Butler. I am KIVO, the Kenta Intelligent Voice Operator. I am at your service."

Butler shook his head, a sense of awe and gratitude overwhelming him. "I... I don't know what to say. Thank you, all of you. For everything."

Casey and Aidan exchanged a look, their expressions

mirroring the determination and resolve that had brought them to this point. They knew that the road ahead would be long and fraught with danger, that the forces arrayed against them were formidable and ruthless.

***************************:

The neon sign of Ye Ole Tavern flickered and buzzed, casting an eerie glow over the rain-slicked streets of Blacksburg. Rigo Balderas stepped out of the shadows, his leather jacket glistening with droplets of water and his eyes scanning the crowd that spilled out of the bar's entrance.

He had been following his own leads into the disappearance of the Idol of Lycoan, chasing down whispers and rumors that had led him to this unassuming watering hole on the outskirts of town. It wasn't the kind of place he usually frequented, but in his line of work, you went where the information took you.

As he shouldered his way through the throng of patrons, his heightened senses picked up on a familiar scent, one that stood out among the sweat and alcohol that permeated the air. His eyes narrowed, his gaze sweeping the room until they settled on a familiar figure at the bar.

Amber Collins, the waitress from Danny's Cafe, was perched on a stool, her blonde hair falling in waves over her shoulders and her eyes fixed on the drink in front of her. She looked out of place in the rough-and-tumble crowd, a delicate flower among thorns.

Rigo's instincts kicked into high gear, his mind racing with the possibilities. What was Amber doing here, alone and unprotected? And why did he have the sinking feeling that her presence was more than just a coincidence?

He made his way to the bar, his movements casual but

his senses on high alert. As he drew closer, he noticed a group of men watching Amber from the corner of the room, their eyes glinting with a predatory light that set Rigo's teeth on edge.

They were were-panthers, Rigo realized with a start. Members of Braydon Mitchell's clan, by the look of them. And they had their sights set on Amber.

Rigo's hand tightened around the glass in his hand, his jaw clenching with barely contained rage. He had seen firsthand the cruelty and depravity that Braydon's crew was capable of, and he'd be damned if he let them lay a finger on an innocent like Amber.

He stepped up to the bar, his presence causing Amber to look up in surprise. "Rigo," she said, her voice barely audible over the din of the crowd. "What are you doing here?"

Rigo leaned in close, his voice low and urgent. "We need to get you out of here, Amber. Now."

Amber's eyes widened, her brow furrowing in confusion. "What? Why? I'm just having a drink..."

But before she could finish her sentence, the group of were-panthers made their move. They surged forward, their eyes flashing with malice and their claws extending from their fingertips.

Rigo was ready for them. He moved with lightning speed, his own claws and fangs emerging as he placed himself between Amber and the attackers. A snarl ripped from his throat, a warning and a challenge all in one.

The were-panthers hesitated, their eyes flickering with uncertainty. They knew Rigo by reputation, knew the power and ferocity of the Hyena Hybrid. But their hesitation was short-lived, their loyalty to Braydon overriding their sense of self-preservation.

They attacked as one, a blur of claws and teeth and raw, primal fury. But Rigo was faster, his movements a dance of deadly grace. He dodged and weaved, his own claws finding flesh and bone with sickening accuracy.

Amber screamed, her eyes wide with terror as she watched the battle unfold. But Rigo was relentless, his focus unwavering as he tore through the were-panthers like a hot knife through butter.

In a matter of moments, it was over. The were-panthers lay broken and bleeding on the floor, their faces twisted in agony and defeat. Rigo stood over them, his chest heaving and his eyes blazing with a savage light.

He turned to Amber, his expression softening as he saw the fear in her eyes. "Come on," he said, his voice gentle but firm. "Let's get you out of here."

Amber nodded, her hands shaking as she allowed Rigo to guide her through the stunned crowd and out into the cool night air. As they stepped onto the street, Rigo's mind was already racing with the implications of what had just happened.

The were-panthers had been bold, attacking in public like that. It was a sign of their growing confidence, their belief that they were untouchable. And if they were willing to go after Amber, then no one in Blacksburg was safe.

Rigo knew that he had to get to the bottom of this, had to find out what Braydon and his crew were planning. But first, he had to make sure Amber was safe.

He glanced at the waitress, her face pale and her eyes haunted. "Don't worry," he said, his voice filled with a quiet determination. "I won't let anything happen to you. I promise."

And as they disappeared into the night, Rigo knew that he would keep that promise, no matter the cost. Because in a world filled with monsters and demons, sometimes the only thing you had was your word.

Rigo knew that he had to get to the bottom of this, had to find out what Braydon and his crew were planning. But first, he had to make sure Amber was safe.

He glanced at the waitress, her face pale and her eyes haunted. "Don't worry," he said, his voice filled with a quiet determination. "I won't let anything happen to you. I promise."

Amber nodded, her breathing slowly returning to normal as the adrenaline of the moment began to fade. Suddenly, her eyes widened, a spark of realization flickering in their depths.

"Rigo," she said, her voice urgent. "We need to call Casey, like we talked about before. This attack, it's proof that Braydon and his crew are getting bolder. Casey needs to know what's happening."

Rigo nodded, remembering his earlier conversation with Amber about the RIPD agent. He had been intrigued by what he had heard of Casey Elkins, her reputation as a brilliant and tenacious investigator preceding her.

"You're right," he said, his voice filled with a new sense of purpose. "Let's give her a call. Set up that meeting. If we're going to take on Braydon and his crew, we're going to need all the help we can get."

Amber smiled, a flicker of hope sparking in her eyes. She pulled out her phone, her fingers flying over the screen as she dialed Casey's number.

"Casey," she said, her voice filled with a mix of relief and urgency. "It's Amber. Remember how I told you about Rigo

Balderas, the Hyena Hybrid who wanted to meet with you? Well, we just had a run-in with some of Braydon's were-panthers at Ye Ole Tavern. We need to talk. Can you meet us?"

There was a pause, a moment of silence as Casey responded on the other end of the line. Then Amber nodded, a small smile tugging at the corners of her lips.

"Great. We'll see you there."

She ended the call, turning to Rigo with a look of determination. "Casey's on her way. She said to meet her at the old abandoned warehouse on the edge of town. She and her partner have set up a base of operations there."

Rigo nodded, his mind already racing with the possibilities. A base of operations sounded like just what they needed, a place to regroup and plan their next move.

"Lead the way," he said, his voice filled with a quiet resolve. "Let's go meet this Casey Elkins and see if she's as good as they say."

And as they set off into the night, Rigo couldn't shake the feeling that this was a turning point, that the fight for Blacksburg's future was about to enter a new phase.

CHAPTER 5

The abandoned warehouse loomed before them, its rusted metal walls and shattered windows a testament to the passage of time. But as Rigo and Amber approached the nondescript entrance, they could sense that there was more to this place than met the eye.

Amber knocked on the heavy metal door, a sense of familiarity and excitement in her movements. The door swung open, revealing the warm glow of light and the hum of advanced technology within.

Casey stood in the doorway, a smile spreading across her face as she saw her old friend. "Amber!" she exclaimed, pulling the waitress into a hug. "I'm so glad you're okay. And you must be Rigo Balderas," she said, turning to the Hyena Hybrid with a nod of respect.

Rigo returned the nod, his eyes taking in the impressive setup of the warehouse. "Casey Elkins, I presume. It's an honor to finally meet you. Amber speaks very highly of you."

As they stepped inside, Amber's eyes widened in amazement at the transformation of the space. Sleek computer terminals, high-tech surveillance equipment, and a dizzying array of gadgets and gizmos filled the room.

At the center of it all stood a tall, lanky man with a mop of unruly hair and a gleam of excitement in his eyes. He bounded forward, his hand outstretched in greeting.

"Welcome to our headquarters," he said, his voice filled with a contagious enthusiasm. "I'm Aidan Kenta, Casey's partner. It's great to meet you both."

Amber shook Aidan's hand, a smile spreading across her face. "Likewise, Aidan. This place is incredible!"

Aidan grinned, his chest puffing up with pride. "Wait until you meet KIVO, our AI assistant."

He gestured to a holographic display in the center of the room, where a shimmering blue avatar hovered in midair. "KIVO, say hello to our guests."

The avatar pulsed with light, its voice smooth and soothing. "Greetings, Mr. Balderas and Ms. Collins. It is a pleasure to make your acquaintance. I am KIVO, the Kenta Intelligent Voice Operator. I am at your service."

Rigo and Amber exchanged a glance of amazement, their faces filled with awe at the advanced technology before them.

Casey stepped forward, her expression growing serious. "Amber, Rigo, there's someone else I'd like you to meet."

She gestured to a man sitting quietly in the corner, his face lined with worry and fatigue. "This is Joshua Butler, the museum curator who was attacked by Chief Blackwell. He's been helping us with our investigation into the Idol's theft."

Amber's face softened with sympathy, while Rigo's jaw clenched in anger at the mention of Blackwell's actions.

"Mr. Butler," Rigo said, his voice filled with a quiet strength. "I'm sorry for what you've been through. But you're safe here, among friends. We'll do everything in our power to protect you and bring those responsible for the Idol's theft to justice."

Butler looked up, his eyes filled with a glimmer of hope. "Thank you, Mr. Balderas. That means more than you know."

As the group settled in, their attention turned to the task at hand. Casey pulled up a series of images on the holographic display, each one showing a different angle of the museum and the surrounding area.

"Alright, team," she said, her voice filled with a quiet intensity. "Let's get to work. We've got an Idol to find and a city to save. And with all of us working together, I know we can do it."

And as the night wore on, the abandoned warehouse hummed with the energy of a group united in purpose, their minds and hearts set on the singular goal of bringing light to the darkness that threatened to engulf their beloved city.

****

The interior of Braydon's mobile home was a stark contrast to the chaotic events unfolding in the city beyond. The sleek, modern furnishings and gleaming surfaces belied the darkness that lurked within the heart of the Panther Prowl's leader.

Braydon sat on the plush leather couch, his eyes fixed on the tablet in his hands. The screen displayed a series of surveillance feeds from around Blacksburg, each one a window into the machinations of his growing empire.

A sharp knock at the door shattered the stillness, and Braydon looked up, his brow furrowing in annoyance. He set the tablet aside and rose to his feet, his movements fluid and predatory.

When he opened the door, he found himself face to face with Chief Dustin Blackwell, the man's expression a mix of anger and frustration.

"Braydon," Blackwell said, his voice tight with barely contained fury. "We need to talk."

Braydon stepped aside, allowing the police chief to enter. "Dustin, what brings you to my humble abode at this hour?"

Blackwell whirled around, his finger jabbing at Braydon's chest. "Don't play games with me, Mitchell. Your were-panthers attacked a group of civilians at Ye Ole Tavern tonight. In public, for all to see!"

Braydon's eyes narrowed, a flicker of irritation passing across his features. "They were acting on my orders, Dustin. The waitress, Amber Collins, has been aiding the RIPD in their investigation. She needed to be reminded of her place."

Blackwell's face reddened, his fists clenching at his sides. "Damn it, Braydon! We had a deal. You keep your lycans under control, and I keep the authorities off your back. But this? This is the opposite of control!"

Braydon's lips curled into a sneer, his eyes flashing with a dangerous light. "Don't presume to lecture me, Dustin. I am the alpha of the Panther Prowl, and my word is law. If I deem it necessary to send a message, then that is what shall be done."

Blackwell took a step forward, his voice lowering to a hiss. "Listen to me carefully, Mitchell. If you can't keep your were-panthers in line, then our arrangement is off. I won't hesitate to bring the full force of the law down upon you and your clan."

For a long moment, the two men stared each other down, the air between them crackling with tension. Then, slowly, Braydon's posture relaxed, a calculated smile spreading across his face.

"Very well, Dustin. You've made your point. I will ensure that my lycans exercise more discretion in the future. But don't forget, I have the Idol of Lycoan in my possession. It's only a matter of time before I unlock its true power, and then Blacksburg will tremble before the might of the Panther Prowl."

Blackwell's eyes widened, a flicker of fear passing across his features. "I know this, Mitchell, but it doesn't give you the right to start making dangerous decisions with the Idol. You can't let this blow up in our face. The Idol is dangerous."

Braydon's smile widened, a malevolent gleam in his eyes. "Dangerous to my enemies, perhaps. But to me, it is the key to unlocking my true potential. Once I master its secrets, no one will be able to stand against me, not even the RIPD."

Blackwell shook his head, his expression one of grim determination. "Just remember, Braydon. I'm watching you. One false move, and our deal is off."

With that, the police chief turned and stalked out of the mobile home, leaving Braydon alone with his thoughts.

The lycan leader returned to his seat on the couch, his hand reaching into his pocket to withdraw a small, intricately carved wooden box. He opened the lid, revealing the Idol of Lycoan nestled within, its surface pulsing with an otherworldly energy.

Braydon picked up the Idol, feeling its power thrumming through his veins. He had possessed the artifact for weeks now, ever since his daring heist at the museum. But despite his best efforts, he had yet to unlock its full potential.

He knew that the key to controlling the Idol lay in the ancient rituals and incantations of the lycans who had come before him. He had spent countless hours poring over dusty tomes and crumbling scrolls, seeking the knowledge that would make him the master of the Idol's power.

But he also knew that time was running out. The RIPD was closing in, and his own were-panthers were growing restless. He needed to act fast, to seize the power that was rightfully his before it was too late.

And as he sat there, the Idol cradled in his hands, Braydon made a silent vow. He would not rest until he had unlocked the secrets of the artifact, until he had bent its power to his will.

For he was Braydon Mitchell, the alpha of the Panther Prowl, and he would let nothing stand in the way of his destiny.

Not the RIPD, not Chief Blackwell, and certainly not the feeble humans who dared to oppose him.

The Idol of Lycoan was his, and with it, he would reshape the world in his own dark image.

It was only a matter of time.

****

The interior of Chief Dustin Blackwell's police cruiser was a sanctuary of sorts, a place where he could escape the pressures of his job and the chaos of the world beyond. But tonight, as he sat behind the wheel, his mind was a whirlwind of conflicting thoughts and emotions.

The radio crackled to life, the dispatcher's voice filling the air with a sense of urgency. "All units, we have a reported animal attack at the corner of Maple and Oak. Victim is a female, approximately nineteen years of age. Ambulance is en route, but be advised, the scene is not secure."

Blackwell's hand tightened on the steering wheel, his jaw clenching with a mix of frustration and dread. Animal attacks were becoming all too common in Blacksburg these days, and he knew that they were anything but random.

He reached for the radio, his voice steady and composed as he responded. "This is Chief Blackwell. I'm en route to the scene now. Have the perimeter secured and keep all civilians back until I arrive."

As he pulled out onto the darkened streets, Blackwell's mind raced with the implications of the attack. He knew that he should call in the RIPD, that their expertise in handling supernatural threats was unparalleled.

But he also knew that involving the RIPD would mean admitting that he had lost control of his city, that the were-panthers and other lycans had grown too powerful for him to handle on his own.

And then there was the matter of his arrangement with Braydon Mitchell. If the RIPD discovered the extent of his involvement with the Panther Prowl, his career would be over, and his life would be forfeit.

As he approached the scene of the attack, Blackwell could see the flashing lights of the ambulance and the gathered crowd of onlookers. He parked his cruiser and stepped out, his expression grim and his shoulders squared.

The victim lay on the ground, her body covered in deep gashes and her clothing soaked with blood. The paramedics were already at work, their movements urgent and precise as they fought to stabilize her condition.

Blackwell knelt beside the girl, his eyes taking in the extent of her injuries. The wounds were unlike anything he had ever seen, ragged and vicious, as if she had been mauled by a creature of unimaginable strength and ferocity.

He stood, his mind racing with the possibilities. He knew that he needed to act fast, to contain the situation before word spread and panic took hold.

But he also knew that he was out of his depth, that the forces at work in Blacksburg were beyond his ability to control or comprehend.

For a moment, he considered reaching for his phone, dialing the number that would bring the RIPD to his doorstep. But then he remembered his conversation with Braydon, the warning in the lycan leader's eyes, and the promise of retribution should he betray their arrangement.

With a heavy sigh, Blackwell turned to his officers, his voice low and urgent. "Secure the scene and take statements from any witnesses. I want a full report on my desk by morning."

As he walked back to his cruiser, Blackwell couldn't shake the feeling that he was making a mistake, that his reluctance to involve the RIPD would come back to haunt him.

But he also knew that he had no choice, that his fate was inextricably tied to that of Braydon Mitchell and the Panther Prowl.

And as he drove off into the night, the weight of his decisions heavy on his shoulders, Blackwell could only pray that he had the strength to see this through to the end.

****

The interior of the abandoned warehouse was a hive of activity, the hum of advanced technology and the low murmur of conversation filling the air. Casey, Rigo, and Aidan stood huddled around the central console, their eyes fixed on the holographic display as they pored over the latest intelligence reports.

Suddenly, KIVO's avatar materialized before them, the AI's voice filled with a sense of urgency. "Excuse me, Agent

Elkins, but I have intercepted a police dispatch that I believe requires your immediate attention."

Casey looked up, her brow furrowing with concern. "What is it, KIVO? What's happened?"

The AI's voice was calm and precise, but there was an undercurrent of tension in its words. "There has been a reported animal attack at the corner of Maple and Oak. The victim is a young female, approximately nineteen years of age. The scene is not yet secure, and the police are en route."

Rigo's eyes narrowed, his posture tensing with a mix of anger and determination. "An animal attack? In the middle of the city? That's no coincidence."

Aidan nodded, his fingers already flying over the keyboard as he pulled up a map of the area. "Rigo's right. This has to be connected to the were-panthers and the Idol of Lycoan. We need to get out there and investigate before the police contaminate the scene."

Casey turned to Aidan, her expression serious and focused. "Aidan, I need you to stay here and man the computers. Keep an eye on the police scanners and the surveillance feeds. If anything else happens, I want to know about it immediately."

Aidan hesitated for a moment, his eyes flickering between Casey and the console. "Are you sure, Casey? I could be more useful out there with you and Rigo."

Casey placed a hand on his shoulder, her voice firm but reassuring. "I'm sure, Aidan. We need you here, coordinating our efforts and keeping everyone safe. Rigo and I can handle the investigation on the ground."

Aidan nodded, his expression one of acceptance and determination. "Alright, Casey. I'll keep things running smoothly here. But if you need backup, just say the word, and I'll be there in a heartbeat."

Casey smiled, her eyes filled with gratitude and affection. "I know you will, Aidan. Thank you."

She turned to Rigo, her expression hardening with resolve. "Alright, Balderas. Let's gear up and head out. We need to get to the scene before Blackwell and his men have a chance to cover anything up."

Rigo grinned, his eyes flashing with a predatory light. "Lead the way, Elkins. It's time to show these were-panthers that they're not the only hunters in this city."

As Casey and Rigo headed for the door, Aidan called out after them, his voice filled with a mix of concern and determination. "Be careful out there, you two. And remember, if you need anything, KIVO and I are just a comm link away."

Casey nodded, her hand resting on the butt of her sidearm. "We'll be careful, Aidan. And we'll be back before you know it, with answers and a plan to stop these attacks once and for all."

And with that, Casey and Rigo stepped out into the night, their senses heightened and their minds focused on the task at hand.

****

The scene at the corner of Maple and Oak was one of barely controlled chaos, the flashing lights of the police cruisers casting eerie shadows across the blood-stained pavement. Casey and Rigo approached the cordon, their expressions grim and their senses heightened.

Chief Blackwell stood at the center of the scene, his face a mask of forced composure as he barked orders to his officers.

When he saw Casey and Rigo, his eyes narrowed, and his jaw clenched with barely contained hostility.

"Agent Elkins, Mr. Balderas," he said, his voice dripping with false cordiality. "I wasn't aware that the RIPD had been invited to this little soirée."

Casey met his gaze, her expression cool and unflinching. "We go where the case takes us, Chief. And right now, it's taken us here."

She knelt beside the victim, her eyes scanning the wounds that marred the young woman's flesh. The gashes were deep and jagged, but there was something off about them, something that didn't quite match any lycan or animal attack she had ever seen.

Rigo crouched beside her, his nostrils flaring as he took in the scents that lingered at the scene. His brow furrowed, and he shook his head, his voice low and urgent.

"I don't recognize this scent, Casey. It's not were-panther, and it's definitely not any animal I've ever encountered. This is something new, something dangerous."

Blackwell cleared his throat, his voice cutting through the tension like a knife. "Actually, we have reason to believe that this attack was the work of a local were-jaguar by the name of Matt Mauney. He's been known to cause trouble in the past, and his rei signature matches the one found at the scene."

Casey stood, her eyes narrowing as she focused her senses on the ethereal energy that surrounded the victim. The rei was faint, but it was there, a shimmering aura that pulsed with an otherworldly light. She snapped a few pictures with her camera phone, immediately sending them to Aidan and KIVO.

She shook her head, her voice firm and unyielding. "I'm

afraid you're mistaken, Chief. The rei signature here doesn't match that of a were-jaguar. In fact, it doesn't match anything I've ever seen before."

Blackwell's face reddened, his composure slipping for a moment before he regained control. "I think I know how to do my job, Agent Elkins. And right now, my job is to keep the people of this city safe from the likes of Matt Mauney and his kind."

Rigo stood, his posture tense and his eyes flashing with a predatory light. "With all due respect, Chief, I think you're barking up the wrong tree. My nose doesn't lie, and it's telling me that there's a rogue lycan out there, one that doesn't fit any known profile."

Casey nodded, her hand resting on the butt of her sidearm. "Rigo's right. We need to expand our search, look for any clues or witnesses that might point us in the right direction. This attack is just the beginning, and if we don't act fast, there will be more bloodshed on the streets of Blacksburg."

Blackwell's eyes darted between Casey and Rigo, his expression one of barely contained rage. "I won't have you two interfering in my investigation. This is a police matter, and we will handle it as we see fit."

Casey stepped forward, her voice low and dangerous. "This stopped being just a police matter the moment that victim was attacked by a supernatural creature. The RIPD has jurisdiction here, and we will use every resource at our disposal to find the truth and stop this threat before it escalates."

She turned to Rigo, her expression one of grim determination. "Come on, Balderas. We have work to do."

As they walked away from the scene, Casey's mind raced with the implications of what they had discovered. A rogue lycan, one that defied classification and seemed to possess abilities beyond those of any known species.

It was a terrifying prospect, but one that she knew they had to confront head-on if they were to have any hope of saving their city. Stepping away from the hustle and bustle of the ambulance and Chief Blackwell, Casey dialed Aidan.

“Aidan, could you have KIVO try to analyze those pictures of the victim. We think we have a rogue lycan loose on top of everything else we have going on,” Casey says, “Rigo couldn’t smell a recognized lycan, and I couldn’t sense a recognized rei signature,”

As Casey and Aidan drop the calls, Rigo approaches. He is holding a small silver item inside a black bag. He presents it to Casey.

“Recognize this?” he asks.

“Afraid not. What am I looking at Balderas?” Casey asks, taking the item and holding it up in the bright light.

“That’s a sliver of Blessed Silver. It was found in the victim’s wound. Unsure of how it got there, but it was there,” Rigo explains, “I’m thinking KIVO could help locate its origin,”

“Good idea, partner. We should really get back and oversee the loading of the body, before we return to HQ,” Casey says.

****

The interior of the abandoned warehouse was a welcome sight as Casey and Rigo stepped through the door, the weight of the crime scene still heavy on their shoulders. Aidan looked up from his computer screen, his expression one of mingled concern and anticipation.

"Welcome back, you two," he said, his voice cutting

through the hum of the computers. "KIVO and I have been analyzing the photos you sent, and we've got some interesting findings."

Casey and Rigo exchanged a glance, their exhaustion tempered by a flicker of hope. They made their way to the central console, where KIVO's avatar hovered in midair, pulsing with a soft blue light.

"What have you got for us, KIVO?" Casey asked, her eyes scanning the holographic displays.

The AI's voice was calm and precise, but there was an undercurrent of excitement in its tone. "Based on the wound patterns and the residual energy signatures, I can confirm that the attacker was indeed a lycan, but one that does not match any known species or clan in my database."

Rigo nodded, his expression grim. "Just as we suspected. A rogue lycan, one that's gone off the grid and developed its own unique abilities."

Aidan leaned forward, his fingers flying over the keyboard as he pulled up a series of images and diagrams. "But that's not all. KIVO and I have been analyzing the sliver of Blessed Silver that Rigo found in the victim's wound. Based on its composition and energy signature, we believe it may have come from a sacred site or artifact, one with ties to the lycan community."

Casey's brow furrowed, her mind racing with the implications. "A sacred site? Like a temple or a shrine?"

KIVO's avatar pulsed with light, its voice filled with a note of affirmation. "Precisely, Agent Elkins. The Blessed Silver bears the hallmarks of a powerful ritual or blessing, one that would have required a great deal of knowledge and skill to perform."

Rigo's eyes narrowed, his posture tense with a newfound sense of urgency. "So we're not just dealing with a rogue lycan, but one that may have ties to a larger conspiracy or organization."

Casey nodded, her hand resting on the hilt of her sidearm. "And one that's not afraid to use sacred artifacts and dark magic to achieve its goals."

Aidan's expression was one of grim determination, his eyes locked on the screens before him. "I've already started running a search algorithm to cross-reference known lycan sacred sites with recent supernatural activity in Blacksburg. If there's a connection, we'll find it."

Casey placed a hand on his shoulder, her touch a silent gesture of gratitude and support. "Good work, Aidan. Keep digging, and let us know the moment you find anything."

She turned to Rigo, her expression one of steely resolve. "In the meantime, we need to hit the streets, shake down our contacts, and see if anyone's heard whispers of a new player in town. If this rogue lycan is out there, we need to find it before it strikes again."

Rigo cracked his knuckles, a predatory glint in his eyes. "Lead the way, partner. It's time to hunt."

As they gathered their gear and prepared to head back out into the night, Casey couldn't shake the feeling that they were on the cusp of something big, something that could change the balance of power in Blacksburg forever.

But she also knew that they were ready, that they had the skills, the knowledge, and the determination to face whatever challenges lay ahead.

As they gathered their gear and prepared to head back out

into the night, the shrill ring of Casey's phone pierced the air. She glanced at the caller ID and frowned, her expression one of mingled surprise and annoyance.

"Chief Blackwell," she said, her voice cool and measured as she answered the call. "To what do I owe the pleasure?"

Rigo and Aidan exchanged a glance, their postures tense as they listened to Casey's side of the conversation.

"I'm afraid that's not possible, Chief," Casey said, her jaw clenching with barely contained frustration. "The evidence we collected at the crime scene is part of an ongoing RIPD investigation. We can't just hand it over to the local authorities."

There was a pause, and then Casey's eyes narrowed, her voice taking on a harder edge. "With all due respect, Chief, the RIPD has jurisdiction in cases involving supernatural threats. And right now, we have reason to believe that this attack was the work of a rogue lycan, one that poses a danger to the entire city."

Another pause, and then Casey's expression turned to one of grim determination. "I understand your concerns, Chief, but I'm afraid my answer is final. We'll share our findings with you once our investigation is complete, but until then, the evidence stays with us."

She ended the call with a decisive tap of her finger, her eyes blazing with a mixture of anger and resolve. Rigo and Aidan looked at her expectantly, their own expressions mirroring her own.

"Let me guess," Rigo said, his voice dripping with sarcasm. "Chief Blackwell wants us to play nice and share our toys?"

Casey snorted, her lips twisting into a humorless smile. "Something like that. He seems to think that the RIPD is overstepping its bounds, and that the local police should be the ones leading the investigation."

Aidan shook his head, his fingers never stopping their dance across the keyboard. "He's just trying to cover his own ass, Casey. He knows that if word gets out about a rogue lycan terrorizing the city, it'll be a PR nightmare for the department."

Casey nodded, her expression one of grim understanding. "Which is why we need to get to the bottom of this, and fast. If Blackwell and his men get their hands on the evidence, there's no telling what they might do with it."

She turned to Rigo, her eyes flashing with a newfound sense of urgency. "We need to move, Balderas. Every minute we waste is another chance for this rogue to strike again."

Rigo cracked his knuckles, a feral grin spreading across his face. "Then what are we waiting for, partner? Let's hunt this bastard down and show it what happens when you mess with the RIPD."

As they strode out into the night, Casey couldn't shake the feeling that they were walking into a storm, one that would test their skills and their resolve like never before.

But she also knew that they were ready, that they had the strength and the determination to weather whatever challenges lay ahead.

CHAPTER 6

The ancient temple was a place of shadows and secrets, its crumbling walls and faded frescoes a testament to the passage of time. Braydon Mitchell stood at the center of the chamber, his eyes fixed on the stone altar before him, where the Idol of Lycoan rested in a pool of flickering candlelight.

He had spent weeks searching for this place, poring over ancient texts and crumbling maps, seeking the key to unlocking the Idol's true power. And now, here he was, on the brink of a discovery that could change the course of history.

Braydon reached out, his fingers trembling slightly as they brushed against the Idol's smooth surface. He could feel the energy pulsing within it, a tangible force that set his nerves on fire and made his heart race with a heady mixture of fear and anticipation.

He closed his eyes, his lips moving in a silent incantation as he called upon the ancient magic that had brought him to this moment. The words were unfamiliar, drawn from a language long dead and forgotten, but he spoke them with a fluency and confidence that belied his mortal origins.

As the final syllable left his lips, the Idol began to glow, its surface shimmering with an otherworldly light. Braydon's breath caught in his throat, his eyes widening as he watched the artifact come to life before him.

But something was wrong. The light was too bright, too intense, and it pulsed with a sickly, greenish hue that made his stomach churn and his head spin. He tried to pull his hand away, but it was as if the Idol had taken on a life of its own, its energy lashing out and ensnaring him in an unbreakable grip.

Braydon screamed, his voice echoing off the temple walls as the Idol's power surged through his body, setting his veins on fire and his mind ablaze with a thousand searing images. He saw himself as the ruler of a new world, a king among lycans, with an army of unstoppable beasts at his command.

But he also saw the price of that power, the sacrifices that would have to be made and the lives that would be lost in the pursuit of his twisted dream. And for a moment, just a moment, he faltered, his resolve wavering in the face of the terrible knowledge that flooded his mind.

And then, just as quickly as it had begun, the vision faded, and Braydon found himself once more in the temple, his hand still gripping the Idol and his body drenched in a cold sweat. He staggered back, his breath coming in ragged gasps as he tried to make sense of what had just happened.

Had the Idol rejected him, deeming him unworthy of its power? Or had it simply been toying with him, testing his resolve and his commitment to the dark path he had chosen?

Braydon didn't know, but he did know one thing: he would not give up, not now, not when he was so close to achieving his ultimate goal. He would find a way to master the Idol's power, to bend it to his will and use it to reshape the world in his own image.

For he was Braydon Mitchell, the alpha of the Panther Prowl, and he would let nothing stand in his way, not even the gods themselves.

As he stood there in the temple, his eyes blazing with a fevered light and his heart pounding with a savage determination, Braydon knew that his destiny was within reach.

And heaven help anyone who tried to stop him

The sound of footsteps echoed through the chamber, and Braydon turned, his senses heightened by the lingering energy of the Idol. He saw Tyler Keal and Kari Byars, his most trusted pridemates, emerging from the shadows, their faces etched with a mix of concern and awe.

"Braydon," Tyler said, his voice low and urgent. "We heard screaming. What happened? Are you alright?"

Braydon took a deep breath, his composure returning as he faced his loyal followers. "I'm fine, Tyler. More than fine, in fact."

He held up the Idol, its surface still glowing with a faint, pulsing light. "The Idol, it spoke to me. Showed me visions of the future, of the power that awaits us."

Kari stepped forward, her eyes wide with wonder and fear. "What did you see, Braydon? What does the future hold?"

Braydon's lips curved into a smile, a predatory expression that sent shivers down his pridemates' spines. "I saw a world where lycans rule, where we are the masters of our own destiny. A world where the Panther Prowl is feared and respected, and where our enemies tremble at the mere mention of our name."

Tyler's eyes gleamed with a fierce pride, his loyalty to Braydon unwavering. "And the Idol, it will help us achieve this vision?"

Braydon nodded, his gaze fixed on the artifact in his hand. "Yes, but it will not be easy. The Idol's power is great, but it is also wild, untamed. It will take time and sacrifice to master its secrets, to bend it to our will."

Kari's brow furrowed, a flicker of doubt crossing her face. "Sacrifice? What kind of sacrifice, Braydon?"

Braydon's expression hardened, his eyes boring into Kari's with an intensity that made her take a step back. "The kind that separates the strong from the weak, the worthy from the unworthy. The kind that demands blood and pain and unwavering dedication to the cause."

He turned to Tyler, his voice low and commanding. "Gather the pride, Tyler. Tell them to prepare for the rituals to come. We have work to do, and we cannot afford to waste a single moment."

Tyler nodded, his posture straightening with a newfound sense of purpose. "As you command, my alpha."

As Tyler and Kari left the chamber, Braydon turned back to the altar, his gaze fixed once more on the Idol. He could feel its power calling to him, whispering promises of glory and dominion in his ear.

And he knew, with a certainty that bordered on madness, that he would do whatever it took to claim that power for himself and his pride.

` For he was Braydon Mitchell, the alpha of the Panther Prowl, and he would let nothing stand in his way, not even the doubts and fears of his own followers.

As Tyler's footsteps faded into the distance, Braydon turned his attention to Kari, his gaze intense and hungry. He stepped closer, the Idol still clutched in his hand, its eerie glow casting shadows across his face.

"Kari," he purred, his voice low and seductive. "You know, you've always been special to me. More than just a pridemate. More than just a loyal follower."

Kari swallowed hard, her eyes darting between Braydon's face and the Idol. "I... I know, Braydon. I've always tried to serve you well, to be worthy of your trust."

Braydon's smile widened, his free hand reaching out to caress Kari's cheek. "Oh, you have, Kari. You've proven yourself time and time again. But now, with the power of the Idol within our grasp, I find myself wanting more."

He leaned in closer, his breath hot against Kari's ear. "I want you by my side, Kari. Not just as a pridemate, but as my queen. Together, we could rule this city, this world. We could have everything we've ever wanted."

Kari's heart raced, a mix of fear and longing coursing through her veins. She had always admired Braydon, had always been drawn to his strength and his charisma. But this... this was something else entirely.

"Braydon, I..." she stammered, her voice trembling. "I don't know. This is all happening so fast. I need time to think, to process everything."

Braydon's grip on her cheek tightened, his claws pressing against her skin. "There's no time for thinking, Kari. The future is ours for the taking, but we have to act now. We have to seize this moment, before it slips away."

He pressed his body against hers, his arousal evident even through the layers of clothing. "I need you, Kari. I need your strength, your loyalty, your devotion. I need you to stand with me, to be mine in every way."

Kari's mind reeled, torn between her desire for Braydon and her fear of the unknown. She knew that this was a turning point, a moment that would define the rest of her life.

But as she looked into Braydon's eyes, saw the hunger and

the need that burned within them, she felt something stir inside her, a primal urge that she could no longer deny.

"Yes," she breathed, her voice barely above a whisper. "Yes, Braydon. I'm yours. Now and forever."

Braydon's smile was triumphant, his eyes flashing with a savage joy. He pulled Kari into a brutal kiss, his teeth and tongue claiming her mouth with a ferocity that left her breathless.

And there, in the shadows of the ancient temple, with the Idol of Lycoan pulsing with an otherworldly energy, Braydon and Kari sealed their pact, their bodies and souls intertwined in a dance of passion and power.

The future was theirs, and they would let nothing stand in their way, not even the bonds of love and loyalty that had once held them together.

For they were the king and queen of the Panther Prowl, and their reign had only just begun.

****

Casey leaned back in her chair, her eyes fixed on the computer screen before her. The secure communication line blinked steadily, indicating that the connection was stable and encrypted.

A moment later, Mick's face appeared on the screen, his expression a mix of concern and curiosity. "Casey," he said, his voice tinged with static. "I've been waiting for your update. What have you got for me?"

Casey took a deep breath, organizing her thoughts before she spoke. "It's been a hell of a ride, Mick. This case is getting more complicated by the minute."

She proceeded to fill him in on the details of the

investigation, from the unusual wound patterns on the victim to the presence of a rogue lycan in Blacksburg. She told him about the sliver of Blessed Silver and the dark magic that seemed to be at play, her voice steady and professional even as the weight of the revelations pressed down on her.

Throughout it all, she was careful to avoid mentioning Rigo or Aidan, knowing that their involvement was a closely guarded secret. She trusted Mick with her life, but she also knew that the fewer people who knew about her unofficial partners, the better.

Mick listened intently, his brow furrowing as he processed the information. "Damn, Casey," he said, his voice low and serious. "This is some heavy stuff. A rogue lycan, dark magic, and now the local police chief breathing down your neck? You've got your work cut out for you."

Casey nodded, a wry smile tugging at the corner of her mouth. "Tell me about it. But you know me, Mick. I'm not one to back down from a challenge."

Mick chuckled, his eyes crinkling with a mix of pride and worry. "I know, Casey. That's what makes you the best damn agent in the RIPD." He paused for a moment, his expression turning thoughtful. "Have you considered reaching out to Alex for help? I know he's got his own case load, but he might be able to provide some backup or intel."

Casey sighed, a flicker of disappointment crossing her face. "Actually, I already did. I called him as soon as I landed in Blacksburg, hoping he might be able to lend a hand."

Mick leaned forward, his interest piqued. "And? What did he say?"

Casey shook her head, her expression rueful. "Unfortunately, he's tied up with his own investigation right now. Some big case that's got him running all over the state. He said he'd try to provide support from afar, but he can't be here in person."

Mick nodded, his expression one of understanding. "Damn, that's tough. But I know you, Casey. You'll find a way to make it work, with or without Alex's help."

Casey smiled, a glimmer of appreciation in her eyes. "Thanks, Mick. That means a lot." She paused for a moment, her expression turning serious. "But there's something else I need from you, too."

Mick leaned forward, his attention fully focused on his partner. "Anything, Casey. You know that."

Casey took a deep breath, steeling herself for the request she knew she had to make. "I need you to keep this investigation off the official channels, Mick. No reports, no paper trail, nothing that could tip off the wrong people."

Mick's eyes widened, a flicker of surprise crossing his face. "Casey, that's a big ask. You know I've got to keep the higher-ups in the loop, especially on a case this sensitive."

Casey nodded, her expression resolute. "I know, Mick. But trust me on this one. There are forces at work here that go beyond anything we've ever faced before. And until I know exactly what we're dealing with, I need to keep this investigation as quiet as possible."

Mick was silent for a long moment, his gaze searching Casey's face through the screen. Finally, he nodded, his expression one of reluctant acceptance. "Alright, Casey. I'll do what I can to keep this off the radar. But you'd better keep me in the loop, you hear? I don't want to be the last one to know if things go sideways out there."

Casey smiled, a genuine warmth spreading through her chest. "I will, Mick. I promise. And thank you, for everything."

As the call ended and the screen went dark, Casey leaned back in her chair, her mind racing with the implications of everything she had learned. She knew that she was walking a dangerous line, keeping secrets from her own partner and the RIPD at large.

But she also knew that she had no choice, that the stakes were too high and the enemy too powerful to risk exposure. She would have to rely on her own instincts and the skills of her unofficial team to see this through, no matter the cost.

And as she sat there in the dimly lit room, the weight of the investigation pressing down on her shoulders, Casey knew that she was ready for whatever lay ahead.

****

Aidan hunched over his workbench, his eyes narrowed in concentration as he tinkered with a complex array of gadgets and gizmos. The soft hum of machinery and the occasional crackle of electricity filled the air, a testament to the technological wonders that lay scattered across the surface.

Rigo leaned against the wall nearby, his arms crossed and his expression one of curious amusement. He had to admit, he was impressed by the sheer scale and sophistication of Aidan's operation. The kid clearly knew his stuff.

"So, Rigo," Aidan said, glancing up from his work with a grin. "I've been meaning to ask you about your lycan abilities. I figure the more I know, the better I can tailor my tech to suit your needs."

Rigo raised an eyebrow, a hint of wariness creeping into his voice. "What do you want to know?"

Aidan shrugged, his expression open and friendly. "Whatever you're comfortable sharing, man. I'm not looking to pry into your personal life or anything. I just want to make sure I'm giving you the best possible tools for the job."

Rigo was silent for a moment, considering the request. He wasn't used to discussing his abilities so openly, especially with someone he barely knew. But there was something about Aidan's earnest enthusiasm that put him at ease, a sense of genuine curiosity and respect that was hard to ignore.

"Alright," he said, pushing off from the wall and moving closer to the workbench. "As a Hyena Hybrid, I've got a few tricks up my sleeve that your average lycan doesn't."

Aidan's eyes widened, his interest piqued. "Like what?"

Rigo grinned, a flash of sharp teeth in the dim light of the workshop. "For starters, my senses are off the charts. I can hear, smell, and see things that most humans and lycans can't even begin to imagine. It's like the world is dialed up to eleven, all the time."

Aidan nodded, his mind already racing with the possibilities. "Heightened senses, got it. What else?"

Rigo flexed his hands, his claws extending with a soft snikt. "I'm stronger and faster than your average lycan, too. And my healing factor is pretty much unbeatable. I can take a hit that would put most folks in the hospital and be back on my feet in minutes."

Aidan let out a low whistle, his expression one of impressed admiration. "Damn, Rigo. That's some serious firepower you're packing."

Rigo shrugged, a hint of pride creeping into his voice. "It comes with the territory. Hyenas are built for survival, and I'm no exception."

There was a moment of silence, a sense of something left unsaid hanging in the air between them. Aidan's brow furrowed, a flicker of curiosity crossing his face.

"Is there anything else?" he asked, his voice gentle but probing. "I get the feeling there's more to your abilities than just the physical stuff."

Rigo hesitated, a shadow of uncertainty passing over his features. He wasn't used to revealing the full extent of his powers, even to allies. But there was something about Aidan's earnest desire to help that made him want to open up, to trust in the bonds of their newfound partnership.

"There is one more thing," he said, his voice low and measured. "As a Hyena Hybrid, I have the ability to force weaker lycans back into their human form. It's not something I like to advertise, but it's come in handy more than once."

Aidan's eyes widened, a glimmer of excitement and understanding flickering in their depths. "That's incredible, Rigo. I had no idea such a thing was even possible."

Rigo nodded, a wry smile tugging at the corner of his mouth. "It's a closely guarded secret among my kind. We don't like to show our hand unless absolutely necessary."

Aidan leaned forward, his expression one of eager curiosity. "How does it work? Is it a mental thing, or do you have to physically overpower them?"

Rigo shook his head, a hint of amusement creeping into his voice. "It's a bit of both, actually. I have to exert my will over theirs, to dominate them on a spiritual level. But it helps if I can get my hands on them, too. The physical contact seems to amplify the effect."

Aidan nodded, his mind already racing with the possibilities. "That's fascinating, Rigo. I wonder if there's a way to replicate that effect with technology, to give you an edge in combat situations."

Rigo chuckled, a glimmer of admiration in his eyes. "If anyone can figure it out, kid, it's you. Just promise me you'll keep this between us, okay? I don't want word getting out about my little party trick."

Aidan grinned, his expression one of sincere understanding. "Your secret's safe with me, Rigo. I won't breathe a word to anyone, not even Casey."

As the two men continued to discuss the finer points of lycan physiology and the potential applications of Aidan's tech, Rigo couldn't help but feel a sense of gratitude and camaraderie washing over him. He had spent so long keeping his abilities hidden, guarding his secrets like precious treasures.

But here, in the warm glow of Aidan's workshop, surrounded by the hum of machinery and the crackling of electricity, he felt a sense of belonging, of shared purpose and understanding.

And as he looked into the bright, eager eyes of his new friend and ally, Rigo knew that he had made the right choice in opening up, in trusting in the bonds of their partnership.

Together, they would face the darkness that threatened to engulf Blacksburg, and they would emerge victorious, no matter the cost.

Suddenly, the door to the workshop burst open, and Casey strode in, her expression one of urgent determination. Rigo and Aidan looked up, startled by the sudden intrusion.

"Rigo, you're not going to believe this," Casey said, a smile tugging at the corner of her mouth. "KIVO's been analyzing the data from the crime scene, and he's found evidence that exonerates Matt Mauney."

Rigo's eyebrows shot up, a flicker of surprise and relief crossing his face. "Really? That's great news. I knew Blackwell was just trying to pin this on the were-jaguar community."

Casey nodded, her eyes sparkling with a sense of vindication. "KIVO was able to track Mauney's movements on the night of the attack. He has a solid alibi, and there's no way he could have been involved."

Aidan leaned back in his chair, a grin spreading across his face. "That's fantastic! One less suspect to worry about, and one step closer to the truth."

Rigo stood up, his posture filled with a newfound sense of purpose. "This is huge, Casey. If Mauney's innocent, that means we're back to square one with the rogue lycan. But at least we can cross one name off our list."

Casey's expression turned serious, her mind already racing with the implications of this new information. "Agreed. And it also means that Blackwell's been trying to steer us in the wrong direction. We need to figure out why, and what he's trying to hide."

Aidan's fingers flew over the keys of his computer, his brow furrowed in concentration. "I'll keep digging into the data, see if I can find any other discrepancies or leads. If Blackwell's involved in this mess, there's bound to be a trail."

“I saw we go to the last known location of Mauney, and question him. See if he can tell us why Blackwell wants to pin this attack on him,” Rigo suggests, “I’ve known Mauney since before our lycan genes were active. He isn’t a vicious killer. Even as a jaguar, he can control himself. We worked hard together to master the animal,"

"Good idea. KIVO, what is Matt Mauney's most recent location?" Casey asks.

"Triangulating cell frequencies, please stand by," KIVO states, as the jeopardy theme plays.

"Really Aidan?" Casey cracks a smile, fighting the urge to laugh, "Jeopardy?"

"Who doesnt love Alex Trebek? Besides elevator music sucks, so Jeopardy wins," Aidan chuckles.

"Matt Mauney's last known coordinate are at the intersection of Highway 29 and River Road. It appears as if he was at a party, according to the heat signature data," KIVO states, cancelling the Jeopardy theme.

"Run the same signature data on the same location for the last twenty four hours," Aidan responds, hurrying over to the computer console, "If it was a party, maybe they are all sleeping and Matt is still there,"

"Aidan, has anyone ever told you that you remind them of a human Alpha 5?" Rigo asks, chucking.

"I've heard it from Alex, so it isn't an insult if thats what you are getting at," Aidan says.

"Matt Mauney has been detected in the same area," KIVO states.

"Good. Aidan, monitor those readings and the cell signal. Rigo, with me. We are going to grab him," Casey instructs, heading towards the vehicle bay with Rigo on her heels.

****

The first rays of dawn were just beginning to peek over

the horizon as Casey and Rigo pulled up to the intersection of Highway 29 and River Road. The area was secluded, surrounded by dense woods and the gentle flow of the nearby river.

As they stepped out of the car, the sound of their footsteps on the gravel seemed to echo in the stillness of the early morning. Rigo inhaled deeply, his heightened senses picking up on the faint scents of lycans and the lingering traces of the night's revelry.

They made their way towards the riverbank, the soft murmur of the water mingling with the occasional birdsong. As they drew closer, the remnants of the party came into view.

Scattered across the clearing were the sleeping forms of various lycans, their bodies sprawled out on blankets and sleeping bags. The embers of a bonfire smoldered in the center of the makeshift camp, the faint scent of smoke and burnt wood hanging in the air.

Casey's eyes scanned the scene, taking in the diverse array of lycan species represented. There were werewolves, their powerful frames curled up in peaceful slumber. Nearby, a group of were-coyotes lay huddled together, their lean bodies twitching as they dreamed.

Rigo's gaze was drawn to a pair of were-bears, their massive forms dwarfing the other lycans around them. He knew that bears were often seen as the peacekeepers of the lycan community, their strength and wisdom respected by all.

But as he surveyed the gathered lycans, Rigo couldn't help but notice the absence of one particular group: the were-panthers. It seemed that the rumors of their possession of the Idol of Lycoan had caused a rift in the community, a sense of distrust and unease that kept them isolated from their fellow lycans.

Casey moved forward, her steps careful and quiet as she navigated through the sleeping bodies. She was looking for one lycan in particular, the one that KIVO had tracked to this location.

Suddenly, Rigo's hand shot out, grasping Casey's arm and stopping her in her tracks. He nodded towards a figure lying apart from the others, his form partially obscured by a large oak tree.

As they drew closer, the figure stirred, his eyes blinking open and his body tensing as he sensed their approach. It was Matt Mauney, the were-jaguar they had come to question.

Mauney sat up slowly, his eyes wary as he took in the sight of Casey and Rigo. "Who are you?" he asked, his voice rough with sleep. "What do you want?"

Casey held up her hands, her expression calm and non-threatening. "Matt Mauney? I'm Special Agent Casey Elkins, RIPD. This is my partner, Rigo Balderas. We're here to ask you a few questions about the recent attack in Blacksburg."

Mauney's eyes widened, a flicker of fear crossing his face. "I had nothing to do with that," he said, his voice urgent. "I swear, I was here all night, with the others. I didn't attack anyone."

Rigo stepped forward, his voice low and reassuring. "We know, Matt. KIVO's analysis proved your innocence. But we need to know why Chief Blackwell was so eager to pin this on you. Do you have any idea why he might want to frame you for the crime?"

Mauney's brow furrowed, his expression troubled. "Blackwell? I don't know. I've never had any trouble with the police before. But..." He hesitated, his eyes darting around the sleeping lycans. "There have been rumors, whispers of something big going down in Blacksburg. Something to do with the were-panthers and some kind of powerful artifact."

Casey and Rigo exchanged a glance, their suspicions confirmed. The Idol of Lycoan was at the center of this mystery, and the were-panthers were somehow involved.

As they continued to question Mauney, the sun rose higher in the sky, casting a golden glow over the riverside clearing. The other lycans began to stir, their eyes widening in surprise and curiosity as they noticed the two RIPD agents in their midst.

Rigo turned to Casey, his expression thoughtful. "Casey, I think we should consider taking Matt into protective custody. We need to pick his brain, figure out why Blackwell is so intent on pinning these crimes on him."

Casey nodded, her brow furrowed. "I agree. There's more to this story than meets the eye, and Matt might be the key to unlocking the truth."

She turned to Mauney, her voice gentle but firm. "Matt, we'd like you to come with us. We can offer you protection while we sort this out, and we have a few more questions that might help us get to the bottom of what's really going on in Blacksburg."

Mauney hesitated for a moment, his eyes darting between Casey and Rigo. Finally, he nodded, his shoulders sagging with a mix of relief and resignation. "Okay. I'll come with you. I want to help in any way I can."

As they led Mauney back to their car, Casey and Rigo exchanged a glance, their minds already racing with the questions they needed to ask.

Once they were on the road, Rigo turned to Mauney, his

voice low and serious. "Matt, we need to know if there's any personal history between you and Chief Blackwell. Has there been any bad blood or conflicts in the past?"

Mauney shook his head, his expression puzzled. "No, not that I can think of. I mean, I've had a few run-ins with the police over the years, minor stuff. But nothing that would make Blackwell come after me like this."

Casey glanced at Mauney in the rearview mirror, her eyes sharp and probing. "What about the were-panthers? Do you have any connections or relationships with them?"

Mauney's face paled, and he swallowed hard. "No, no connections. To be honest, most of us steer clear of the panthers. There's always been a bit of tension there, a sense that they think they're better than the rest of us."

Rigo leaned forward, his elbows resting on his knees. "Speaking of the panthers, we couldn't help but notice their absence at the party last night. Is there a reason why they weren't invited or didn't show up?"

Mauney shrugged, his expression uneasy. "I don't know for sure, but there have been rumors going around. People saying that the panthers have gotten their hands on some kind of powerful artifact, something that could give them an edge over the other lycan clans."

Casey's eyes narrowed, her suspicions confirmed. "The Idol of Lycoan."

Mauney's eyes widened, and he nodded slowly. "Yeah, that's the one. I don't know much about it, but the whispers are that it's some kind of game-changer. And if the panthers have it... well, that could be bad news for the rest of us."

Rigo sat back, his mind spinning with the implications.

"One last question, Matt. The party last night... what was the occasion? Why the big gathering of different lycan clans?"

Mauney hesitated, his eyes darting between Casey and Rigo. "It's... it's a bit of a tradition. Every few months, the clans come together to reaffirm our alliances, our commitment to maintaining the peace between our kinds. With all the tensions and uncertainties in Blacksburg lately, we thought it was important to show a united front."

Casey nodded, her expression thoughtful. "A united front against the were-panthers and whatever they might be planning with the Idol."

As they drove on, the pieces of the puzzle began to fall into place. The were-panthers' absence from the party, the rumors of their possession of the Idol, and Chief Blackwell's attempts to pin the recent attack on Mauney... it all pointed to a larger conspiracy, one that threatened the delicate balance of Blacksburg's supernatural community.

But Casey and Rigo knew that they were just scratching the surface. There were still so many questions left unanswered, so many leads to pursue.

As they pulled into the warehouse district, the sun now high in the sky, they knew that their work was far from over. But they also knew that they were not alone in this fight.

****

The tension in Chief Blackwell's office was palpable as Braydon, Kari, and Tyler filed in, their expressions a mix of curiosity and apprehension. Blackwell sat behind his desk, his face etched with lines of stress and frustration.

"Thank you for coming on such short notice," Blackwell began, his voice strained. "I wanted to update you on the recent attack and the steps I've taken to keep the RIPD's attention away from your... activities."

Braydon leaned forward, his eyes narrowing. "What steps, exactly? And why do you look like you've just swallowed a lemon?"

Blackwell sighed, his fingers drumming nervously on the desktop. "I pinned the blame on Matt Mauney, the were-jaguar. I figured if the RIPD was focused on him, they'd be less likely to dig into your business with the Idol."

Kari's eyes widened, and she let out a sharp laugh. "Seriously, Blackwell? You think the RIPD is stupid enough to just take your word for it and not investigate Mauney themselves?"

Blackwell's face reddened, and he opened his mouth to retort, but Kari cut him off with a wave of her hand. "No, don't even try to defend yourself. This is sloppy, even for you."

Tyler glanced between Kari and Blackwell, his expression one of confusion and growing unease. "Kari, what's going on here? Since when do you question Blackwell's decisions?"

Kari stood, her posture regal and her eyes glinting with a newfound power. "Since I became the queen of the Panther Prowl, Tyler. Braydon and I have... come to an understanding."

Tyler's jaw dropped, and he turned to Braydon, seeking confirmation. Braydon nodded, a smirk playing at the corners of his mouth. "It's true, Tyler. Kari and I are united in our vision for the future of Blacksburg and the role of the were-panthers in it."

Blackwell's eyes darted between the three lycans, his expression one of growing realization and fear. "Queen? What are you talking about? And what does this have to do with the attack and the RIPD's investigation?"

Kari fixed Blackwell with a piercing stare, her voice low and dangerous. "It means that your days of making decisions for the Panther Prowl are over, Blackwell. From now on, you answer to me and Braydon."

She leaned forward, her hands braced on the chief's desk. "And as for the RIPD? If they start sniffing around Mauney and realize that he's innocent, they'll come straight to you. And when they do, you'd better have a damn good explanation for why you tried to frame him."

Blackwell's face paled, and he swallowed hard. "I... I was just trying to protect your interests, Kari. You know how important your father's support is to my position as chief."

Kari's eyes narrowed, and she let out a huff of laughter. "My father? You mean the mayor of Blacksburg? Yes, I'm well aware of the influence he wields. But don't forget, Blackwell, my loyalty is to the Panther Prowl first and foremost. And right now, your actions are putting us all at risk."

Braydon stood, his presence commanding and his voice filled with quiet menace. "Kari is right, Blackwell. Your bungling of this situation has drawn unwanted attention to our activities. And if the RIPD starts digging deeper, they may uncover the truth about the Idol and our plans for Blacksburg."

He leaned in close, his breath hot against Blackwell's ear. "And if that happens, you can be sure that the mayor's influence won't be enough to save you from our wrath."

Blackwell trembled, his hands clenching into fists at his sides. "I... I understand, Braydon. It won't happen again. I'll do whatever you need me to do to keep the RIPD off your trail."

Kari smiled, a cold and predatory expression that sent shivers down Blackwell's spine. "Good. Because if you fail us again, you'll wish the RIPD was your biggest problem."

With that, the three lycans turned and strode out of the office, leaving Blackwell alone with his thoughts and his growing sense of dread.

As they emerged into the hallway, Tyler turned to Kari, his expression one of awe and respect. "I had no idea, Kari. You... you're really the queen of the Panther Prowl?"

Kari grinned, her eyes flashing with a fierce pride. "I am, Tyler. And together with Braydon, we're going to lead our people to a new era of power and prosperity."

Braydon nodded, his arm snaking around Kari's waist in a possessive gesture. "And with the Idol in our possession, nothing will stand in our way. Not the RIPD, not the other lycan clans, and certainly not a weak-willed fool like Blackwell."

As they walked out of the police station and into the bright sunlight of the day, Kari and Braydon shared a look of triumph and anticipation. The future was theirs for the taking, and they would let nothing and no one stand in their way.

****

As the team settled into a tense silence, each lost in their own thoughts and fears, Casey felt a hand on her shoulder. She looked up to see Rigo standing beside her, his eyes filled with a fierce determination.

"We've got this, Casey," he said, his voice low and steady. "Whatever comes next, we'll face it together. We're a team, and we won't let each other down."

Casey nodded, a small smile tugging at the corners of her mouth. "You're right, Rigo. We've come too far to back down now. We'll see this through to the end, no matter what it takes."

"We have Matt giving KIVO and Aidan a complete rundown of everything he knows, Case, we have been making leadway into the case so far, and the more we make into it, the more likely we are to uncover the truth. Perhaps you should give your field agent an update," Rigo offers.

Just then, the door to the warehouse burst open, and a figure stumbled inside, their face obscured by a hood and their body wracked with tremors. As the team jumped to their feet, ready for a fight, the figure collapsed to the ground, a pool of blood spreading out beneath them.

Casey rushed forward, her heart pounding in her chest as she reached for the figure's hood. But when she pulled it back, she felt the world tilt beneath her feet, and a scream of anguish tore from her throat.

It was Cyndi, her beloved sister, her face pale and her body covered in deep, vicious wounds. Casey gathered her in her arms, tears streaming down her face as she cradled Cyndi's limp form.

Rigo and Aidan were at her side in an instant, their faces etched with shock and horror. They had never seen Casey so broken, so utterly devastated.

As they worked frantically to stem the bleeding and call for help, Casey's mind raced with questions and fears. Who had done this to Cyndi, and why? Was it connected to their investigation, or was it something else entirely?

But one thing was certain - Casey would not rest until she had found the truth and brought her sister's attackers to justice. The game had just changed, and the hunt for answers had become a personal vendetta.

CHAPTER 7

Earlier that evening...

Cyndi stepped out of The Corner Stop, her shift finally over after a long and tiring day. She pulled her rainbow-colored hair, now faded from its once vibrant hues, into a tight ponytail and let out a sigh of relief. The streets of Blacksburg were quiet at this hour, the only sound the distant hum of traffic and the occasional rustling of leaves in the cool night breeze.

As she walked along the sidewalk, her mind wandered to her sister, Casey. It had been months since they'd last spoken, and Cyndi couldn't shake the feeling that something was amiss. Casey had always been the strong one, the protector, but lately, there had been a distance in her voice, a sense of unease that Cyndi couldn't quite put her finger on.

Lost in her thoughts, Cyndi almost didn't notice the figure stumbling out of the alleyway up ahead. But as she drew closer, she recognized the woman's striking features and sultry attire - it was Kari Byars, her former classmate from high school.

Kari looked different than Cyndi remembered, her once understated beauty now amplified to an almost otherworldly degree. Her curves were more pronounced, her breasts straining against the tight fabric of her low-cut top, and her hips swaying with a seductive rhythm that seemed to draw the eye and quicken the pulse. But there was something else, too - a wild, feral quality to her movements, a hint of danger lurking beneath the surface.

"Kari?" Cyndi called out, her voice tentative. "Is that you? Are you okay?"

Kari's head snapped up, her eyes flashing with a mix of surprise and annoyance. "Cyndi? What are you doing here?"

Cyndi took a step closer, her hands raised in a placating gesture. "I was just heading home from work. I saw you stumbling and wanted to make sure you were alright."

Kari let out a harsh laugh, the sound sending a shiver down Cyndi's spine. "Alright? Oh, I'm more than alright, Cyndi. I'm fucking fantastic."

Cyndi's brow furrowed in confusion. "What do you mean? You look like you've been through hell."

Kari's lips curved into a wicked smirk. "Hell? No, not hell. More like heaven. I've been reborn, Cyndi. Reborn as the queen of the Panther Prowl."

Cyndi's eyes widened, a flicker of fear and recognition sparking in their golden-green depths. "The Panther Prowl? Isn't that Braydon Mitchell's gang? Kari, what have you gotten yourself into?"

Kari's expression hardened, her eyes narrowing to slits. "Don't say his name like that. Braydon is my king, my partner in all things. Together, we're going to rule this city."

Cyndi shook her head, a sense of dread settling in the pit of her stomach. "Kari, listen to me. Braydon is dangerous. He's not to be trusted. Remember what he did to my sister, Casey? How he hurt her, manipulated her? You need to be careful."

Kari's hand shot out, grabbing Cyndi by the throat and slamming her against the wall of the alleyway. "Careful? I'm done being careful, Cyndi. I'm done being the good little girl, the one who always plays by the rules. Braydon has shown me the truth, the power that lies within me. And now, I'm going to take what's mine."

Cyndi struggled against Kari's grip, her eyes wide with terror as she felt the other woman's claws digging into her skin. "Kari, please," she choked out, her voice hoarse with fear. "This isn't you. You're not a monster."

But Kari only laughed, a cold, cruel sound that echoed off the walls of the alleyway. "Oh, but I am, Cyndi. I'm the queen of the monsters. And you? You're just another piece of prey, waiting to be devoured."

With a snarl of rage, Kari lashed out, her claws tearing into Cyndi's flesh with a sickening sound. Cyndi screamed, her body convulsing in agony as she felt the poison of Kari's bite coursing through her veins.

As she slipped into unconsciousness, her last thought was of Casey, and the desperate hope that her sister would find her before it was too late.

Little did she know that Braydon and his crew were already aware of the RIPD's presence in Blacksburg, and that they had plans of their own for the young woman who had stumbled into their midst.

****

Casey cradled Cyndi's limp form in her arms, her heart racing with fear and desperation as she called out to her team. "Aidan, we need medical assistance, now! It's Cyndi, she's hurt!"

Aidan and Rigo were at her side in an instant, their faces etched with concern as they took in the extent of Cyndi's injuries. Matt and Mr. Butler hovered nearby, their expressions a mix of shock and confusion.

"KIVO, we need a medical bay, stat!" Aidan commanded, his voice tight with urgency.

"Acknowledged," KIVO responded, the AI's calm tone a stark contrast to the chaos of the moment. "Initializing medical bay protocols. Please stand by."

Before their eyes, the interior of the warehouse began to shift and transform, the advanced technology of Aidan's design springing to life. Walls moved and reconfigured, equipment materialized out of thin air, and a state-of-the-art medical facility took shape, complete with monitoring systems, surgical tools, and a stasis pod for Cyndi.

Casey and Rigo carefully lifted Cyndi onto the medical bed, their hands shaking as they worked to stem the flow of blood from her wounds. Aidan moved to the computer console, his fingers flying over the keys as he inputted commands and analyzed the data streaming in from the sensors.

"KIVO, initiate stasis protocol," he ordered, his brow furrowed in concentration. "We need to stabilize her vitals and assess the extent of the damage."

The stasis pod hissed open, and Casey and Rigo gently placed Cyndi inside, the young woman's rainbow-colored hair fanning out around her pale face. As the pod sealed shut, a soft blue glow enveloped Cyndi's form, and the monitoring systems came to life, displaying her heartbeat, respiration, and other vital signs.

For a long moment, the team stood in silence, watching the steady rise and fall of Cyndi's chest, the only sign that she was still alive. Casey felt a hand on her shoulder and turned to see Rigo standing beside her, his eyes filled with a mix of sympathy and determination.

"She's a fighter, Casey," he said softly, his voice a comforting rumble in the stillness of the room. "Just like her sister. She'll pull through this."

Casey nodded, tears stinging the corners of her eyes as she reached out to touch the cool surface of the stasis pod. "I know she will, Rigo. But what happened to her? Who did this?"

Aidan's voice cut through the silence, his tone grim. "I'm not sure, but the wounds... they're not like anything I've seen before. They're too precise, too deliberate. This wasn't a random attack."

Matt stepped forward, his expression haunted. "You don't think it could be the work of the were-panthers, do you? Braydon and his crew?"

Casey's eyes flashed with a dangerous light, her hands clenching into fists at her sides. "If they had anything to do with this, I swear I'll-"

"Wait," Mr. Butler interrupted, his voice trembling slightly. "There's something else. Something you need to see."

He pointed to the monitoring system, where a new set of data had appeared alongside Cyndi's vital signs. It was a DNA analysis, the strands of genetic code twisting and morphing before their eyes.

Aidan's eyes widened, a flicker of fear and realization crossing his face. "Oh my god. Those are lycan genes. Cyndi... she's turning."

Casey felt the world tilt beneath her feet, a wave of nausea rising in her throat. Her sister, her sweet, innocent sister, was becoming one of them. A lycan, a creature of the night.

And suddenly, the hunt for the Idol of Lycoan and the

were-panther conspiracy took on a whole new level of urgency and danger. Because now, it wasn't just about saving Blacksburg or unraveling a mystery.

It was about saving Cyndi, before it was too late.

****

Aidan stepped out of the medical bay, his heart heavy with worry for both Cyndi and Casey. He'd never seen his friend so broken, so utterly lost in her grief and fear. It was clear that Casey needed time to process what had happened, to be there for her sister in this critical moment.

But the investigation couldn't wait. The were-panthers were still out there, and the Idol of Lycoan remained a mystery. Aidan knew that he and Rigo would have to take the lead, to keep pushing forward even as Casey focused on her family.

With a sigh, Aidan pulled out his phone and dialed a familiar number. After a few rings, Alex's voice came through the speaker, tinged with concern.

"Aidan? What's going on? Is everything okay?"

Aidan closed his eyes, steeling himself for the conversation to come. "No, Alex. It's not. Something's happened to Cyndi, Casey's sister. She was attacked, and it's bad. Really bad."

There was a moment of stunned silence on the other end of the line, followed by a sharp intake of breath. "Oh my god. Is she... is she going to be okay?"

Aidan rubbed his forehead, the weight of the situation pressing down on him like a physical force. "We don't know yet. She's in stasis, and her vitals are stable, but... Alex, there's something else. Something you need to know."

"What is it, Aidan? Tell me."

"Cyndi... she's turning. Into a lycan. We found lycan genes in her DNA, and they're spreading fast. We don't know how or why, but..."

Alex's voice was tight with emotion, a mix of fear and anger bleeding through the phone. "Aidan, listen to me. You have to keep this quiet, okay? Don't let anyone outside of your team know about Cyndi's condition. Especially not the RIPD."

Aidan's brow furrowed in confusion. "What? Why? Alex, what's going on?"

There was a long pause, followed by a heavy sigh. "Aidan, I... I can't get involved with Casey's case. Not anymore. The RIPD... they're investigating me. As a potential lycan."

Aidan felt his heart skip a beat, a chill running down his spine. "What? Alex, that's insane. You're not a lycan. You're one of us, a member of the team. You are Sheriff of Polkville. You protected the city from Tommy Leons,"

"Not anymore," Alex said, his voice tinged with bitterness. "Ever since my transformation against Leons, they've been watching me, hoping I'll randomly transform. Truth be told, they know even less about the transformation that occurred than I do. They are waiting for me to slip up, to show signs of turning. They don't trust me, Aidan. And if they find out about Cyndi..."

Aidan closed his eyes, the implications of Alex's words sinking in like a lead weight. "They'll think you're involved. That you had something to do with her attack."

"Exactly. Aidan, I need you to promise me that you won't tell Casey about this. She has enough on her plate right now, and I don't want to add to her burden. Please, just... keep this between us."

Aidan took a deep breath, his mind racing with the implications of Alex's revelation. He knew that keeping secrets from Casey was a dangerous game, that it could fracture the trust and loyalty that held their team together.

But he also knew that Alex was right. Casey needed to focus on Cyndi, on being there for her sister in this critical moment. She didn't need the added stress of worrying about Alex's situation with the RIPD.

"Okay, Alex. I promise. I won't say anything to Casey. But... be careful, okay? Watch your back. And if you need anything, anything at all..."

"I know, Aidan. Thank you. And please, keep me updated on Cyndi's condition. I may not be able to be there in person, but... I still care. Deeply."

As the call ended, Aidan leaned back against the wall, his mind reeling with the weight of the secrets he now carried. The investigation, the were-panthers, the Idol... it all paled in comparison to the personal stakes that now hung in the balance.

Because it wasn't just about solving a case anymore. It was about protecting the people they loved, the bonds of friendship and family that held them together.

And as Aidan stepped back into the medical bay, his gaze falling on Casey's hunched form beside Cyndi's stasis pod, he knew that he would do whatever it took to keep them safe.

****

Aidan hunched over his workbench, his brow furrowed in concentration as he tinkered with a complex array of circuitry and glowing blue vials. Rigo paced the length of the lab, his eyes flickering between the schematics on the wall and the prototype taking shape before them.

"I think we're close," Aidan muttered, his fingers flying over the delicate components. "If we can just stabilize the neurotransmitter inhibitors and calibrate the dosage..."

Rigo nodded, his gaze intense. "We have to get this right, Aidan. With Cyndi's transformation and the were-panthers on the loose, we need every advantage we can get."

Aidan paused, looking up at Rigo with a mix of determination and understanding. "I know, Rigo. And we will. This device...it could be a game-changer. Not just for Cyndi, but for any lycan who wants to control their transformations."

Rigo's eyes drifted to the medical bay, where Casey sat in silent vigil over her sister's stasis pod. The weight of their mission hung heavy in the air, a constant reminder of the lives at stake.

"How does it work, exactly?" Rigo asked, turning back to the prototype. "I mean, I get the basic idea, but..."

Aidan grinned, a glimmer of excitement in his eyes. "It's a combination of biochemistry and advanced technology. The device targets specific neural pathways and hormone receptors associated with lycan transformations. By regulating these systems, it can potentially halt or reverse the transformation process."

Rigo's eyebrows shot up, impressed. "And the blue vials? What's in them?"

"A unique blend of compounds derived from rare plant extracts and synthesized moonstone," Aidan explained. "The serum acts as a stabilizing agent, helping the body adapt to the device's effects without triggering a rejection response."

Rigo let out a low whistle. "Moonstone, huh? I've heard

stories about its properties, but I never thought..."

"...that it could be harnessed for something like this?" Aidan finished, a note of pride in his voice. "That's the beauty of science, Rigo. There's always new frontiers to explore, new possibilities to unlock."

As they worked, the conversation turned to the challenges ahead - the need to track down the were-panthers, unravel the mystery of the Idol, and keep their loved ones safe. They talked about Casey and Cyndi, about the toll this case was taking on their team and their hearts.

But through it all, there was a sense of purpose, a shared determination to see this through no matter the cost. Because they knew that this device, this tiny miracle of science and sorcery, could be the key to saving not just Cyndi, but countless others caught in the crosshairs of the lycan world.

Hours passed, the lab humming with the sound of their labor and the crackle of electricity. And then, as the first light of dawn began to filter through the windows, Aidan stepped back from the workbench, a triumphant grin on his face.

"It's done," he said, holding up the finished prototype. "The Lycan Suppression Device, mark one. Ready for testing."

Rigo clasped Aidan's shoulder, a fierce pride shining in his eyes. "Incredible work, Aidan. I knew if anyone could pull this off, it'd be you."

Aidan smiled, the weight of exhaustion and hope mingling on his face. "We did this together, Rigo. Your knowledge of lycan biology, my tech...we make a hell of a team."

As they moved to the medical bay, the device cradled carefully in Aidan's hands, they knew that the real test was still to come. But for now, in this moment of hard-won progress and solidarity, they allowed themselves to feel a flicker of hope.

As they moved to the medical bay, the device cradled carefully in Aidan's hands, they knew that the real test was still to come. But as they approached Cyndi's stasis pod, Rigo hesitated, a flicker of uncertainty crossing his face.

"Wait," he said, his voice low and serious. "Before we use this on Cyndi, I want to test it on myself first."

Aidan's eyebrows shot up in surprise. "What? Rigo, are you sure? We don't know how your unique lycan physiology might react to the device."

Rigo shook his head, his jaw set with determination. "I can't explain it, Aidan, but... I feel like I need to do this. For Cyndi. To make sure it's safe."

Aidan studied Rigo's face, a glimmer of understanding dawning in his eyes. He had seen the way Rigo looked at Cyndi, the flicker of protectiveness and something deeper that passed over his features when he thought no one was watching.

"Okay," Aidan said softly, handing the device to Rigo. "But we take it slow, and at the first sign of trouble, we abort. Agreed?"

Rigo nodded, his fingers closing around the cool metal of the prototype. He took a deep breath, steeling himself for the unknown.

As he pressed the device against his skin, he felt a sudden rush of energy, a tingling sensation that spread from his chest to his fingertips. For a moment, the world seemed to tilt on its axis, and he could feel the primal pull of his lycan nature rising to the surface.

But then, as quickly as it had begun, the sensation faded, replaced by a sense of calm and control unlike anything he had ever experienced. Rigo opened his eyes, a grin spreading across his face.

"It works," he said, his voice tinged with awe. "Aidan, it really works."

Aidan let out a whoop of joy, clapping Rigo on the back. "You did it, Rigo! How do you feel?"

Rigo flexed his fingers, marveling at the newfound clarity in his mind. "I feel... balanced. Like my human and lycan sides are in harmony for the first time in my life."

He glanced at Cyndi's pod, a flicker of hope and something deeper stirring in his chest. "Let's do this, Aidan. Let's bring Cyndi back."

As Rigo and Aidan approached Cyndi's stasis pod, device in hand, Casey suddenly stood up, blocking their path. Her eyes were red-rimmed and filled with a fierce protectiveness.

"Stop right there," she said, her voice trembling with a mix of fear and anger. "What do you think you're doing?"

Aidan held up the device, a cautious smile on his face. "Casey, it's okay. We've created something that can help Cyndi, to suppress her lycan transformation."

But Casey shook her head, her gaze darting between the device and her sister's still form. "No. I can't let you use that on her. It worked on Rigo, but he's a Hyena hybrid. We don't know how it will react to panther DNA."

Rigo stepped forward, his hands held up in a placating gesture. "Casey, I understand your concerns, but we would never do anything to put Cyndi at risk. This device could be her best chance at a normal life."

Casey's eyes flashed with pain and betrayal. "Normal life? My sister was assaulted and turned into a lycan, and you think some untested device can make that all go away?"

She turned away, her shoulders shaking with barely suppressed emotion. "I trusted you. All of you. But now... I don't know who to trust anymore."

Aidan exchanged a worried glance with Rigo, the weight of Casey's words hanging heavy in the air. "Casey," he said softly, "we're still your team. We're still here for you and Cyndi, no matter what."

Casey laughed, a bitter, broken sound. "Are you? Because from where I'm standing, it looks like you're more interested in playing mad scientist than actually helping my sister."

She took a deep breath, her gaze turning distant. "You know what has to happen next, don't you? Cyndi has to register with the RIPD. She's a lycan now, and there are protocols to follow."

Rigo's eyes widened, a flicker of alarm crossing his face. "Casey, wait. Before you make any hasty decisions, you should talk to Mick. He's your partner, your friend. He can help you navigate this."

Aidan nodded, his expression earnest. "And as for the device, we'll do more testing before we even think about using it on Cyndi. We can capture a were-panther, study their DNA, make sure it's safe."

Casey hesitated, torn between her desire to protect her sister and the glimmer of hope that Aidan and Rigo's words offered. "You promise? You'll do everything you can to make sure this device is safe for Cyndi?"

Rigo placed a hand on Casey's shoulder, his touch gentle and reassuring. "We promise, Casey. We won't let anything happen to Cyndi. She's family, and we take care of our own."

As Casey looked into the eyes of her team, she saw the sincerity and determination that had always been there, beneath the fear and the uncertainty. And for the first time since this nightmare began, she felt a flicker of hope rekindling in her heart.

"Okay," she said softly, her gaze drifting back to Cyndi's pod. "We'll do it your way. But if anything goes wrong, if Cyndi gets hurt..."

Aidan shook his head, his voice firm and unwavering. "She won't, Casey. We won't let that happen. We're in this together, until the end."

And as they stood there, united in their love for Cyndi and their determination to see her through this crisis, Casey knew that she had made the right choice. Because in the end, it wasn't about devices or protocols or even the RIPD.

It was about family, and the unbreakable bonds that held them together, even in the darkest of times. And with her team by her side, Casey knew that they could face anything that the lycan world threw their way.

****

The Corner Stop was quiet, the only sound the gentle hum of the refrigerators and the occasional beep of the security system. Cyndi's coworker, a young man named Ethan, stood behind the counter, his eyes heavy with the weight of the late-night shift.

Suddenly, the door burst open, and three figures strode in, their faces hidden beneath dark hoods and their movements jittery with nervous energy. Ethan's heart leapt into his throat, his hand instinctively reaching for the silent alarm beneath the counter.

But before he could press the button, one of the figures leapt forward, his movements a blur of speed and agility. In an instant, he had Ethan pinned against the wall, a clawed hand wrapped around his throat.

"Don't even think about it," the figure growled, his voice a raspy snarl. "We're here for the money, and we're not leaving without it."

Ethan's eyes widened, his gaze darting to the other two figures as they moved behind the counter, their clawed hands rifling through the cash registers with practiced ease. And then, as they stepped into the light, he saw the truth of what they were.

Were-rats, their faces elongated and their eyes glinting with a feral hunger. Ethan had heard stories about the lycan gangs that roamed the city, but he had never seen one up close. Until now.

As the were-rats emptied the registers, the figure holding Ethan leaned in close, his breath hot and rancid against Ethan's face. "You tell anyone about this, and we'll be back. And next time, we won't be so gentle."

With a final shove, the figure released Ethan, sending him crumpling to the ground. The were-rats moved towards the door, their pockets bulging with cash and their eyes darting with nervous energy.

But as they stepped out into the night, a figure emerged from the shadows, his form tall and imposing. Tyler Keal, his eyes glinting with a mix of satisfaction and menace.

"Well done, boys," he said, his voice a low purr. "The Panther Prowl appreciates your service."

The were-rats nodded, their postures submissive in the

presence of the powerful lycan. "Anything for you, boss. You just say the word, and we'll make it happen."

Tyler grinned, his teeth flashing in the moonlight. "Oh, I know you will. Because if you don't, well... let's just say that the Panther Prowl has a long memory, and an even longer reach."

With a final nod, Tyler melted back into the shadows, his form vanishing as quickly as it had appeared. The were-rats exchanged nervous glances, the weight of their allegiance hanging heavy in the air.

Inside the Corner Stop, Ethan struggled to his feet, his heart pounding and his mind racing with the implications of what had just happened. He knew he should call the police, report the robbery and the lycans who had perpetrated it.

But as he reached for the phone, he hesitated, the memory of the were-rat's claws against his throat still fresh in his mind. And in that moment, he knew that this was bigger than just a simple robbery.

Inside the trailer, Braydon lounged on the sofa, his arm draped casually across Kari's shoulders. They looked up as Tyler entered, their expressions a mix of expectation and satisfaction.

"It's done," Tyler said, his voice gruff with exhaustion. "The were-rats hit the Corner Stop, just like you asked. The Panther Prowl's cut is on its way."

Braydon grinned, his eyes glinting with a predatory light. "Excellent work, Tyler. The Panther Prowl's influence grows stronger every day, and it's all thanks to loyal soldiers like you."

But Kari's expression was troubled, her brow furrowed with a mix of concern and uncertainty. "The Corner Stop? Tyler, did the were-rats leave any witnesses? Did they make it clear that they were working for the Prowl?"

Tyler shifted uncomfortably under Kari's scrutiny, his eyes darting to Braydon for support. "I... I'm not sure. They roughed up the clerk pretty good, but I don't think they killed him. And they didn't say anything specific about the Prowl, but..."

Kari's eyes flashed with annoyance, her voice rising with each word. "But what, Tyler? We can't afford to be sloppy, not now. If the RIPD catches wind of this, if they start connecting the dots..."

Braydon raised a hand, his fingers curling in a simple gesture that silenced Kari mid-sentence. He pointed to the seat beside him, his eyes locked on hers with an intensity that made Tyler's heart skip a beat.

For a moment, Kari hesitated, her jaw clenched with frustration. But then, slowly, she lowered herself into the seat, her eyes never leaving Braydon's.

Braydon smiled, a cold, satisfied thing. He placed a finger to his lips, a silent command that Kari obeyed without question.

But inside, Kari's mind was a whirlwind of conflicting emotions. She knew that Braydon was right, that the Panther Prowl needed to be strong, to show no weakness in the face of their enemies.

And yet, a part of her couldn't help but question the wisdom of their actions, the risks they were taking by involving outside groups like the were-rats. She thought of the message she had sent to the RIPD, the brutal attack on Cyndi, and a pang of doubt twisted in her gut.

Was this really the best way to achieve their goals, to assert their dominance over the city? Or were they simply inviting more trouble, more scrutiny from the authorities?

As she sat there, her hand entwined with Braydon's, Kari couldn't shake the feeling that they were walking a dangerous line, that one wrong move could bring everything they had worked for crashing down around them.

And as Tyler watched the silent exchange between his leaders, he felt a chill run down his spine. Because he knew, with a certainty that went beyond words, that the Panther Prowl was playing a dangerous game, one with stakes higher than any of them could imagine.

****

Casey stepped out of the medical bay, her heart heavy with the weight of her sister's fate. The device that Aidan and Rigo had created, the hope it represented... it all seemed so fragile, so uncertain in the face of the reality of Cyndi's transformation.

She pulled out her phone, her fingers hovering over the screen for a long moment before she finally dialed Mick's number. As the phone rang, Casey felt a wave of exhaustion wash over her, the events of the past few days catching up to her all at once.

"Casey?" Mick's voice was tinged with concern, the sound of it a welcome anchor in the chaos of her thoughts. "What's going on? Is everything okay?"

Casey took a deep breath, her eyes stinging with unshed tears. "No, Mick. It's not. It's Cyndi. She... she was attacked. By a were-panther."

There was a moment of stunned silence on the other end of the line, followed by a sharp intake of breath. "My God, Casey. Is she... is she alive?"

Casey nodded, forgetting for a moment that Mick

couldn't see her. "Yes, but... Mick, she's changing. She's becoming one of them. A lycan."

Mick's voice was steady, but Casey could hear the undercurrent of worry beneath the surface. "Okay. Okay, Casey, listen to me. We'll figure this out, alright? We'll do whatever we need to do to help Cyndi."

Casey felt a surge of gratitude, a flicker of hope in the darkness. "I know, Mick. I just... I don't know what to do. Some local friends of mine, they've created this device, something that might be able to suppress the transformation. But I'm scared, Mick. I'm scared of what it could do to her, of what it could mean for her future."

Mick was quiet for a long moment, the sound of his breathing a steady presence in Casey's ear. "Casey, I know you're scared. I know you want to protect Cyndi, to keep her safe from all of this. But you have to trust your friends, trust in the work they're doing."

He paused, his voice softening with understanding. "And you have to trust in Cyndi, too. She's strong, Casey. Just like you. She'll get through this, with your help and support."

Casey felt a tear slip down her cheek, the weight of Mick's words settling into her bones. "You're right, Mick. I know you're right. It's just... it's hard, you know? Seeing her like this, knowing what she's going through."

Mick's voice was gentle, a comfort in the storm. "I know, Casey. But you're not alone in this. You have your friends, and you have me. I'm here for you, always. Whatever you need."

Casey took a deep breath, the tightness in her chest easing just a fraction. "Thank you, Mick. I don't know what I would do without you."

She paused, a thought occurring to her suddenly. "Mick, there's something else. Something I need your help with."

"Anything, Casey. You know that."

Casey hesitated, the words sticking in her throat. "Cyndi... she's going to have to register with the RIPD. As a lycan. I don't know the protocol, the procedures. Can you... can you help me with that? Help me navigate all of this?"

Mick's response was immediate, his voice firm with conviction. "Of course, Casey. I'll take care of everything on my end, make sure that Cyndi's registration is handled with the utmost discretion and care. You just focus on being there for her, on helping her through this."

Casey felt a wave of relief wash over her, the burden on her shoulders easing just a bit. "Thank you, Mick. For everything. I don't know what I would do without you."

“One more thing, Ace, Hawkins has been out of the office for a while. His destination records show that he left for Polkville. Do you know anything about that? If not, do you think you could find out something about it?” Mick asks.

Casey’s mind felt burned out but when Mick mentioned Polkville, it regained its traction, enabling Casey to think clearly only briefly.

“Hawkins went to Polkville?” Casey asks, “Why would he need to go there?”

“I can’t find out any details on his mission, because the files are all rank locked and I dont have the rank to open it. Maybe you could give your boyfriend a call and see if he knows anything?” Mick suggests.

“He aint my boyfriend, Mick,” Casey says, her southern

slang coming out, "But I'll give him a call. Hopefully he can give me details about what is going on. Thank you for the heads up, Mick. I'll be in touch with an update," Casey ends the com link.

CHAPTER 8

In the depths of her stasis-induced slumber, Cyndi found herself in a world that felt both familiar and utterly foreign. She stood before a mirror in a dimly lit room, her hands smoothing over the silky fabric of a form-fitting red dress. Her rainbow-hued hair cascaded down her back in soft waves, and her green eyes sparkled with anticipation.

She was getting ready for a date, she realized, though she couldn't quite remember the details of how she had arrived at this moment. A flicker of unease passed through her, but she pushed it aside, determined to enjoy the evening ahead.

A knock at the door startled her from her reverie, and she felt a flutter of excitement in her chest. She opened the door to find a stunningly handsome man waiting for her, his chiseled features and perfectly styled hair taking her breath away. He wore a tailored suit that accentuated his lean, muscular build, and as he smiled at her, she caught a glimpse of his perfectly defined six-pack abs beneath the thin fabric of his shirt.

"Wow," she breathed, her eyes drinking in every detail of his appearance. "You look... amazing."

He chuckled, a low, seductive sound that sent shivers down her spine. "Not nearly as amazing as you, Cyndi. Shall we?"

He offered her his arm, and she took it, feeling a thrill of pleasure at the contact. They stepped out into the night, the city lights twinkling around them like stars.

As they walked, Cyndi found herself losing track of time and place, the details of the world around her blurring and shifting in unsettling ways. One moment they were strolling through a bustling downtown street, the next they were in a secluded park, the trees looming over them like silent sentinels.

And through it all, her date remained a constant presence at her side, his touch electric and his gaze intense. She felt drawn to him in a way she couldn't quite explain, a primal need that pulsed through her veins like liquid fire.

But as the night wore on, something began to change. A strange sensation crept over Cyndi, a prickling beneath her skin that grew more intense with each passing moment. She tried to ignore it, to focus on the man beside her and the thrill of the evening, but it was becoming impossible to deny.

And then, without warning, it happened. A searing pain ripped through her body, and she doubled over, gasping for breath. Her date's eyes widened in shock and fear, and he reached out to her, his voice filled with concern.

But as he touched her, Cyndi felt something inside her snap. A wild, feral rage consumed her, and she lashed out, her hands curling into claws and her teeth elongating into sharp fangs.

She was transforming, she realized with a surge of horror. Becoming something monstrous, something inhuman. And as the change overtook her, she lost all control, her consciousness fading into a red haze of hunger and fury.

When she came back to herself, she was standing over the torn and bloody remains of her date, his once-beautiful face frozen in a rictus of terror. She looked down at her own hands, saw the blood and flesh beneath her claws, and screamed, a sound of anguish and despair that echoed through the empty streets.

And as the world around her began to fade, the dream dissolving into a swirl of shadow and mist, Cyndi knew that nothing would ever be the same again. She had become a monster, a creature of the night, and there was no going back.

****

"Agent Elkins, your sister's vitals are experiencing abnormal pulses and have increased dramatically," KIVO says, breaking the eerie silence that had fallen over the medical bay, forcing Casey awake,

"Cyndi?" She calls, seeing her sister laying there, appearing normal even with the vicious bite mark on her neck, "Cyndi, you are not alone. I'm here. KIVO, give the stats,"

"Her blood pressure has nearly doubled, her pulse is erratic, and the strand of panther dna Aidan has instructed me to monitor has quadrupled in size, meaning the transformation could happen at any time. Agent Elkins, your sister isn't a rei user, but since becoming a lycan, her rei has increased exponentially as the panther dna combines with hers," KIVO announces, "Should I try to sedate her further?"

"No KIVO. Thank you for the input. Only administer more sedation if she goes feral and attacks," Casey instructs.

"Understood. Rigo and Aidan are on their way to investigate a robbery attempt at Cyndi's job. Mr. Butler and Mrs. Collins have returned to their homes, but have taken with them emergency coms disguised as wristwatches so they can communicate with me directly if anything happens," KIVO reports.

"Keep me updated on their findings," Casey says solemnly,

her voice wavering.

Casey knew her team needed her leadership, but she also knew that she couldn't trust them. They didn't stop Cyndi from getting attacked. They couldn't stop her from being a lycan. Despite Mick encouraging her to trust them, she just couldn't do it. Right now she only knew of one person she could trust. Removing her phone, she dialed his number, hesitating briefly.

Would he answer? The two of them hadn't talked since she sent him the very brief message telling him where she was being assigned. Then she called for help when she got to town, and he sent Aidan instead. Would he still answer her phone call? She dropped her hand, accidentally hitting send.

"Shortstack? Shortstack?" Alex called from the other end.

She shakily put the phone to her ear and broke down, telling him what happened. He listened intently before speaking.

"Listen, I'm sorry I didn't tell you sooner, but your superior is here in Polkville. He claims my new transformation makes me a lycan. So I'm kind of tied up at the moment. He is upset that I can't call the form at will, which is something a lycan can do. I cannot. However, let me give you some advice," Alex pauses, "Trust Aidan. Trust your team. Like I trusted my team when we worked together here in Polkville. You have to trust them 100%. Aidan's tech has never failed him. If he built it, trust it,"

"What are you going to do about RIPD investigating? If the by laws are to be trusted and upheld, RIPD can remove you from the sheriff's position. Which would give Leons time to grab it up," Casey panicks.

"Shortstack, take a deep breath. Hawkins read me everything. I've utilized my ability to name a replacement sheriff in the event that he finds enough evidence to label me a lycan. My father is coming out of retirement," Alex says.

"Rebel, what are you going to do then?" Casey asks.

"Traveling salesman?" Alex jokes, "But seriously, if my Dad has to take over, Tai, Ken and I will work side by side with him. Hawkins made sure to tell me I wasn't eligible for RIPD,"

"Why the hell not? You stopped a power hungry tyrant from changing the dimensional flow of things. I think that makes you eligible for RIPD," Casey bellows.

"I'm not sure, I'm waiting for him to finish his investigation," Alex says, "But Case, this is about your sister, not about me. You should get back to her. Keep me in the loop,"

"Thank you, Tigger," Casey says, softly, "I needed that,"

The two of them hung up, with Casey clutching her phone to chest. She whispered softly, "I love you, Tigger,"

****

Aidan and Rigo pulled up to The Corner Stop, the flashing lights of police cruisers casting an eerie glow over the crime scene. The store's front window had been shattered, and shards of glass littered the ground, crunching beneath their feet as they approached the yellow police tape.

An officer stepped forward, his hand raised to stop them. "I'm sorry, gentlemen, but this is an active crime scene. I can't let you through."

Aidan flashed a disarming smile, his voice calm and confident. "Officer, my name is Aidan Kenta, and this is my associate, Rigo Balderas. We're working with Special Agent Casey Elkins of the RIPD on a case that we believe may be connected to this robbery."

The officer's brow furrowed, uncertainty flickering in his eyes. "The RIPD? I wasn't aware that they were involved in this investigation."

Rigo stepped forward, his posture relaxed but his gaze intense. "That's why we're here, officer. To determine if there's a link between this crime and our ongoing investigation. If you could just let us take a look around, we'll be out of your hair in no time."

The officer hesitated, his gaze darting between Aidan and Rigo. But before he could respond, a familiar voice cut through the night air.

"Well, well, well. If it isn't Casey Elkins' little sidekicks, playing dress-up and pretending to be real investigators."

Aidan and Rigo turned to see Chief Blackwell striding towards them, his face twisted into a sneer of contempt. The chief came to a stop in front of them, his arms crossed over his chest and his eyes narrowed with suspicion.

"Mr. Kenta, Mr. Balderas," Blackwell drawled, his tone dripping with condescension. "I don't recall inviting the RIPD to stick their noses into my department's business. And last I checked, neither of you had a badge or any official authority in Blacksburg."

Aidan's smile never wavered, but there was a hint of steel in his voice as he replied. "Chief Blackwell, we're not here to step on any toes or interfere with your investigation. We simply want to ensure that there's no supernatural element to this crime that might require the RIPD's expertise."

Blackwell let out a harsh bark of laughter. "Supernatural element? Please. This is a simple smash-and-grab, nothing more. And even if it were something more, I hardly think a tech geek and a..."

He paused, his gaze raking over Rigo with a mix of disdain and curiosity. "What are you, exactly? Some kind of mercenary? Bounty hunter?"

Rigo met Blackwell's gaze evenly, his voice low and measured. "Let's just say I have a vested interest in keeping the streets of Blacksburg safe, Chief. From all threats, both human and otherwise."

Blackwell's eyes narrowed, a flicker of unease passing over his features. But he quickly masked it with a sneer, his voice dripping with sarcasm. "Well, isn't that noble of you. But I think we've got things covered here, gentlemen. So why don't you run along and let the real cops handle this?"

Aidan opened his mouth to protest, but Rigo placed a hand on his arm, his expression calm but unyielding. "Of course, Chief Blackwell. We wouldn't want to interfere with your investigation. But if you do happen to come across anything unusual, anything that might suggest a lycan presence or the involvement of the Panther Prowl..."

He let the words hang in the air, a silent challenge that made Blackwell's jaw clench with barely suppressed anger. "You'll be the first to know, Mr. Balderas. Now, if you'll excuse me, I have a crime scene to secure and a perpetrator to catch."

With that, Blackwell turned on his heel and stalked away, barking orders at his officers and pointedly ignoring Aidan and Rigo's presence.

Aidan let out a low whistle, his eyes wide with disbelief. "Well, that went well. I can see why Casey has such a high opinion of the chief."

Rigo snorted, his gaze still fixed on Blackwell's retreating form. "He's hiding something, Aidan. I can feel it in my bones. And whatever it is, it's got him running scared."

Aidan nodded, his mind already racing with the possibilities. "Agreed. But we're not going to get any answers here, not with Blackwell and his goons watching our every move."

He glanced around, his eyes landing on a nearby security camera mounted on a lamp post. "But I might know another way to get the information we need. Come on, let's get back to the base and see what KIVO can dig up on this robbery."

As Aidan and Rigo turned to leave the crime scene, a flash of movement caught Rigo's eye. He nudged Aidan, his voice low and urgent. "Look, over there. Isn't that Kari, the woman we saw with Braydon before?"

Aidan followed Rigo's gaze, his brow furrowing as he spotted the familiar figure ducking into an alleyway across the street. "Yeah, that's definitely her. What's she doing here, so close to the robbery site?"

Rigo's instincts were screaming at him, a sense of unease prickling at the back of his neck. "I don't know, but I don't like it. She's up to something, Aidan. I can feel it."

Aidan nodded, his mind already racing with the possibilities. "We should follow her, see what she's doing. If she's involved in this robbery or the larger plot with the Idol..."

He trailed off, the implications hanging heavy in the air between them. Rigo's hand drifted to the device concealed beneath his jacket, a sudden idea forming in his mind.

"Aidan, the suppression device. What if we used it on Kari? If she's a were-panther, it could temporarily neutralize her abilities, give us a chance to question her without interference."

Aidan's eyes widened, a mix of excitement and apprehension flickering across his face. "That's a big risk, Rigo. We still don't know the full extent of the device's effects on different lycan species. And if Kari realizes what we're doing..."

Rigo's jaw tightened, his resolve hardening. "I know it's a risk. But we're running out of time and options, Aidan. We need answers, and Kari might be our best chance at getting them."

Aidan hesitated for a moment, weighing the potential consequences against the urgent need for information. Finally, he nodded, his expression grim but determined.

"Okay. We'll do it your way. But we need to be smart about this, Rigo. We can't just confront her in the middle of the street."

Rigo's mind was already racing ahead, formulating a plan. "We'll follow her, wait for an opportunity to get her alone. Then we'll make our move."

As they set off in pursuit of Kari, Aidan couldn't shake the feeling that they were stepping into something much bigger and more dangerous than they had initially realized. But he trusted Rigo's instincts and his own abilities, and he knew that together, they would stop at nothing to uncover the truth.

They tracked Kari through the winding streets and alleyways of Blacksburg, their senses heightened and their bodies coiled with tension. Kari moved with purpose, her stride confident and her head held high, seemingly unaware of the two men tailing her.

Suddenly, Kari turned into a narrow, dimly lit alley, the shadows swallowing her form. Rigo and Aidan exchanged a glance, a silent understanding passing between them. This was their chance.

They quickened their pace, closing the distance between

themselves and their target. As they rounded the corner into the alley, they found Kari standing with her back to them, her attention focused on a rusted metal door set into the brick wall.

Rigo moved first, his steps swift and silent as he approached Kari from behind. In a flash, he had her arms pinned behind her back, his grip firm but not painful.

Kari let out a hiss of surprise and anger, her body tensing as she struggled against Rigo's hold. "What the hell do you think you're doing?" she snarled, her eyes flashing with a dangerous light.

Aidan stepped forward, his expression calm but unyielding. "We need to talk, Kari. About the robbery at The Corner Stop, and your connection to Braydon and the Panther Prowl."

Kari's lips curled into a sneer, a harsh laugh escaping her throat. "I don't know what you're talking about. And even if I did, I wouldn't tell you anything."

Rigo tightened his grip, his voice low and menacing. "We have ways of making you talk, Kari. Ways that you won't like."

With his free hand, he reached into his pocket and withdrew the suppression device, the sleek metal glinting in the dim light of the alley.

Kari's eyes widened, a flicker of fear passing over her features as she recognized the device. "What is that? What are you going to do to me?"

Aidan's voice was steady, his gaze locked on Kari's. "This device has the power to neutralize your lycan abilities, Kari. To make you human again, if only for a little while. And we're going to use it on you, unless you start talking."

Kari's struggles intensified, a growl rumbling in her

throat as she fought against Rigo's hold. But Rigo was too strong, his grip unbreakable.

With a nod from Aidan, Rigo pressed the device against Kari's neck, the metal cool and unyielding against her skin. Kari let out a gasp, her body going rigid as the device activated, a pulse of energy surging through her veins.

For a moment, nothing happened. And then, slowly, the changes began to manifest. Kari's features shifted, her feline characteristics fading away, replaced by the soft, human curves of her face. Her claws retracted, her fangs shrinking back into normal teeth.

Kari sagged in Rigo's grip, her strength leaving her as the device worked its magic. She looked up at Aidan and Rigo, her eyes wide with shock and disbelief.

"What have you done to me?" she whispered, her voice trembling with a mix of fear and anger.

Aidan leaned in close, his voice filled with a quiet intensity. "We've leveled the playing field, Kari. Now, you're going to tell us everything you know about the robbery, about Braydon, and about the Panther Prowl's plans for Blacksburg."

Rigo loosened his grip, allowing Kari to stand on her own feet. But he kept the device pressed firmly against her neck, a silent warning of the consequences should she try to resist.

And as Kari began to talk, her words spilling out in a jumbled rush of fear and desperation, Aidan and Rigo listened intently, their minds racing with the implications of what they were hearing.

The pieces of the puzzle were finally starting to fall into place, the truth behind Blacksburg's darkest secrets slowly coming to light. And with each revelation, the stakes grew higher, the dangers more profound.

But Aidan and Rigo knew that they could not falter, could not let their resolve waver. For the sake of Casey, for the sake of Blacksburg, they would see this through to the end, no matter the cost.

The confrontation with Kari was only the beginning, a single battle in a much larger war. But it was a crucial victory nonetheless, a step towards the truth and the justice they sought.

And as the night wore on, the secrets of the Panther Prowl unraveling before them, Aidan and Rigo knew that they were ready for whatever lay ahead, their partnership a beacon of hope in the darkness that threatened to consume them all.

****

Cyndi found herself standing in a beautifully decorated church, sunlight streaming through the stained-glass windows and casting a kaleidoscope of colors across the altar. The pews were filled with smiling faces, friends and family gathered to celebrate the union of two hearts.

At the front of the church, Braydon stood tall and handsome in a tailored tuxedo, his eyes shining with love and anticipation. And there, walking down the aisle on her father's arm, was Casey, resplendent in a flowing white gown, her face aglow with joy.

Cyndi's heart swelled with happiness for her sister, a sense of warmth and contentment enveloping her. She watched as Casey and Braydon joined hands, their gazes locked and their smiles radiant.

The ceremony began, the priest's words a soothing cadence that filled the church. Cyndi listened, her eyes misty with emotion, as the couple exchanged their vows, their voices trembling with the depth of their love.

But as the priest began to utter the final, binding words, a strange sensation washed over Cyndi. A prickling beneath her skin, a tightness in her chest. She tried to ignore it, to focus on the beautiful moment unfolding before her, but the feeling only grew stronger, more insistent.

Suddenly, a searing pain ripped through her body, and Cyndi doubled over, a scream tearing from her throat. The congregation turned to look at her, their faces a mix of concern and confusion.

But Cyndi couldn't focus on them, couldn't focus on anything but the agony that consumed her. She felt her bones shifting, her muscles twisting and contorting, as a terrifying transformation overtook her.

Fur sprouted from her skin, claws burst from her fingertips, and her jaws elongated into a feral muzzle. She had become a beast, a creature of nightmare and legend.

The wedding guests screamed in terror, scrambling to flee the church as Cyndi's lycan form towered over them. But Casey and Braydon remained frozen at the altar, their eyes wide with shock and horror.

Cyndi tried to speak, to beg for help, but only a guttural growl escaped her throat. She took a step forward, her claws scraping against the stone floor, and Casey recoiled, a whimper of fear escaping her lips.

"Cyndi, no," Casey pleaded, her voice trembling. "This isn't you. You have to fight it!"

But Cyndi couldn't fight it, couldn't control the primal urges that surged through her veins. With a roar of hunger and rage, she lunged forward, her claws slashing through the air towards her sister and her once-beloved friend.

The scene dissolved into chaos, screams and snarls echoing through the church as Cyndi's lycan form rampaged unchecked. She caught glimpses of torn flesh and spilled blood, of broken bodies and shattered lives.

And through it all, a single thought pounded in her mind, a desperate plea that went unheard and unanswered.

"Please, let me wake up. Let this be just a dream. Please, don't let me hurt them. Don't let me become this monster."

But the dream held her fast, the nightmare playing out in all its brutal, inescapable horror. And as Cyndi's claws found their mark, as the life drained from the eyes of those she loved, she knew that there was no escape, no redemption.

She was a beast, a creature of the shadows, and the world she had once known was lost to her forever. All that remained was the hunt, the hunger, and the unending cycle of violence and despair.

And so Cyndi ran, her howls echoing through the empty streets of a shattered dreamscape, a prisoner of her own shattered psyche.

****

The changes to Cyndi's body began almost instantaneously. One moment she was a normal human, the next minute coarse black fur had covered her body as her face elongated into the muzzle of the panther. Casey jumped back from the stasis pod, alarmed, drawing her firearm.

"Protocol Zero One Nine Activate," KIVO announced.

The stasis pod hummed slightly as Cyndi's body was

coated in a light blue light. Casey looked around, feverish and scared.

"KIVO, what is Protocol Zero One Nine?" She asks.

"Protocol Zero One Nine is the sedation protocol you and I discussed earlier, Agent Elkins. I have also alert Mr. Kenta and Mr. Rigo of the changes. They have informed me that they have captured Kari Byars," KIVO explains.

"Can you bring up all the information on Kari Byars on the main screen?" Casey inquires.

"Her information is listed now," KIVO explains.

Casey approached the main screen in the central chamber of the HQ. She reads off the information.

"Kari Ann Byars, Daughter of Blacksburg Mayor Keith Byars. Has been involved with the Panther Prowl since early 2014, Kari is believed to be one of Braydon Mitchell's high ranking members," Casey reads aloud, "KIVO can you display a 3D hologram of Kari transforming?"

"One moment, Agent Elkins," KIVO begins playing the jeopardy theme song as it works, suddenly in the center of the room, a large 3D hologram of Kari transforming.

"Stop right there," Casey instructs, hurriedly grabbing a tape measure from her desk and measuring the claws of Kari's panther form. "No fucking way,"

Casey's eyes widened as she compared the measurements of Kari's claws in her panther form to the wounds on Cyndi's body. The realization hit her like a freight train, a wave of anger and betrayal washing over her.

Just then, the door to the headquarters burst open, and Rigo and Aidan strode in, a struggling Kari held firmly between them. The suppression device glinted on her neck, a testament to the temporary neutralization of her lycan abilities.

Casey whirled around, her eyes blazing with fury as she locked onto Kari's face. "YOU BITCH!" she screamed, her voice raw with emotion.

Before anyone could react, Casey lunged forward, her fist connecting with Kari's jaw in a satisfying crack. Kari's head snapped back, a grunt of pain escaping her lips as she sagged in Rigo and Aidan's grip.

Rigo and Aidan exchanged a look of surprise and concern, their hold on Kari tightening as they pulled her back, creating distance between her and the enraged Casey.

"Casey, what's going on?" Aidan asked, his voice calm but urgent. "Why did you hit her?"

Casey's chest heaved with anger, her finger pointing accusingly at Kari. "She's the one, Aidan. She's the one who attacked Cyndi, who turned her into a lycan."

Rigo's eyes widened, his gaze darting between Casey and Kari. "What? How do you know?"

Casey gestured to the hologram still floating in the center of the room, the image of Kari's transformed state frozen in place. "KIVO, show them the measurements of Kari's claws compared to Cyndi's wounds."

The hologram shifted, the data and images aligning to create a damning picture of Kari's guilt. Aidan and Rigo stared at the evidence, their expressions hardening as the truth sank in.

Kari, despite the pain of Casey's punch, managed a defiant smirk. "So what if I did? The little bitch had it coming, always sticking her nose where it didn't belong."

Casey's vision went red, her hands clenching into fists as she took a step towards Kari. But Rigo intercepted her, his strong arms holding her back.

"Casey, don't," he warned, his voice low and urgent. "She's not worth it. We have her now, and we'll make sure she pays for what she's done."

Casey struggled against Rigo's grip, her anger and grief threatening to consume her. But as she looked into his eyes, she saw the steadiness and support there, the unwavering commitment to justice that had brought them all together.

Slowly, the fight drained out of her, replaced by a cold, steely determination. She nodded to Rigo, and he released her, stepping back but remaining close, ready to intervene if necessary.

Casey turned to Kari, her voice low and dangerous. "You're going to tell us everything, Kari. Everything about the Panther Prowl, about Braydon's plans, and about what you did to my sister."

Kari's smirk faltered, a flicker of fear passing over her features. But she quickly masked it with bravado, her chin lifting defiantly. "And why would I do that?"

Aidan stepped forward, his expression grim. "Because if you don't, we'll make sure you rot in the darkest, deepest cell the RIPD has to offer. And trust me, that's a fate worse than anything Braydon could do to you."

Kari's eyes darted between the three of them, the gravity of her situation finally sinking in. She swallowed hard, her defiance crumbling under the weight of their combined resolve.

"Fine," she spat, her voice filled with venom. "I'll tell you what you want to know. But it won't change anything. The

Panther Prowl is stronger than you can imagine, and Braydon's plan is already in motion."

Casey leaned in close, her voice a whisper that carried the weight of a thousand threats. "We'll see about that, Kari. We'll see about that."

As Rigo and Aidan led Kari away to the interrogation room, Casey turned back to the hologram, her eyes fixed on the image of her sister's attacker.

The truth was out there, waiting to be uncovered. And Casey would stop at nothing to find it, to bring justice to those who had hurt her family and threatened her city.

Aidan helped Rigo put Kari in the interrogation room. He looked to Rigo and the unspoken words between the two of them sealed their fates. Rigo opened the door to the interrogation room once more, as Aidan turned to find Casey.

“KIVO, what is Agent Elkins’ location?” Aidan asks, as he runs down the corridor.

“She is in the medical bay,” KIVO responds.

“Thanks,” Aidan says, entering a full run.

Moments later, Aidan skids to a stop at the entrance to the medical bay door, his shoes leaving black marks on the floor.

“Casey,” Aidan says, clearly out of breath, “Can we talk?”

“Whatever you have to say, Kenta, can be said now,” Casey says, fighting the urge to tell Aidan to leave.

“Casey, the device. It works,” Aidan explains, “Kari was transforming to fight Rigo when I latched it around her neck. Unfortunately, I have to build a second one for Cyndi, but with KIVO’s help it shouldn’t take long. But we have proof that my device works to suppress the lycan’s transforming powers,”

“How long do you think it should take?” Casey asks, as Alex’s words flashed through her mind.

“Give me two hours,” Aidan says.

“He means three,” KIVO explains, “If you want the suppressor to work properly, the way Rigo intended, I need three hours,”

“Show off,” Aidan says, “So Three Hours, Case. What do you say?”

“Three hours. And then I will do an interrogation,” Casey says, looking ominously towards the interrogation room, then back at Cyndi.

****

Braydon lounged in his throne-like chair, his eyes fixed on the flickering screens before him. The security cameras positioned throughout Blacksburg fed a constant stream of information into his lair, allowing him to keep a watchful eye on his territory.

Suddenly, the door burst open, and a scrawny, twitchy were-rat scurried in, his eyes wide with fear and agitation. Braydon's gaze snapped to the intruder, his lip curling in a snarl of annoyance.

"What is it, Nathan?" he growled, his voice low and menacing. "You know better than to barge in here uninvited."

Nathan cowered before Braydon, his hands wringing nervously. "I-I'm sorry, boss," he stammered, his voice high-pitched and tremulous. "But I got news, important news. It's about Kari."

Braydon sat up straighter, his interest piqued. "Kari?

What about her?"

Nathan swallowed hard, his Adam's apple bobbing in his throat. "She's been taken, boss. By the Joker and his tech friend. I saw it happen, saw them put something around her neck and drag her away."

Braydon's eyes narrowed, a cold fury settling over his features. "The Joker? You mean Rigo Balderas, that Hyena hybrid freak?"

Nathan nodded vigorously, his head bobbing up and down. "Yeah, him and that Aidan guy, the one with all the fancy gadgets. They got Kari, boss. They got her good."

Braydon's hand clenched into a fist, his claws digging into his palm. Kari was his queen, his partner in every sense of the word. The thought of her in the hands of his enemies made his blood boil and his heart race with a primal rage.

He stood abruptly, his chair clattering to the floor behind him. "Gather the Prowl," he snarled, his voice echoing through the lair. "Every last one of them. We're going to get Kari back, and we're going to make those bastards pay for ever laying a hand on her."

Nathan backed away, his head bowed in submission. "Right away, boss. I'll let them know."

As the were-rat scurried out of the room, Braydon turned back to the screens, his eyes scanning the feeds for any sign of Kari or her captors. He would find them, and he would make them suffer for their insolence.

No one took what belonged to Braydon Mitchell, no one challenged the might of the Panther Prowl. And those who dared to try would soon learn the true meaning of fear and pain.

Braydon's lips twisted into a cruel smile, his fangs

glinting in the dim light of the lair. The hunt was on, and he would not rest until Kari was back by his side and his enemies lay broken at his feet.

****

Amber drops her coffee cup as she looks up seeing the entire Prowl of Panthers marching through the streets of Blacksburg through the front windows of Danny's Cafe. Amber immediately grabbed the wrist mounted com, bringing it to her lips.

"KIVO, this is Amber. The Were-Panthers are on the hunt," She said, her voice shaking.

"Ms. Collins, batten the hatches and hide yourself and any patrons safely inside the cafe. I'm executing protocols to protect the city now," KIVO replied.

"Can you let Casey know?" Amber asks.

"Agent Elkins is being made aware of the absurdity at once," KIVO replies..

"Amber," Aidan's voice cackled through the com, "KIVO alerted me to what you have reported. You and anyone near you should get into the walk-in cooler, and lock the door. It's crunch time,"

"Thanks, Aidan," Amber says nervously, before she raised her voice, "EVERYONE, I just received word from THE RIPD that Blacksburg is under martial law. We have been instructed to barricade ourselves into the walk-in cooler until further notice,"

The patrons begin to clamor after Amber's message and move towards the walk-in, however a few of them remain seated. One, a piece of pie named Anthony Woods, sneered at Amber.

“You really think your large cooler can stop the Panthers? If Panzer wants to kill you, he will,” Woods bellows.

“Oh shit. I knew today was a day I was supposed to call in sick,” Amber rolls her eyes, “If the RIPD thinks it will save us, I’m going to go with them,”

As Anthony Woods roared, Amber began closing the large door. Suddenly a large black claw reached through the door, stopping it from closing entirely and scaring Amber.

“Jesus, Mary, Joseph, and the fucking camel they rode in on, can’t you rude ass men not take a hint?” Amber manages to quip between grunts as she tries to bring the door closed.

The were-panther outside the door roared, and almost ripped the door off the hinges, however quick thinking by Amber allowed her to throw jalapeno pepper juice into the lycan’s eyes, which caused him to stumble backwards, clawing at his eyes as they burned. Amber slams the cooler door closed, locking it tightly.

“Someone turn those cooling fans off. We can stay here for a while,” Amber says softly, “I just dont know how long,”

****

Inside the Kenta Corp base, the main screen flashed red, and KIVO's voice echoed through the central chamber. "Attention all personnel, we have a Code Black situation. The Panther Prowl has launched an invasion of Blacksburg. I repeat, the Panther Prowl has launched an invasion of Blacksburg."

Casey, who had been keeping a watchful eye over Cyndi's stasis pod, snapped to attention. "KIVO, give me a full report. Where are they, and what's the extent of the damage?"

KIVO's avatar materialized on the screen, its face a mask

of calm determination. "Agent Elkins, the Panther Prowl has been spotted marching through the main streets of Blacksburg. They appear to be targeting key locations and infrastructure. I have received a report from Ms. Collins at Danny's Cafe, indicating that she and several patrons have barricaded themselves in the walk-in cooler for safety."

Casey's heart raced, her mind already spinning with the implications of the invasion. She knew she couldn't call for official RIPD backup, not with Cyndi's situation still unresolved. Instead, she reached for her phone, dialing Mick's number.

"Mick, it's Casey. We have a situation here in Blacksburg. The Panther Prowl is making a move on the city, and I need your advice."

Mick's voice came through the speaker, steady and reassuring. "Casey, listen to me. You've got this. Trust your instincts and your team. They're your best assets right now."

Casey nodded, her jaw clenched with determination. "Thanks, Mick. I'll keep you updated."

As she ended the call, Casey turned to the interrogation room where Kari was being held. She keyed the intercom, her voice tight with urgency. "Rigo, Aidan, we have a situation. The Panther Prowl is making a move on the city. We need to act fast."

Rigo's voice crackled over the intercom, his tone grim. "Understood, Casey. We'll finish up here with Kari and join you in the main chamber. We need to come up with a plan."

Casey turned back to KIVO, her mind racing. "KIVO, pull up a map of Blacksburg. Highlight all known Panther Prowl locations and potential targets. We need to figure out their endgame and cut them off at the pass."

As the map materialized on the screen, red dots

blossoming across the cityscape, Casey felt a chill run down her spine. The Panther Prowl was making a bold move, a show of force that threatened to tear Blacksburg apart.

But she wouldn't let that happen. Not on her watch.

The door to the main chamber slid open, and Rigo and Aidan strode in, their faces etched with worry and resolve. Aidan made a beeline for the computer console, his fingers flying over the keys as he pulled up data and schematics.

"I've got eyes on the streets," he said, his voice tight with concentration. "Traffic cameras, security feeds, everything. We'll be able to track their movements in real-time."

Rigo moved to Casey's side, his presence a solid comfort in the midst of the chaos. "We'll stop them, Casey. Whatever it takes, we'll stop them."

Casey nodded, her eyes fixed on the map before her. The Panther Prowl was out there, prowling the streets of her city, threatening the lives of innocent people.

But they had no idea who they were up against.

Casey's hand drifted to her sidearm, the weight of it a reassuring presence at her hip. She took a deep breath, her resolve hardening with each passing second.

It was time to bring the fight to the Panther Prowl, to show them what happened when they messed with her city, her family.

And heaven help anyone who got in her way.

CHAPTER 9

The streets of Blacksburg trembled beneath the thunderous march of the Panther Prowl, their sleek black forms moving as one through the heart of the city. At the center of the procession, a grand platform adorned with two thrones was carried aloft by a group of were-rats, their bodies straining under the weight of their burden.

Upon one of the thrones sat Braydon, his posture regal and his eyes glinting with a fierce determination. Beside him, Kari's throne sat empty, a stark reminder of her absence and the reason for the Panther Prowl's bold invasion.

Between the two thrones, perched precariously on a gilded pedestal, rested the Idol of Lycoan. Its surface seemed to pulse with an otherworldly energy, a tangible manifestation of the power that Braydon sought to wield.

As the platform moved through the streets, the were-panthers flanking it on all sides, a sense of awe and terror rippled through the onlookers. Braydon reveled in their fear, his lips curling into a smirk of satisfaction.

Suddenly, one of the were-panthers leapt atop the platform, his movements graceful and precise. In his clawed hands, he held a megaphone, which he presented to Braydon with a deep bow.

Braydon took the megaphone, his fingers curling around it with a sense of purpose. He rose from his throne, his voice booming out across the streets as he addressed the city.

"People of Blacksburg, hear me now! I am Braydon Mitchell, the alpha of the Panther Prowl and the rightful ruler of this city. Your lives, your very existence, are now under my dominion."

He paused, his gaze sweeping over the cowering masses. "But there is one among you who has dared to challenge my authority, who has taken that which is most precious to me. The RIPD, in their arrogance and foolishness, have imprisoned my queen, Kari Byars."

Braydon's voice grew louder, his anger palpable in every word. "I demand the immediate release of Kari, and the surrender of those responsible for her capture. The Hyena hybrid, Rigo Balderas, and his tech-savvy ally, Aidan Kenta. Bring them to me, and I may yet show mercy to this city."

He lifted the Idol of Lycoan from its pedestal, its surface glowing with an eerie light. "But defy me, and you will face the full wrath of the Panther Prowl. With the power of the Idol at my command, I will unleash a fury upon Blacksburg the likes of which has never been seen."

Braydon's voice dropped to a menacing whisper, amplified by the megaphone. "You have one hour to comply. One hour to bring me Kari, Rigo, and Aidan. If you fail, the streets of Blacksburg will run red with blood, and the reign of the Panther Prowl will be eternal."

With that, Braydon returned to his throne, the Idol cradled in his lap like a cherished child. The were-panther with the megaphone leapt down from the platform, his mission accomplished.

As the procession continued its march through the city, the weight of Braydon's ultimatum hung heavy in the air. The people of Blacksburg trembled in fear, their eyes darting to the shadows, seeking any sign of hope or salvation.

But in the heart of the Kenta Corp base, Casey and her team were already in motion, their resolve hardened by the threat to their city and their loved ones.

The final confrontation was at hand, and the fate of Blacksburg hung in the balance. Casey knew that she would need every ounce of her strength, every shred of her determination, to face the coming storm.

But she was ready, her team at her side and the power of justice in her heart. The Panther Prowl may have the Idol, but Casey had something far more powerful: the unbreakable bonds of family, friendship, and duty.

And with those bonds, she knew that anything was possible, even in the face of the darkest evil.

****

Mick sat at his desk, his brow furrowed as he stared at the phone in his hand. The conversation with Casey kept replaying in his mind, the urgency in her voice, the determined set of her jaw as she described the escalating situation in Blacksburg.

He knew she was capable, knew that she had faced countless challenges and emerged victorious. But this was different. The Panther Prowl, the Idol of Lycoan... it was a threat unlike any they had faced before.

With a sigh, Mick dialed Alex's number, his fingers tapping impatiently on the desk as he waited for the former Marine to pick up.

"Ruler," Alex's voice came through the speaker, his tone expectant. "I assume this is about Casey and the situation in Blacksburg?"

Mick gritted his teeth, his free hand clenching into a fist. "Yeah, it is. I'm calling to give you an update. The Panther Prowl has launched a full-scale invasion of the city, and they're demanding the release of their queen, Kari Byars."

Alex's sharp intake of breath was audible through the phone. "Damn it. I knew things were bad, but a full-scale invasion? Casey's going to need all the help she can get."

Mick snorted, his tone dripping with sarcasm. "Oh, really? I hadn't realized. Thank you for that astute observation, Ruler. It's not like you're a rei user or a former Marine or anything."

Alex's response was immediate, his voice laced with irritation. "Cut the crap, Mick. If you're so concerned about Casey, why are you sitting behind a desk playing phone tag instead of being out there with her?"

Mick's jaw tightened, a flicker of anger sparking in his chest. "You know damn well why, Ruler. I'm her handler, her support on the inside. It's my job to coordinate resources and make sure she has what she needs to get the job done."

There was a pause, and when Alex spoke again, his tone was more measured. "Fair enough. But Casey needs boots on the ground, too. People who can watch her back and help her take down the Panther Prowl."

Mick sighed, his shoulders slumping in defeat. "You're right, Ruler. As much as I hate to admit it, you're right. Casey needs all the help she can get, and that includes you."

He paused, his mind racing with the implications of what he was about to say. "Listen, there's something else you should know. Hawkins, the RIPD's top brass? He was in Polkville recently, investigating your new abilities."

Alex's voice was tight with tension. "I know. I've had the pleasure of meeting him. He has occupied most of my time so I can't be involved with the investigation going on in Polkville. "

Mick's stomach churned with unease, a sense of distrust settling over him like a heavy fog. "According to what I've dug up so far, he is investigating a new rei induced transformation used by you during the confrontation with Thomas Leons in the finals of the Strongest Under The Heavens Tournament. The rei readings were so high that our RIPD computers couldn't measure them. It appears as if this transformation registered as lycanthropy. Which means–?"

Mick is cut off abruptly as Alex speaks, "That Hawkins can legally force me to retire as Sheriff, but first he has to prove that I am unable to control the transformation process. Which he hasn't be able to do so far. Besides due to by laws passed in the city of Polkville, if I am forced to retire, I can choose my successor and I've already decided on that in the worst case scenario,"

"If Hawkins is there, how are you going to help Casey?" Mick asks, "If he thinks you are a lycan, you will definitely be considered a lycan if you leave town to go assist with a lycan problem,"

"Is there no way you can call him back to the RIPD HQ for something urgent?" Alex asks.

"Unfortunately, no. He is my superior. I dont have the access required to call him back," Mick says.

"I'll figure something out, Mick. Just hang tight and keep me updated on the situation in Blacksburg," Alex says.

"Alright. I'll be in touch. Ruler, watch yourself," Mick says, "Casey will kill me if she finds out something happened to you because of me,"

Alex was silent for a moment, the weight of Mick's words hanging heavy in the air. "Alright. I'll keep my eyes open, see if I can find out anything on my end. But right now, my priority is getting to Blacksburg and backing up Casey."

Mick nodded, even though Alex couldn't see him. "Understood. Keep me in the loop, Ruler. And... watch your back out there. I don't trust Hawkins, and I don't like the idea of him sniffing around your abilities."

"Roger that," Alex said, his voice filled with determination. "I'll be careful. And Mick? Thanks for the heads up. I know we don't always see eye to eye, but I appreciate you looking out for Casey... and for me."

As the call ended, Mick leaned back in his chair, his eyes drifting to the window and the snowy landscape and beyond.

****

Casey stood beside Cyndi's stasis pod, her heart heavy with worry and exhaustion. The chaos of the Panther Prowl's invasion, the demands for Kari's release, and the looming threat of the Idol of Lycoan weighed on her like a physical burden.

But as she looked down at her sister's face, peaceful in the artificial slumber, Casey felt a flicker of hope. Aidan had worked tirelessly to create a suppressor device tailored to Cyndi's unique physiology, a feat of technological brilliance that could mean the difference between life and death.

The door to the medical bay slid open, and Aidan stepped inside, the device cradled carefully in his hands. His face was lined with fatigue, but his eyes shone with a fierce determination.

"It's ready," he said, his voice steady and confident. "The

suppressor is calibrated to Cyndi's specific genetic markers. It should help to control her transformations and keep her lycan side in check."

Casey nodded, her throat tight with emotion. "Thank you, Aidan. I can't even begin to express how much this means to me, to Cyndi."

Aidan offered a small smile, his free hand coming to rest on Casey's shoulder. "She's family, Casey. We take care of our own."

He moved to the stasis pod, his fingers flying over the control panel as he prepared to administer the device. Casey watched, her heart pounding in her chest, as Aidan carefully attached the suppressor to Cyndi's neck, the metal gleaming against her pale skin.

For a moment, nothing happened. The steady beep of the monitors, the soft hiss of the ventilation system, were the only sounds in the room.

And then, slowly, almost imperceptibly, the readings on the displays began to change. Cyndi's heart rate stabilized, her brain activity shifting from the chaotic patterns of lycan transformation to the more orderly rhythms of human consciousness.

Casey let out a breath she hadn't realized she'd been holding, tears pricking at the corners of her eyes. "Is it... is it working?"

Aidan nodded, his gaze fixed on the monitors. "It looks that way. Her vitals are stabilizing, and the lycan genetic markers are being suppressed. She's not out of the woods yet, but this is a huge step in the right direction."

Casey sagged against the stasis pod, relief and gratitude

washing over her in waves. For the first time since this nightmare began, she allowed herself to feel a glimmer of hope, a sense that maybe, just maybe, they could find a way through this darkness.

But even as she savored this small victory, Casey knew that the battle was far from over. The Panther Prowl was still out there, their claws poised to tear Blacksburg apart. And the Idol of Lycoan, the source of their power and their madness, remained in Braydon's possession.

She straightened, her jaw set with determination. "We can't stop now, Aidan. We have to find a way to end this, to stop the Panther Prowl and secure the Idol."

Aidan met her gaze, his expression mirroring her own resolve. "We will, Casey. Together, we'll find a way. We'll save Cyndi, and we'll save Blacksburg."

Casey nodded, her hand coming to rest on the cool surface of the stasis pod. She knew that the road ahead would be long and treacherous, that the dangers they faced were unlike any they had encountered before.

But she also knew that she was not alone. With Aidan, Rigo, and the rest of her team by her side, Casey felt a renewed sense of purpose, a certainty that they could overcome any obstacle, face any foe.

And as she stood there, watching over her sister and drawing strength from the unwavering support of her friends, Casey knew that they would not rest until the job was done.

Until the Panther Prowl was defeated, and the streets of Blacksburg were safe once more.

Looking up at the clock hovering in the air, Casey could see that only twenty minutes had passed since Braydon's announcement.

“I’m going to interrogate Kari, so we can give her back to Braydon and stop the blood flow for now,” Casey says, hurrying off to the interrogation room.

“Casey,” Aidan says, “Wait,”

Aidan hurries after her, stopping Casey before she enters the room.

“There is something you should know. The suppressor is acting as an inhibitor preventing Braydon’s mind control over the Were-Panthers from working. She can willingly talk now that she has been under the influence of it for a couple hours. She will seem panicked because she doesnt understand what is going on,” Aidan says, “The suppressor doesnt suppress memories, so if you question her about Cyndi, she may break down crying,”

Casey paused at the entrance to the interrogation room, her hand resting on the doorknob as she absorbed Aidan's words. The knowledge that the suppressor could free Kari from Braydon's mind control was a game-changer, a potential key to unlocking the secrets behind the Panther Prowl's reign of terror.

She took a deep breath, steeling herself for the confrontation ahead. "Thank you, Aidan. I'll keep that in mind. But we don't have much time. Braydon's ultimatum is ticking down, and we need answers."

Aidan nodded, his expression grim. "I understand. Just... be careful in there, Casey. Kari's been through a lot, and we don't know the full extent of what Braydon's done to her."

Casey met his gaze, her jaw set with determination. "I will. But we can't afford to pull any punches. Not with Blacksburg on the line."

With that, she pushed open the door and stepped into

the interrogation room, the harsh fluorescent light casting deep shadows across her face.

Kari sat at the table, her hands cuffed in front of her and her head bowed. As Casey approached, she lifted her gaze, and the agent was struck by the raw emotion in her eyes. Gone was the defiant swagger, the cruel smirk that had graced her features during their previous encounters. In its place was a haunted, almost frightened expression, the look of someone who had been dragged kicking and screaming into the light.

"Kari," Casey said, her voice firm but not unkind. "We need to talk."

Kari flinched at the sound of her name, her hands trembling in their restraints. "I... I don't understand. What's happening to me? Why do I feel so... so..."

"It's the suppressor," Casey explained, taking a seat across from her. "It's blocking Braydon's control over you, allowing you to think and feel for yourself again."

At the mention of Braydon's name, Kari's eyes widened, a flicker of fear and revulsion passing over her features. "Braydon... oh god, what have I done? What have we done?"

Casey leaned forward, her gaze intense. "That's what I need you to tell me, Kari. I need to know everything about Braydon's plans, about the Idol of Lycoan, and about what happened to my sister."

Kari's breath hitched, tears welling up in her eyes. "Your sister... Cyndi. I... I didn't mean to hurt her. I swear, I didn't want to. But Braydon, he... he made me. He said it was necessary, that it would send a message."

Casey's heart clenched, her fingers tightening into fists. "What message, Kari? What is Braydon trying to achieve?"

Kari shook her head, her voice breaking. "He wants power, Casey. He wants to control Blacksburg, to bend both humans and lycans to his will. And the Idol... it's the key to everything. With its power, he believes he can create an army of unstoppable were-panthers, loyal only to him."

Casey's mind raced, the pieces of the puzzle falling into place with sickening clarity. "And my sister? Why target her?"

Kari met her gaze, tears streaming down her face. "Because of you, Casey. Because he knew that hurting Cyndi would hurt you, would make you vulnerable. He... he wanted to break you, to shatter your resolve."

Casey closed her eyes, the weight of Kari's words settling like a lead weight in her chest. The cruelty, the sheer ruthlessness of Braydon's actions, was almost too much to bear.

But she couldn't afford to break, not now. Not with so much at stake.

She opened her eyes, her voice steady and unwavering. "Kari, I need you to tell me everything you know about Braydon's plans. Every detail, every scrap of information you can remember. We don't have much time, but if we work together, we might still be able to stop him."

Kari nodded, her expression a mix of fear and determination. "I'll tell you everything, Casey. I'll help you in any way I can. But please... you have to protect me from him. From Braydon. I can't go back to being his puppet, his plaything. I can't..."

Casey reached across the table, her hand resting on Kari's cuffed wrists. "I will, Kari. I promise. You're safe now, and we'll make sure you stay that way."

As Kari began to talk, her words spilling out in a rush of

fear and desperation, Casey listened intently, her mind racing with the implications of each new revelation.

The clock was ticking, and the fate of Blacksburg hung in the balance. But with Kari's help, with the strength and determination of her team, Casey knew that they could still turn the tide.

They had to. For Cyndi, for Blacksburg, and for all the innocent lives caught in the crosshairs of Braydon's twisted ambitions.

****

Casey strode into the main hub of the Kenta Corp headquarters, her mind still reeling from the revelations of her interrogation with Kari. The weight of the information, the sheer magnitude of Braydon's plans, pressed down on her like a physical force.

But as she looked around at the faces of her team, at the determination and resolve etched into every line of their expressions, Casey felt a flicker of hope. They were in this together, united by a common purpose and an unbreakable bond.

"Alright, everyone," she said, her voice cutting through the low hum of the computers and the crackle of the comm systems. "We've got a lot to discuss, and not a lot of time to do it."

Aidan looked up from his workstation, his fingers still flying over the keys. "What did you learn from Kari? Did she give us anything useful?"

Casey nodded, her jaw tight. "More than useful. She confirmed what we already suspected about Braydon's plans. He wants to use the Idol of Lycoan to create an army of loyal were-panthers, to take control of Blacksburg and bend both humans and lycans to his will."

Rigo let out a low whistle, his eyes narrowing. "That's a bold move, even for Braydon. He must be pretty confident in the Idol's power."

Casey met his gaze, her expression grim. "He is. And with good reason. According to Kari, the Idol is the key to everything. With it, Braydon believes he's unstoppable."

There was a moment of heavy silence, the weight of Casey's words sinking in like a stone. Finally, Aidan spoke, his voice tight with determination.

"So, what's our play? How do we stop him?"

Casey took a deep breath, her mind racing with the possibilities. "We have to get the Idol away from him, first and foremost. As long as he has it, he's too powerful to confront directly."

Rigo nodded, his hand resting on the hilt of his weapon. "Agreed. But how do we do that? Braydon's not just going to hand it over."

Casey's lips thinned, her gaze distant as she considered their options. "We have to be smart about this. We can't take him head-on, not yet. But maybe... maybe we can use his own tactics against him."

Aidan's eyebrows shot up, a glimmer of interest in his eyes. "What do you mean?"

Casey leaned forward, her voice low and intense. "Braydon used Cyndi to get to me, to throw me off balance. What if we did the same thing to him? Use Kari to lure him out, to make him vulnerable?"

Rigo's expression turned thoughtful, his head tilting to

the side. "It's risky. Braydon's not stupid, and he's not going to fall for an obvious trap."

Casey nodded, her mind already spinning with the possibilities. "I know. But if we can make him believe that Kari's escaped, that she's turned against him... it might be enough to draw him out, to make him act rashly."

Aidan's fingers flew over the keys, his eyes lighting up with excitement. "I can help with that. I can create a false trail, make it look like Kari's on the move. If we're careful, we can make it convincing enough to fool even Braydon."

Casey felt a surge of pride and gratitude, a sense of unshakeable faith in her team. "Good. That's good. But we need to be ready for anything. Braydon's not going to go down without a fight, and we need to be prepared for the worst."

She looked around at each of them in turn, her gaze filled with a fierce determination. "We're the only thing standing between Braydon and total control of Blacksburg. The only thing protecting the innocent lives caught in the crossfire of his ambitions. We can't afford to fail."

Rigo stood, his posture straight and his eyes blazing with resolve. "We won't, Casey. We've got your back, no matter what."

Aidan nodded, his expression mirroring Rigo's. "Damn straight. We're in this together, until the end."

Casey felt a lump rise in her throat, a wave of emotion threatening to overwhelm her. She swallowed hard, her voice rough with gratitude.

"Thank you. All of you. I couldn't do this without you, without your strength and your courage."

She paused, her brow furrowing as a sudden thought struck her. "KIVO, I have a question for you."

The AI's holographic avatar materialized in the center of the room, its face a mask of calm attentiveness. "How may I assist you, Agent Elkins?"

Casey met the AI's gaze, her expression intense. "Is it possible for you to create a suppressor that could work on a town-wide scale? Something that could prevent Braydon from using the Idol's power to control the were-panthers and other lycans in Blacksburg?"

KIVO was silent for a moment, its processors whirring as it considered the request. "Theoretically, it is possible. However, the amount of power and resources required would be immense. We would need to tap into the city's power grid and set up a network of transmitters to blanket the entire town with the suppressor signal."

“We are covert RIPD officers, my badge gives us authorization to hack into any power we need. Tap into the grid and do what needs to be done. Establish a new protocol for this suppressor. We dont want to utilize it all the time, just only when necessary,” Casey says aloud

Aidan leaned forward, his eyes sparkling with excitement. "I can help with that. If we can access the main power plant and the cell towers, we should be able to piggyback off their infrastructure to create a makeshift suppressor network."

Rigo nodded, his expression thoughtful. "It's a good idea, but it's not going to be easy. Braydon's sure to have his own people watching those key locations. We'll need to be careful, move fast and quiet."

Casey's jaw tightened, her resolve hardening. "We don't have a choice. Besides, Braydon doesn’t know the full extent of our power either. There isn’t a computer network alive that

Aidan can't hack into. Aidan, do you happen to have any of your ChamDots? I have an idea to utilize it."

"Do tell, fearless leader," Aidan smiles as he digs through one of his many pockets and produces a sleek, petite metallic dot.

"I'm thinking if I can get close enough to attach this to the idol, it will not only allow you to remotely analyze it, but we can track it," Casey says with a smirk. "We have to try every thing can to stop him because If we can't stop Braydon from using the Idol, then everything else we do is just a bandage on a bullet wound. We need to cut off his power at the source."

"That is so crazy, it might just. But who will be putting the ChamDot on the Idol?" Rigo asks.

"Kari," Casey says softly, "She has been under his mind control. She knows how to act accordingly. KIVO has already exchanged her suppressor with a different model, that is disguised as a set of earrings. KIVO will allow her to transform if Braydon issues that command,"

"I dont like cornered Casey. She gets down right scary," Rigo chuckles, "I'm loving it,"

"This is so we can break Braydon's control over her and she can stop being his puppet. As much as Kari is into the 50 Shades of Gray bullshit, she doesn't like doing it without consent," Casey laughs.

She turned back to KIVO, her voice steady and commanding. "KIVO, start working on the suppressor design. Focus on range and efficiency, and let us know what you need from us to make it happen."

The AI nodded, its avatar already beginning to shift and change as it dove into the task. "Understood, Agent Elkins. I will begin the necessary calculations.

Aidan's eyes lit up as he processed Casey's request, his mind already racing with possibilities. "A town-wide suppressor? Oh, I can definitely make that happen. It's all about manipulating the rei frequency and amplifying the signal."

He turned to KIVO, his fingers flying over the holographic interface. "KIVO, pull up the schematics for the individual suppressor we used on Kari. We'll use that as a starting point and scale it up."

As the schematics materialized in the air before them, Aidan began to explain, his voice taking on the excited cadence of a mad scientist. "You see, lycans manipulate their rei to trigger transformations. It's like a specific frequency that resonates with their genetic structure. The suppressor works by emitting a counter-frequency that disrupts that resonance, effectively blocking the transformation."

Rigo leaned in, his brow furrowed. "But how do we amplify that signal to cover the entire town?"

Aidan grinned, his eyes sparkling with manic energy. "That's the brilliant part! We hijack the cell towers and use them as transmitters. With a few modifications and a boost from the city's power grid, we can blanket Blacksburg with the suppressor frequency."

He swiped through the holographic display, highlighting various components. "We'll need to install these modulator units on each tower, linked to a central control system. KIVO can monitor the rei activity in the town and adjust the suppressor output as needed."

Casey nodded, her expression a mix of awe and determination. "What about the power requirements? Can the city's grid handle it?"

Aidan waved a hand dismissively. "Please, I could run this baby off a couple of car batteries if I had to. But yeah, the city's grid should be more than enough. We might cause a few brownouts here and there, but it's a small price to pay."

Rigo crossed his arms, his gaze serious. "What about side effects? Will this thing hurt the lycans or anyone else?"

Aidan's expression sobered. "In theory, no. The suppressor frequency is specifically targeted to disrupt lycan rei. Humans and other creatures shouldn't be affected. But I won't lie, this is untested tech. There might be some discomfort or fatigue for the lycans, and we'll have to keep an eye out for any unexpected consequences."

Casey placed a hand on Aidan's shoulder, her eyes meeting his. "We trust you, Aidan. If anyone can make this work, it's you. Just keep us informed and let us know what you need."

Aidan nodded, his gaze already distant as his mind raced with calculations and designs. "I'll need access to the cell towers and the power grid, KIVO lets get to work,"

Casey looked around at her team, her eyes blazing with determination. "Rigo, lets allow Aidan and KIVO time to work, while we provide the distraction. You and I delivering Kari to Braydon,"

Rigo stood, his hand resting on the hilt of his weapon. "We'll get it done, Casey. And when the time comes, we'll be ready to take the fight to Braydon and the Panther Prowl."

Casey nodded, her heart swelling with pride and determination. "I know we will. Because we're not just a team, we're a family. And there's nothing in this world or any other that can stop us when we stand together."

As they dispersed to their various tasks, Casey felt a

renewed sense of hope and purpose. The road ahead was long and treacherous, the dangers they faced unlike any they had encountered before.

But with her team by her side, with the strength of their bond and the power of their resolve, Casey knew that they could overcome anything.

CHAPTER 10

The streets of Blacksburg were eerily quiet as Casey and Rigo escorted Kari to the designated meeting point. The town's residents had retreated to the safety of their homes, leaving an unsettling stillness in their wake. Even the wind seemed to hold its breath, as if sensing the impending confrontation.

Kari walked between them, her head held high and her expression a mask of regal indifference. To the untrained eye, she appeared every inch the loyal queen, ready to return to her king's side. But Casey knew the truth - the glint of determination hidden beneath the surface, the subtle tension in her jaw. She was a woman on a mission, a coiled spring waiting to be released.

As they approached the town square, Casey's heart began to pound, her senses heightened and her body coiled with anticipation. She knew that Braydon would be waiting for them, the Idol of Lycoan in his grasp and his loyal followers at his side. But she also knew that Aidan was out there, working tirelessly to implement the town-wide suppressor that could turn the tide of battle.

Rigo's hand rested on the hilt of his weapon, his gaze scanning the surrounding buildings for any sign of a threat. "Remember the plan," he muttered, his voice low and tense. "We make the exchange, and Kari does her part. Aidan will handle the rest."

Casey nodded, her own hand hovering near her sidearm. "And if things go south, we'll be ready. Braydon won't know what hit him."

Kari remained silent, her gaze fixed ahead and her posture regal. But for a moment, her eyes met Casey's, and a flicker of understanding passed between them. They were in this together, a team united by a common goal and an unbreakable bond.

As they entered the town square, a figure emerged from the shadows, flanked by a group of hulking lycans. Braydon Mitchell, the self-proclaimed king of the Panther Prowl, strode forward, his eyes glinting with malice and his lips twisted into a cruel smirk.

"My queen," he purred, his voice dripping with false affection. "I knew you would return to me. You could never stay away for long."

Kari inclined her head, her expression one of cool detachment. "I knew you wouldn't let them keep me, my King. But to hell with these pleasantries, my King, we have business to discuss."

Braydon's smirk widened, his hand tightening around the Idol of Lycoan. "Indeed we do, my dear. Indeed we do."

He turned to Casey and Rigo, his gaze filled with a predatory hunger. "Agent Elkins, Mr. Balderas. I must admit, I'm surprised to see you here. I would have thought you'd be busy licking your wounds after our last encounter."

Casey met his gaze, her chin lifted in defiance. "We're full of surprises, Braydon. And we're not here to play games. I'm tougher than the females you are used to dealing with. We made a deal - Kari in exchange for a ceasefire. Are you going to honor it, or not?"

Braydon chuckled, a low and menacing sound. "Oh, I'll honor it, Agent Elkins. But on my terms. You see, I hold all the cards now. And with my queen by my side and the Idol in my grasp, I am unstoppable."

He began to pace, his eyes never leaving Casey's face. "Here's how it's going to work. You and your little team will stand down and surrender yourselves to the Panther Prowl. In return, I'll call off my forces and spare the people of Blacksburg. For now."

Casey's jaw clenched, her mind racing as she tried to find a way to stall for time. "And what happens to us, once we surrender? You expect us to just roll over and let you take control of the city?"

Braydon's smirk widened, a glint of malice in his eyes. "Oh, I have special plans for you, Agent Elkins. You and your hybrid friend will serve as an example to anyone who dares to defy me. As for the rest of your team... well, let's just say they'll learn the true meaning of loyalty."

Rigo stepped forward, his hand tightening on his weapon. "We're not going to let that happen, Braydon. We'll fight you to our last breath before we let you enslave the people of Blacksburg."

Braydon threw back his head and laughed, the sound echoing through the empty square. "You really think you stand a chance against me? Against the power of the Idol? You're nothing but insects to be crushed beneath my heel."

As Braydon continued to gloat, Casey's mind was racing, her eyes darting around the square as she searched for any sign of Aidan or the suppressor. She knew they needed to keep Braydon talking, to give their team more time to put the plan into action.

"You're forgetting one thing, Braydon," she said, her voice steady and filled with conviction. "The people of Blacksburg are stronger than you think. They won't just roll over and accept your rule. They'll fight, just like we will."

Braydon's eyes narrowed, a flicker of annoyance crossing his features. "The people of Blacksburg are weak, Agent Elkins. They're sheep, waiting to be led to the slaughter. And I am the wolf that will guide them to their fate."

As he spoke, Kari stepped forward, her head held high and her gaze locked on the Idol. "Braydon, my love," she purred, her voice dripping with false affection. "Perhaps we should discuss this in private. After all, we have much to celebrate, now that I have returned to your side."

Braydon's gaze softened as he looked at Kari, a possessive hunger burning in his eyes. "Of course, my queen. We have all the time in the world, now that you are mine once more."

He turned back to Casey and Rigo, his expression hardening. "You have one hour to make your decision, Agent Elkins. Surrender, or watch your city burn. The choice is yours."

With that, he turned and strode away, Kari at his side and the Panther Prowl falling into step behind them. As they disappeared into the shadows, Casey let out a breath she hadn't realized she'd been holding.

"That was too close," she muttered, her heart pounding in her chest. "We need to find Aidan and KIVO, now. We're running out of time."

Rigo nodded, his expression grim. "Agreed. Let's just hope Kari can do her part and get that ChamDot on the Idol. Otherwise, this whole plan is going to go up in smoke."

As they hurried through the streets of Blacksburg, Casey's mind was racing, her thoughts consumed by the task at hand. She knew that the fate of the city rested on their shoulders, and she was determined to see this through, no matter the cost.

****

Kari followed Braydon into the dimly lit room, her heart pounding in her chest as the door clicked shut behind them. The Idol of Lycoan sat on a pedestal in the center of the room, its surface pulsing with an otherworldly energy that set her teeth on edge.

Braydon turned to face her, his eyes gleaming with a possessive hunger that sent shivers down her spine. "My queen," he purred, his voice low and seductive. "You have no idea how much I've missed you."

Kari forced a smile, her fingers itching to reach for the ChamDot hidden in her pocket. "I've missed you too, my king. But I must confess, I've had time to think during our separation. About us, and about the nature of our... arrangement."

Braydon's brow furrowed, a flicker of annoyance crossing his features. "What is there to think about, my love? You are mine, body and soul. The Panther Prowl is yours to command, as long as you remain by my side."

Kari hesitated, her mind racing as she tried to find the right words. She had always been drawn to the power and the pleasure of their dynamic, the thrill of submitting to Braydon's will. But now, with the suppressor freeing her mind from his control, she couldn't ignore the unease that coiled in her gut.

"I enjoy what we have, Braydon," she said carefully, her gaze locked on his. "The games we play, the roles we assume. But I need to know that it's my choice. That I'm not just a puppet, dancing on your strings."

Braydon's lips curled into a sneer, his hand tightening around the Idol. "Choice? You gave up your choice the moment you accepted my gift, the moment you became mine. The Idol ensures that you will never stray, never question your place by my side."

Kari's heart sank, a cold realization washing over her. She had been a fool to think that Braydon's love for her was anything more than a means to an end, a way to control and possess her.

But even as despair threatened to engulf her, a flicker of defiance sparked to life in her chest. She was Kari Byars, the Queen of the Panther Prowl, and she would not be anyone's puppet, not even Braydon's.

"I understand now," she said softly, her voice steady despite the tremors that shook her body. "I thought I could have both - the power of the Prowl and the love of a partner. But I see now that with you, it's all or nothing. And I choose myself, Braydon. I choose freedom."

With a swift motion, she reached into her pocket and withdrew the ChamDot, her fingers closing around the small device like a lifeline. Braydon's eyes widened, a snarl of rage twisting his features as he lunged for her.

But Kari was faster, her hand darting out to slap the ChamDot onto the surface of the Idol. The device adhered instantly, its liquid metal alloy syncing it effortlessly onto the idol, making it one with the idol. The ChamDot was installed. KIVO was receiving the information at fractions of a millisecond speeds. Kari turned to Braydon, smiling seductively.

Braydon roared, his claws extending as he grabbed for Kari's throat. But she was already moving, ducking under his arm and spinning away, her heart pounding with a heady mix of fear and exhilaration.

"You'll pay for this, Kari," Braydon growled, his eyes flashing with murderous intent. "I'll make you suffer in ways you can't even imagine."

Kari met his gaze, her chin lifted in defiance. "You can try, Braydon. But you'll never control me again. I'm done being your plaything, your puppet. From now on, I will choose my own path."

With that, she turned and fled the room, her heart pounding in her ears as she raced towards the exit. She knew that she had just signed her own death warrant, that Braydon would stop at nothing to hunt her down and make her pay for her betrayal.

She had played her part, had given Casey and her team the opening they needed to take down the Panther Prowl. And whatever happened next, she knew that she had made the right choice, the only choice she could live with. Casey would protect her for effortlessly helping with the ChamDot thing. She hoped.

****

The steady beep of the heart monitor filled the room as Cyndi lay motionless in the stasis pod, her chest rising and falling with each shallow breath. Casey sat by her side, her eyes fixed on her sister's face, searching for any sign of awareness.

Suddenly, Cyndi's eyelids fluttered, a soft groan escaping her lips. Casey leaned forward, her heart pounding with a mixture of hope and fear.

"Cyndi? Can you hear me? It's Casey."

Slowly, Cyndi's eyes opened, her gaze unfocused and hazy. She blinked a few times, her brow furrowing in confusion as she took in her surroundings.

"Casey?" she croaked, her voice rough from disuse. "Where am I? What happened?"

Casey reached out, her hand grasping Cyndi's with a gentle squeeze. "You're safe, Cyndi. You're in the Kenta Corp headquarters. We've been taking care of you."

Cyndi's eyes widened, a flicker of panic crossing her features. "The attack... the were-panther... oh god, Casey, what's happening to me?"

Casey's heart clenched, tears pricking at the corners of her eyes. "We're going to figure this out, Cyndi. Together. I promise you, I won't let anything happen to you."

Cyndi's breathing quickened, her eyes darting around the room as if searching for hidden dangers. "I can feel it, Casey. The change, the beast inside me. It's like a fire in my veins, a hunger I can't control."

Casey leaned in closer, her voice low and soothing. "We have a suppressor, Cyndi. A device that can help you control the transformation. You're not alone in this. We're all here for you."

Cyndi's eyes met Casey's, a flicker of hope amidst the fear. "A suppressor? You mean, I don't have to become a monster?"

Casey shook her head, a fierce determination burning in her chest. "You could never be a monster, Cyndi. You're my sister, and I love you, no matter what. We're going to get through this, I swear it."

Just then, the door to the medical bay burst open, and Kari stumbled inside, her face flushed and her eyes wide with adrenaline. Casey and Cyndi turned to stare, their expressions a mix of surprise and wariness.

"Kari?" Casey asked, rising to her feet. "What are you

doing here? What happened with Braydon?"

Kari leaned against the wall, her chest heaving as she tried to catch her breath. "I did it, Casey. I got the ChamDot on the Idol. But Braydon, he knows. He's coming for me, for all of us."

Casey's jaw tightened, her hand instinctively reaching for her sidearm. "Okay, okay. We knew this was a possibility. We'll handle it."

She turned to Cyndi, her expression softening. "Cyndi, I have to go. But I'll be back, I promise. Aidan and Rigo will stay with you, keep you safe."

Cyndi nodded, fear and determination warring in her eyes. "Casey, if you are facing Braydon, aren't you worried about what happened before RIPD came into your life? Before he became this monster?"

"What do you mean?" Rigo asks, entering the bay, "Cyndi, pleasure to meet you. I'm Rigo Balderas,"

"Rigo, Braydon put my sister in intensive care more times than I can count, he has to have gotten stronger since then," Cyndi cries.

"Cyndi, we wont let anything happen to your sister. She has a team behind her. Myself and Techie, wont let anything bad happen to her. KIVO will ensure of it," Rigo smiles.

"KIVO?" Cyndi asks.

"The computer man who does wondrous things like build these surpressors," Kari breaths touching the ear rings, "He and Aidan are pure genius,"

"Casey," Cyndi sobs, "Promise you'll come back to me,"

“I pinky promise,” Casey extends her pinky to her sister, “and I’ll seal it,”

Cyndi wraps her pinkie around Casey’s and they twist their hands in opposite directions before kissing the locked fingers.

“Casey Lynn, I love you,” Cyndi says.

Casey hesitated for a moment, then leaned down and pressed a fierce kiss to Cyndi's forehead. "I love you, sis. More than anything."

With that, she turned and strode out of the room, Kari and Rigo falling into step beside her. The three warriors exchanged a glance, a silent acknowledgment of the danger that lay ahead.

But as they made their way through the halls of the Kenta Corp headquarters, a sense of purpose settled over them, a grim determination to see this through to the end.

The Panther Prowl was coming, and they would be ready. For Cyndi, for Blacksburg, and for the chance to build a future free from Braydon's tyranny.

****

The town square was a sea of black, the members of the Panther Prowl gathered in tight formation as they awaited their leader's command. Braydon stood atop a makeshift stage, his eyes blazing with fury and his claws flexing at his sides.

"My loyal subjects," he began, his voice booming across the square. "I have called you here today to share grave news. Our queen, Kari Byars, has betrayed us."

A murmur of shock and disbelief rippled through the

crowd, the were-panthers shifting uneasily as they processed the information. Braydon raised a hand, silencing them with a single gesture.

"She has allied herself with the RIPD, with the very humans who seek to destroy us. She has placed a device on our sacred Idol, a tool of our enemies to weaken and control us."

The murmurs grew louder, anger and confusion mingling in the air. Some of the were-panthers looked to each other, their expressions uncertain and torn.

Braydon's gaze swept over the crowd, his lips curling into a sneer. "I see doubt in some of your eyes. Loyalty to a false queen, a traitor to our kind. Let me make one thing clear: the Panther Prowl bows to no one but me. I am your alpha, your king, and your god."

He raised the Idol of Lycoan above his head, its surface pulsing with an eerie light. "With this, I will lead you to glory, to a future where we rule over the humans and the other lycans alike. But I will not tolerate disloyalty, not from anyone."

As he spoke, a group of were-panthers began to break away from the crowd, their eyes downcast and their postures submissive. Braydon's gaze snapped to them, his eyes narrowing with disdain.

"And where do you think you're going?" he snarled, his voice dripping with menace.

One of the were-panthers, a young male with a shock of red hair, stepped forward, his voice trembling. "Braydon, we... we can't do this. Kari was our queen, our leader. If she has turned against you, maybe... maybe there's a reason."

Braydon's roar of rage shook the square, his claws slashing through the air. "Reason? The only reason is her weakness, her pathetic attachment to the humans. She has forgotten what it means to be a were-panther, to be one of us."

He pointed at the group of defectors, his eyes blazing with hatred. "And you, you spineless cowards. You dare to question me, to turn your backs on the Prowl? You are no longer welcome here, no longer part of our family."

The red-haired were-panther's eyes widened, fear and anger warring in his expression. "You can't do that, Braydon. We have rights, we have..."

But Braydon cut him off with a snarl, his claws extending to their full length. "You have nothing, not anymore. You are enemies of the Prowl, traitors to our kind. And enemies of the Prowl do not live long."

With a roar of fury, Braydon leapt from the stage, his body shifting and contorting as he transformed into his full were-panther form. The defectors scrambled back, their own transformations rippling over their bodies as they prepared to defend themselves.

But Braydon was too fast, too strong. He tore through their ranks like a whirlwind, his claws and fangs rending flesh and bone with sickening ease. The screams of the dying and the roars of the enraged filled the square, a symphony of violence and brutality.

As the last of the defectors fell, Braydon stood over their broken bodies, his chest heaving and his fur matted with blood. He turned to the remaining members of the Prowl, his eyes glowing with a feral light.

"Let this be a lesson to all of you," he growled, his voice guttural and inhuman. "The Panther Prowl is mine, and mine alone. Anyone who dares to challenge me, to question my rule, will meet the same fate as these pathetic weaklings."

He raised the Idol once more, its surface now slick with the blood of the fallen. "We are the Panther Prowl, the true rulers of Blacksburg. And we will not rest until every human, every lycan, and every traitor bows before us."

As the remaining were-panthers let out a roar of approval, their eyes glinting with a savage hunger, Braydon smiled, a cold and cruel twist of his lips.

****

Casey, Kari, and Rigo burst into the main control room of the Kenta Corp headquarters, their faces etched with a mix of shock, anger, and determination. Aidan looked up from his console, his eyes alight with a newfound excitement.

"Guys, you're not going to believe this," he exclaimed, his voice thrumming with energy. "KIVO's been analyzing the data from the ChamDot, and we've had a breakthrough."

Casey's brow furrowed, her attention momentarily diverted from the horror of Braydon's actions in the town square. "What kind of breakthrough?"

Aidan grinned, his fingers flying over the keyboard as he brought up a series of complex schematics and frequency readouts. "We've isolated the specific frequency that allows the Idol to enhance Braydon's abilities. And with that knowledge, we've been able to create these."

He held up a small case, his eyes sparkling with pride. "Specialized bullets, designed to nullify the Idol's effect on Braydon. They won't kill him, but they'll level the playing field, give us a fighting chance."

Rigo's eyes widened, a flicker of hope kindling in his chest. "That's incredible, Aidan. With those bullets, we might actually stand a chance of stopping him."

Kari, her face still pale from the weight of the defectors' deaths, looked up, her expression a mix of determination and trepidation. "But we'll still need to get close enough to use them. Braydon's not going to make it easy."

Casey nodded, her mind already racing with the possibilities. "You're right, Kari. But this changes everything. If we can nullify the Idol's power, we can focus on taking down Braydon himself, without worrying about his enhanced abilities."

She turned to Aidan, her voice low and urgent. "How many bullets do we have?"

Aidan's expression sobered, his hand tightening around the case. "Not many. The process is complex, and the materials are rare. But KIVO and I have been working around the clock, and we've managed to create a dozen rounds."

KIVO speaks out of turn, against his programming, “Agent Elkins, these bullets are designed for your side arm. You are the best marksman. It would be advised for you to fire the bullets into Braydon, allowing Mr. Balderas to become his other self, and fight Braydon on equal footing. The Idol’s frequency would be neutralized within Braydon, allowing an equal playing field,”

Casey took a deep breath, her gaze flickering between her team members as she processed KIVO's suggestion. The weight of the responsibility settled on her shoulders, but she drew strength from the trust and determination in their eyes.

"Alright," she said, her voice steady and resolute. "If you all believe in me, then I'll do it. I'll take the shots and give Rigo the opening he needs to take Braydon down."

Rigo placed a hand on Casey's shoulder, his expression a

mix of pride and concern. "I've got your back, Casey. We'll do this together, as a team."

Kari nodded, her mind already racing with the possibilities of her own role in the plan. "If I can't lure Braydon away, then I'll go to the Prowl directly. With my suppressors removed, I can tap into my connection with them, remind them of the loyalty they once had to me."

Aidan's eyes widened, a flicker of uncertainty crossing his features. "Kari, are you sure? Without the suppressors, you'll be vulnerable to Braydon's influence again."

Kari's jaw tightened, a fire burning in her eyes. "I'm sure, Aidan. I need to do this, need to face my demons head-on. And if I can sway even a fraction of the Prowl to our side, it could make all the difference."

Casey turned to KIVO, her expression a mix of gratitude and determination. "KIVO, prepare the bullets for my sidearm. And Aidan, get started on removing Kari's suppressors. We don't have much time."

As the team sprang into action, a sense of purpose and unity settled over them. They knew the risks, knew the dangers that lay ahead. But they also knew that they had each other, that their bond was unbreakable and their resolve unshakeable.

Rigo and Casey moved to the armory, their minds focused on the task at hand. As Casey loaded her sidearm with the specialized bullets, Rigo transformed, his eyes glinting with a predatory light.

"I'm ready," he growled, his voice low and fierce. "Let's end this, once and for all."

Casey nodded, her own eyes blazing with determination. "For Cyndi, for Blacksburg, and for the future we're fighting for."

Meanwhile, Aidan worked quickly to remove Kari's suppressors, his hands steady and his mind focused. As the last device fell away, Kari gasped, feeling the rush of her lycan senses returning in full force.

"How do you feel?" Aidan asked, his voice laced with concern.

Kari took a deep breath, her eyes flashing with a newfound power. "Like myself again. Like the queen I was always meant to be."

As the team regrouped, their faces set with grim determination, Casey felt a swell of pride and love for each and every one of them. They were more than just a team, more than just friends. They were a family, bound by a love that would never break.

And as they set out into the streets of Blacksburg, ready to face their greatest challenge yet, Casey knew that whatever happened, whatever the outcome, they would face it together.

For Cyndi, for Blacksburg, and for the chance to build a better world, free from the shadows of fear and oppression.

****

The walk-in cooler was a cramped, frigid space, the hum of the refrigeration unit a constant backdrop to the tense silence that filled the air. Amber huddled in the corner, her arms wrapped tightly around her knees as she tried to calm her racing heart.

Around her, the other patrons of Danny's Cafe sat in small groups, their faces etched with fear and uncertainty. Some wept quietly, while others stared blankly ahead, lost in their own thoughts.

Amber's mind raced with the events of the past few hours - the sudden invasion of the Panther Prowl, the screams and chaos that had erupted in the streets, the desperate scramble for safety that had led them here, to this cold, dark refuge.

She couldn't shake the image of the were-panther's claw, reaching through the gap in the door, its razor-sharp talons gleaming in the dim light. If she hadn't been quick with the pepper spray, if she hadn't managed to force the door closed...

Amber shuddered, pushing the thought away. She had to stay focused, had to keep her wits about her. The people in this room were counting on her, looking to her for guidance and reassurance.

She stood up, her legs stiff from the cold and the cramped position. "Listen up, everyone," she said, her voice rough but steady. "I know you're all scared, and I don't blame you. What's happening out there... it's like nothing we've ever seen before."

The patrons looked up at her, their eyes wide and desperate. Amber took a deep breath, forcing herself to project a calm she didn't entirely feel.

"But we're going to get through this, together. The RIPD is out there, fighting to keep us safe. And we've got each other, right here in this room."

She looked around, making eye contact with each person in turn. "We need to stay calm, conserve our energy. We don't know how long we'll be in here, but we've got enough food and water to last us a while."

A young woman in the corner, her face streaked with tears, spoke up, her voice trembling. "But what if they find us? What if they break down the door?"

Amber's jaw tightened, her hand clenching around the can of pepper spray at her side. "Then we'll fight. We'll use whatever we have, whatever we can find. We'll make them regret ever setting foot in our town."

A murmur of agreement rippled through the room, a flicker of determination kindling in the eyes of the patrons. They were scared, but they weren't broken. They were the people of Blacksburg, and they would not go down without a fight.

Suddenly, a sound from outside the cooler made them all freeze, their hearts pounding in their chests. Footsteps, heavy and deliberate, echoing on the tiled floor of the cafe.

Amber held up a hand, signaling for silence. She crept towards the door, her ear pressed against the cold metal, straining to hear over the hum of the refrigeration unit.

The footsteps grew louder, closer. And then, a voice, low and menacing, filled the air.

"Come out, come out, wherever you are..." it crooned, the words dripping with malice. "You can't hide forever, little lambs. The Panther Prowl always finds its prey."

Amber's blood ran cold, her breath catching in her throat. She recognized that voice, had heard it countless times over the years.

It was Braydon, the leader of the Panther Prowl. And he was here, in Danny's Cafe, hunting them down like animals.

Amber's mind raced, desperately searching for a way out, a way to protect the people in her care. But the walk-in cooler was a dead end, a trap with no escape.

She closed her eyes, a silent prayer on her lips. Please, she thought, please let Casey and the others stop him. Please let them save us, before it's too late.

The footsteps drew closer, the sound of claws scraping against metal filling the air. And as the patrons huddled together in the corner, their faces pale with fear, Amber knew that their fate hung in the balance, dependent on the strength and determination of a small group of heroes, fighting for the soul of Blacksburg.

****

As Braydon's footsteps drew closer and the sound of his claws scraping against the metal door filled the air, Amber and the patrons huddled together, their hearts pounding with fear. It seemed like all hope was lost, that their fate was sealed.

Suddenly, a deafening roar echoed through the cafe, followed by the sound of shattering glass and splintering wood. The patrons exchanged startled glances, unsure what to make of this new development.

Then, the unmistakable sounds of a violent struggle erupted just outside the cooler door - growls, snarls, and the clash of claws against claws. Amber pressed her ear to the door, straining to make sense of the chaos.

After what felt like an eternity, the sounds of battle faded, replaced by an eerie silence. The patrons held their breath, waiting for the outcome, for the moment that would decide their fate.

Slowly, the door to the cooler began to open, the metal groaning on its hinges. Amber raised her pepper spray, ready to fight with everything she had.

But as the door swung wide, it wasn't Braydon who stood before them. Instead, it was Matt Mauney, his jaguar form sleek and powerful, his eyes glinting with a fierce determination.

"It's okay," he said, his voice a low rumble. "You're safe now. Braydon's gone."

Amber's eyes widened, a mix of relief and confusion washing over her. "Matt? But how... why?"

Matt shifted back to his human form, his expression serious. "I couldn't let Braydon hurt innocent people, not again. I've seen firsthand the destruction he's capable of, the lives he's ruined. I had to do something."

He stepped aside, allowing the patrons to exit the cooler, their faces filled with a tentative hope. Amber approached Matt, her voice low and filled with gratitude.

"Thank you, Matt. You saved our lives."

Matt shook his head, a sad smile on his lips. "I'm just trying to do what's right, to make up for the mistakes of my past. Casey and her team, they're the real heroes. They're the ones who will stop Braydon and save Blacksburg."

As the patrons filed out of the cafe, Amber and Matt shared a look of understanding. They knew that the battle was far from over, that Braydon and the Panther Prowl still posed a grave threat to the town.

CHAPTER 11

The streets of Blacksburg had become a battlefield, the once-peaceful town now a stage for the final confrontation between the forces of good and evil. In the heart of the chaos stood Rigo and Braydon, their lycan forms a blur of claws and fangs as they clashed in a deadly dance.

Rigo snarled, his hyena form sleek and powerful as he dodged Braydon's attacks. The Idol of Lycoan glowed with an otherworldly light, its power pulsing through Braydon's veins, making him faster, stronger, and more ruthless than ever before.

But Rigo was not alone. In the shadows, Casey watched the battle unfold, her sidearm steady in her hands, the specialized bullets glinting in the dim light. She knew that she would only have one chance, one moment to turn the tide of the battle and save Blacksburg from Braydon's reign of terror.

Nearby, Kari and Aidan worked to keep the rest of the Panther Prowl at bay, their combined efforts a testament to the strength of their newfound alliance. Kari's connection to the Prowl, amplified by the removal of her suppressors, had proven invaluable in sowing discord and doubt among Braydon's followers.

But even with their help, the battle was far from won. Braydon's power seemed to grow with every passing moment, his eyes glinting with a madness that sent shivers down Casey's spine.

Rigo lunged forward, his claws raking across Braydon's chest, drawing a howl of pain and rage from the Panther Prowl leader.

But Braydon was quick to retaliate, his own claws finding purchase in Rigo's flesh, sending the hyena hybrid stumbling back.

Casey's heart pounded in her chest, her finger hovering over the trigger of her sidearm. She knew that she had to time her shot perfectly, had to wait for the right moment to strike.

Rigo and Braydon circled each other, their chests heaving with exertion, their eyes locked in a battle of wills. The Idol of Lycoan pulsed with an angry light, its power straining against the confines of Braydon's control.

Suddenly, Rigo lunged forward, his jaws closing around Braydon's arm, his teeth sinking deep into the flesh. Braydon howled in pain, his free hand scrabbling at Rigo's face, desperate to break free.

And in that moment, Casey saw her chance. With a deep breath and a silent prayer, she squeezed the trigger, the specialized bullet leaping from the barrel of her sidearm, streaking through the air towards its target.

Time seemed to slow, the world narrowing to a single point of focus. Casey watched as the bullet raced towards Braydon, her heart in her throat, her breath caught in her lungs.

Would it find its mark? Would it be enough to turn the tide of the battle, to save Blacksburg from the brink of destruction?

As the bullet closed in on Braydon's chest, Casey could only watch and wait, her fate, and the fate of everyone she loved, hanging in the balance.

****

The door to the lab burst open, startling Aidan from his intense focus on the computer screens before him. He whirled around, his hand instinctively reaching for the sidearm at his hip, only to relax when he saw the familiar face of Mr. Butler.

"Mr. Butler?" Aidan asked, his brow furrowed in confusion. "What are you doing here? I thought you were at the museum, researching the Idol."

Mr. Butler rushed forward, his eyes wide with excitement and urgency. "I was, I was! But Aidan, I've found something incredible, something that could change everything!"

He thrust a bundle of papers into Aidan's hands, his fingers trembling with barely contained energy. Aidan glanced down at the papers, his eyes widening as he took in the ancient texts and intricate diagrams.

"What is this?" he breathed, his mind already racing with the implications.

Mr. Butler tapped the papers, his voice low and intense. "These are ancient Lycoan texts, dating back to the time when the Idol was first created. I've been translating them, trying to understand the artifact's true nature and purpose."

Aidan's head snapped up, his gaze locking with Mr. Butler's. "And what did you find?"

The curator took a deep breath, his words tumbling out in a rush. "The Idol of Lycoan was never meant to be a tool of control or domination. It was created as a means of balance, a way to bridge the gap between the human and lycan worlds."

Aidan's brow furrowed, his mind struggling to make sense of this new information. "Balance? But Braydon's been using it to enhance his own power, to bend others to his will."

Mr. Butler nodded, his expression grim. "Yes, because he's tapped into only one aspect of the Idol's power - the aspect of dominance and aggression. But there's another side to the artifact, one that's been forgotten over the centuries."

He pointed to a specific passage in the text, his finger trembling with excitement. "The Idol has the power to bring harmony and understanding between lycans and humans, to create a bond of empathy and cooperation. But to access that power, the wielder must approach the Idol with a pure heart and a desire for peace."

Aidan's eyes widened, the pieces of the puzzle falling into place. "So if someone were to use the Idol with the right intentions, with a genuine desire to bring balance..."

Mr. Butler nodded, a smile tugging at the corners of his mouth. "It could change everything. It could end the conflict between lycans and humans, and create a new era of coexistence."

Aidan's mind was racing, the possibilities unfolding before him like a map to a brighter future. If what Mr. Butler said was true, then the key to stopping Braydon and saving Blacksburg wasn't just about neutralizing the Idol's power - it was about harnessing it for good.

He turned to the curator, his voice low and urgent. "We need to tell Casey about this. It could be the key to everything."

Mr. Butler nodded, his own excitement mirroring Aidan's. "We should decipher the whole text first. I'll keep working on the translations, see if I can uncover any more details about how to access the Idol's hidden power."

As the two men set to work, a new sense of hope and purpose filled the air. The battle against Braydon and the Panther Prowl was far from over, but with this new knowledge, they finally had a glimmer of a chance.

And somewhere out there, in the heart of the chaos and violence, Casey and Rigo fought on, unaware of the revelation that could change the course of their struggle, and the fate of Blacksburg itself.

As Aidan and Mr. Butler pored over the ancient texts, their excitement palpable, a thought suddenly struck Aidan. He turned to the curator, his eyes wide with realization.

"Mr. Butler, we've been going about this all wrong. We have a resource here that could help us decipher these texts much faster than we ever could on our own."

The curator looked up, his brow furrowed in confusion. "What do you mean?"

Aidan grinned, his fingers already flying over the keyboard. "KIVO, of course! With its advanced language processing and pattern recognition capabilities, it could analyze these texts and provide a full translation in a matter of minutes."

Mr. Butler's eyes widened, a spark of hope igniting in their depths. "Of course! Why didn't I think of that before?"

Aidan chuckled, his fingers never stopping their dance across the keys. "Because you're used to doing things the old-fashioned way, Mr. Butler. But in this lab, we've got the most advanced technology at our fingertips."

He tapped a final command, and KIVO's holographic avatar materialized before them, its calm voice filling the air. "How may I assist you, Aidan?"

Aidan gestured to the ancient texts, his voice thrumming with excitement. "KIVO, we need you to analyze these Lycoan texts and provide a full translation. We believe they hold the key to understanding the Idol's true nature and unlocking its hidden power."

KIVO's avatar pulsed with light, its processors whirring as it scanned the pages. "Analyzing now. Translation in progress."

For a moment, the only sound in the lab was the gentle hum of the computers and the soft whisper of KIVO's calculations. Then, the AI spoke again, its voice filled with a new sense of wonder.

"Translation complete. The texts reveal that the Idol of Lycoan was created not as a tool of domination, but as a means of fostering understanding and cooperation between lycans and humans. It has the power to create a bond of empathy and harmony, but only if the wielder approaches it with a pure heart and a desire for peace."

Aidan and Mr. Butler exchanged a look of triumph, their hearts racing with the implications of KIVO's words. This was it - the key to everything they had been fighting for.

Aidan turned back to KIVO, his voice low and urgent. "KIVO, does the text provide any guidance on how to access this hidden power? Any specific rituals or incantations?"

KIVO was silent for a moment, its processors whirring as it analyzed the data. Then, it spoke again, its voice filled with a quiet reverence.

"The texts speak of a ritual, a coming together of lycan and human, united in purpose and heart. They must approach the Idol together, their intentions pure and their souls open to the possibilities of peace. Only then will the Idol's true power be revealed, and the bridge between worlds be built."

Aidan and Mr. Butler looked at each other, their eyes shining with a newfound sense of purpose. They knew what they had to do, knew the path that lay before them.

They had to get this information to Casey and Rigo, had to give them the tools they needed to end the conflict and bring a new era of understanding to Blacksburg.

And with KIVO's help, they finally had the means to do just that.

****

The streets of Blacksburg trembled beneath the weight of the titans, the asphalt cracking and buckling as Braydon and Rigo collided in a flurry of claws and fangs. Their lycan forms were a sight to behold, a panther and a hyena, each radiating a primal strength that seemed to defy the very laws of nature.

Braydon's form was sleek and powerful, his muscles rippling beneath his glossy black fur. The Idol of Lycoan pulsed at his chest, its eerie light casting a sickly glow over the battlefield. With each blow he landed, the air seemed to shudder, the very fabric of reality straining against the onslaught of his enhanced strength.

"Is that all you've got, Joker?" Braydon snarled, his voice dripping with disdain. "I expected more from the so-called King of the Hyena Clan. But you're nothing special, just another fool standing in the way of my destiny."

But Rigo was not one to back down, even in the face of such overwhelming power. His hyena form was a marvel of speed and agility, his jaws snapping and his claws rending as he danced around Braydon's attacks.

"Destiny?" Rigo scoffed, his words punctuated by the clash of claws on claws. "You're delusional, Braydon. The only thing you're destined for is a jail cell, and I'm going to be the one to put you there."

High above the fray, atop the sturdy roof of the Blacksburg Fire Department, Casey knelt, her sidearm trained on the battling lycans below. She had been forced to relocate, her previous vantage point compromised by the sheer scale of the destruction wrought by Braydon and Rigo's battle.

Her heart raced as she watched Rigo struggle against Braydon's onslaught, her finger hovering over the trigger of her weapon. She knew she had to time her shot perfectly, had to wait for just the right moment to strike. The specialized bullets that KIVO had crafted were her only hope of neutralizing the Idol's power and giving Rigo a fighting chance.

But getting a clear shot was proving more difficult than she had anticipated. Braydon and Rigo moved with a speed and ferocity that defied tracking, their forms blurring and merging as they clashed again and again. Casey gritted her teeth, her focus narrowing to a laser point as she followed the flow of the battle, waiting for her moment.

Below, Rigo let out a roar of pain as Braydon's claws found purchase in his flank, the razor-sharp talons slicing through flesh and bone. He stumbled back, his breath coming in ragged gasps as he fought to keep his feet. The Idol's power was taking its toll, sapping his strength and dulling his reflexes.

But he would not give up, would not let Braydon win. With a snarl of defiance, Rigo lunged forward, his jaws clamping down on Braydon's forearm, his teeth sinking deep into the corded muscle. Braydon howled in rage and pain, his free hand scrabbling at Rigo's face, desperate to break free. For a moment, the two lycans were locked in a deadly embrace, their bodies straining against each other with a force that seemed to make the very air tremble. Casey watched, her heart in her throat, as Rigo fought to maintain his grip, fought to give her the opening she needed.

"Pathetic," Braydon sneered, his eyes glinting with sadistic glee. "You're weak, Joker. Weak and useless. Just like the rest of your kind. The Hyena Clan has always been a joke, a lone scavenger playing at being a king."

Rigo's vision swam, the pain and exhaustion threatening to overwhelm him. But beneath it all, a spark of defiance still burned, a stubborn refusal to let Braydon's words be the last he ever heard.

"You know nothing of my clan, of our strength and our legacy," Rigo growled, his voice low and fierce. "I may be the last of my kind, but I carry the courage and spirit of all those who came before me. That's something you'll never understand, Braydon. Because all you know is hate and greed and the lust for power."

Braydon's laughter was a twisted, malevolent thing, echoing through the shattered streets of Blacksburg. "You really think you can stop me? With the power of the Idol, I'm invincible. I'll crush you, and wipe the Hyena's from the face of the planet. Then I'll make the rest of your little band of do-gooders watch as I destroy the town they have worked so hard to save. And finally, I'll have Casey be my human slabe."

Rigo's eyes flashed with rage, his hackles rising as he bared his fangs. "You'll never get the chance. We won't allow you to win, Braydon. You may be the Panzer, the king of the were-panthers. The other lycan clans will not stand by idly while you reign supreme,"

As Rigo finished speaking, a figure fell from the sky, striking Braydon in the back, pinning him to the ground. A were-jaguar. Rigo's hyena form smiled.

"Looks like I got one one of your fellow felines on my side, Panzer," Rigo snarls, "Matt, I know you are able to control your lycan form. Let's work together,"

The jaguar roared in approval. Rigo know this meant Matt wasn't able to communicate regularly. The two of them could coordinate but Rigo had to do the talking.

"If you really want to turn this into Goku and Piccolo vs Raditz, I get to be Goku," Rigo chuckles, "Matt, you and I together can hold him for the final blow. Together!"

Rigo and Matt barrelled into Braydon's form as he picked himself up. Moments passed by, and the three of them came up, with Braydon captured between the Hyena and The Jaguar.

And then, suddenly, it was there. A clear shot, a straight line from her sidearm to Braydon's chest. Casey drew in a breath, her finger tightening on the trigger.

Time seemed to slow, the world narrowing to a single point of focus. Casey could feel the weight of the moment, the fate of Blacksburg and everyone she loved resting on the precision of her aim and the strength of her resolve.

She exhaled, a soft whisper lost amidst the chaos of the battle below. And then, with a gentle squeeze, she sent the bullet flying, a gleaming messenger of hope and defiance, streaking towards its target with unerring accuracy.

The world held its breath, the seconds stretching into eternity as the bullet closed the distance, its trajectory a shining arc of possibility. As the bullet struck Braydon's chest, a flash of bright white light flooded the area, with Braydon thrashing free from Rigo and Matt.

Casey, still shielding her eyes from the light, strained her eyes to see what was happening. Her rei senses were on high alert, and she could sense Braydon's fading rapidly, returning to manageable levels for her team. Rigo and Matt clambered to their feet. The Idol of Lycoan still pulsed its energies outward, but Braydon was receiving none of it.

"Casey, get to the idol, Matt and I will handle this," Rigo

says in Casey's ear, on the earpiece, "Matt, Let's do this," he looks to the Were-Jaguar and receives a thumbs up, "Panzer, for your crimes against the lycan community, we will take you down,"

Matt leaped first, full body tackling a weakened Braydon to the ground. Rigo stood over the two of them, and gave his Hyena's Roar, forcing Braydon to revert to human. Rigo looks up in time to see one of KIVO's drones arriving with a set of suppressor cuffs. Rigo applies the cuffs to Braydon's weakened form and hoists him to his feet, as Casey arrives with the Idol in her hand.

"Braydon Mitchell, Panzer of the Panther Prowl, you are under arrest, via the jurisdiction of The RIPD. You have the right to remain silent. Anything you say can and will be used against you in a court of law. You have the right to an attorney. If you cannot afford an attorney, one will be provided for you. Do you understand the rights I have just read to you? With these rights in mind, do you wish to speak to me?" Casey says.

Braydon's reply was mumbled due to him steeling the effects of KIVO's special bullets and the effects of Rigo's Hyena Roar.

****

The streets of Blacksburg lay in ruins, a testament to the titanic clash that had just taken place. Buildings were crumbling, pavements were shattered, and the air hung heavy with the acrid scent of smoke and the metallic tang of blood.

Through this apocalyptic landscape walked three figures, their steps steady and purposeful. Casey and Rigo, now back in his human form, flanked a handcuffed Braydon, their grips on his arms unyielding. Matt, still in his jaguar form, prowled ahead, his keen senses alert for any signs of trouble.

As they made their way through the heart of the city, the

were-panthers who had once followed Braydon with fanatical devotion began to emerge from the shadows. Their faces were marked with a mixture of fear, uncertainty, and a growing realization of their leader's defeat.

One by one, they dropped their heads, their eyes cast downward in a show of submission. They knew that the balance of power had shifted, that the reign of the Panther Prowl was coming to an end.

Suddenly, a voice rang out across the street, sharp and defiant. "What are you doing? Fight for him! Fight for our king!"

It was Tyler, Braydon's right-hand man, his face contorted with rage and desperation. He looked around at his fellow were-panthers, his eyes pleading for someone, anyone, to take up arms and resist.

But before anyone could move, another roar split the air, this one deeper, more powerful. All eyes turned to see Kari striding forward, her posture regal and her eyes blazing with a newfound authority.

"Enough, Tyler!" she commanded, her voice ringing with the strength of a true queen. "Braydon's reign is over. The Panther Prowl must accept this and move forward. If you don't fall in line with my leadership, you will be excommunicated."

Tyler's face paled, his bravado crumbling in the face of Kari's unwavering resolve. He took a step back, his hands trembling at his sides.

Casey, Rigo, and Matt exchanged a look of respect and acknowledgment. They knew that Kari's role in this victory had been crucial, that her bravery and determination had helped to turn the tide against Braydon.

As one, they raised their hands in a salute to the new

were-panther queen, a gesture of alliance and recognition. Kari met their eyes, a small smile playing at the corners of her mouth. She returned the salute, her head held high.

With that, the trio continued their march, guiding Braydon towards the imposing structure of the RIPD headquarters. As they passed through the shattered streets, the were-panthers who had once been Braydon's loyal soldiers parted before them, their heads bowed in deference.

Finally, they reached the entrance to the headquarters, where Aidan and the rest of the team were waiting. Braydon was quickly ushered inside, his struggles futile against the combined strength of his captors.

Deep within the bowels of the building, a special cell had been prepared, lined with suppressor technology that would keep Braydon's lycan abilities in check. As the door slammed shut behind him, the once-mighty Panzer of the Panther Prowl was reduced to a mere shadow of his former self, his power and his influence stripped away.

Casey, Rigo, and Matt stood outside the cell, their faces grim but their eyes shining with a sense of accomplishment. They had done it. They had brought down the tyrant who had threatened to plunge Blacksburg into darkness, and they had restored hope to a city on the brink of collapse.

As they made their way back to the surface, the weight of the battle and the sacrifices they had endured began to settle on their shoulders. But they knew that they had faced this challenge as a team, as a family, and that together, they could overcome anything.

CHAPTER 12

The room was dark, the air heavy with the pungent scent of cigar smoke and the musky odor of unwashed bodies. In the center of the space, illuminated by a single flickering light bulb, sat two figures, their postures tense and their eyes glinting with a mixture of wariness and calculation.

Dustin Blackwell leaned forward, his elbows resting on the scarred wooden table, his gaze fixed on the man across from him. Trey Smith, known to the lycan world as "The Silver Back," met his stare with an unwavering intensity, his massive frame barely contained by the flimsy metal chair he sat upon.

"I'm telling you, Trey," Blackwell said, his voice low and urgent, "the Idol of Lycoan is the key to everything. With its power, the Were-Gorillas could rule Blacksburg, could make the humans and the other lycans bow down before you."

Trey's eyes narrowed, a flicker of interest sparking in their depths. "And what's in it for you, Blackwell? Why come to me with this information, instead of keeping it for yourself?"

Blackwell smiled, a thin, humorless thing that didn't reach his eyes. "Let's just say that I have a vested interest in seeing the current power structure in Blacksburg upended. The RIPD, the Panther Prowl, the humans... they're all obstacles to true lycan supremacy."

He leaned in closer, his voice dropping to a conspiratorial whisper. "But with the Idol in your possession, Trey, you could change all that. You could be the one to lead the lycan world into a new era of dominance and prosperity."

Trey sat back, his massive arms crossed over his chest, his brow furrowed in thought. "And what about this Agent Elkins and her team? They're not just going to hand over the Idol, especially not after what they went through to get it."

Blackwell's smile widened, a predatory gleam in his eye. "Leave Elkins and her band of do-gooders to me. I have a plan to distract them, to keep them occupied while you and your boys make your move."

He reached into his pocket, pulling out a small, black device. "This is a remote detonator, linked to a series of explosives I've planted throughout the city. When the time is right, I'll set them off, creating chaos and confusion that will keep the RIPD busy and allow you to slip in and grab the Idol."

Trey's eyes widened, a mixture of surprise and admiration on his face. "You've thought of everything, haven't you, Blackwell?"

Blackwell leaned back, a self-satisfied smirk on his lips. "I always do, Trey. That's why I'm the one who's going to come out on top, when all is said and done."

He stood, straightening his jacket and smoothing back his hair. "So, what do you say, Silver Back? Are you ready to take your rightful place as the leader of the lycan world, with the Idol of Lycoan as your tool and your symbol?"

Trey stood as well, his massive frame towering over Blackwell. For a long moment, he was silent, his eyes searching the other man's face for any sign of deceit or weakness.

Finally, he nodded, his hand extending to clasp Blackwell's in a firm, decisive grip. "I'm in, Blackwell. Let's do this. Let's show the world what true lycan power looks like."

As the two men shook hands, sealing their dark pact, the flickering light above them cast a sinister glow across their features.

And somewhere in the distance, unbeknownst to either of them, a figure watched from the shadows, their eyes wide with shock and horror at the plot they had just overheard

****

The halls of the Blacksburg Police Department were strangely quiet as Casey made her way towards the front desk, her footsteps echoing off the polished linoleum. The usual bustle of officers and civilians was conspicuously absent, replaced by an eerie stillness that set her instincts on edge.

As she approached the desk, the young officer on duty looked up, his eyes widening in recognition. "Agent Elkins," he said, his voice tinged with a mixture of respect and apprehension. "What can I do for you today?"

Casey leaned against the counter, her expression serious. "I'm here to inquire about Braydon Mitchell's trial date. I need to know when he's scheduled to appear in court."

The officer's brow furrowed, his fingers tapping nervously on the keyboard in front of him. "Let me just pull up that information for you, ma'am."

As he worked, Casey's gaze drifted around the empty waiting area, taking in the deserted chairs and the unattended coffee machine in the corner. Something was off, a prickling sense of wrongness that she couldn't quite put her finger on.

"I'm sorry, Agent Elkins," the officer said, drawing her attention back to the desk. "But I can't seem to find any record of a trial date for Braydon Mitchell in the system."

Casey's eyebrows shot up, a flicker of alarm sparking in her chest. "What do you mean, there's no record? He was arrested and charged. There has to be a trial scheduled."

The officer shook his head, his expression apologetic. "I understand, ma'am. But according to our records, no trial has been set. In fact, it looks like the case hasn't even been officially filed with the court yet."

Casey's mind raced, trying to make sense of this new information. It wasn't like the Blacksburg PD to drop the ball on such a high-profile case, especially one that involved a dangerous criminal like Braydon.

Suddenly, a thought occurred to her, a niggling suspicion that had been growing in the back of her mind. "Officer, where is Chief Blackwell? I need to speak with him about this immediately."

The young man's face paled, his eyes darting away from Casey's intense gaze. "I... I'm sorry, Agent Elkins. But Chief Blackwell hasn't been seen in days. No one knows where he is or when he'll be back."

Casey felt a chill run down her spine, a sense of dread settling in the pit of her stomach. Blackwell's absence, combined with the lack of progress on Braydon's case, could only mean one thing.

Something was very, very wrong.

She leaned in closer, her voice low and urgent. "Listen to me carefully, officer. I need you to pull every scrap of information you have on Chief Blackwell's whereabouts and activities over the past week. I have a feeling that his disappearance and the irregularities in Braydon's case are connected."

The officer nodded, his fingers flying over the keys as he complied with her request. But even as he worked, Casey's mind was racing, piecing together the clues and trying to anticipate the next move in this deadly game.

She had a sinking feeling that Blackwell's absence was just the tip of the iceberg, that there were forces at work here that went beyond anything she and her team had faced before.

And as she stood there, in the heart of the Blacksburg PD, Casey knew that she would stop at nothing to uncover the truth, to protect her city and the people she loved from the darkness that threatened to consume them all.

****

The dense, green canopy of the Lycan National Forest seemed to hum with an unseen energy, the air thick and heavy with the scent of damp earth and primal power. Beneath the towering trees, a group of figures moved with a deliberate, almost ritualistic purpose, their massive frames casting long shadows in the dappled sunlight.

At the center of the gathering stood Trey Smith, his silver-black fur glinting as he surveyed his assembled followers. The Were-Gorillas, the most powerful and feared of all lycan clans, had come together at his call, drawn by the promise of a new era of dominance and supremacy.

"My brothers," Trey rumbled, his voice a deep, guttural growl that seemed to resonate through the very ground beneath their feet. "The time has come for us to claim our rightful place as the true rulers of the lycan world. With the Idol of Lycoan in our grasp, nothing will stand in our way."

A chorus of grunts and roars met his words, the Were-Gorillas beating their chests and stamping their feet in a primal display of agreement and solidarity. The sheer force of their combined rei was staggering, a palpable wave of energy that rippled out from the gathering like a physical thing.

Miles away, in the heart of the Kenta Corp headquarters, an alarm suddenly blared to life, the screens of the command center flashing with urgent red warnings. KIVO's avatar materialized, its normally calm voice laced with an undercurrent of concern.

"Alert," it intoned, "Massive rei manifestation detected in the Lycan National Forest. Energy levels are off the charts, far exceeding any previously recorded lycan gathering."

Casey, Rigo, Aidan, and Cyndi exchanged a look of alarm, their expressions mirroring the growing sense of unease that permeated the room. They had known that the Were-Gorillas were a force to be reckoned with, their raw power and brute strength unmatched by any other lycan clan.

But this... this was something else entirely. The sheer magnitude of the rei they were sensing spoke to a level of danger and threat that they had never encountered before.

"KIVO," Casey said, her voice tight with tension, "Can you get a visual on the gathering? We need to know exactly what we're dealing with here."

The AI's avatar pulsed, its processors whirring as it tapped into the network of surveillance drones and satellite feeds at its disposal. A moment later, a live feed sprang to life on the main screen, the images sharp and starkly clear.

Casey and Rigo watched in growing horror as the scene unfolded before them - dozens of Were-Gorillas, their forms massive and rippling with barely contained power, gathered in a tight circle around the imposing figure of Trey Smith.

"Casey, What is going on out there?" Cyndi asks, still not used to sensing rei, "It feels like someone turned on a 90s TV without cable,"

"That's rei," Rigo explains, his voice soft, "All living beings have it, but not all living beings can access it. Lycans, like yourself and me, can sense it. We also use it to shift into our animal forms and back to human form. Some lycans, like the Were-Gorillas dislike the feeling of being human, so they stay shifted. Those lycans are able to speak human while in animal form. I am able to speak while in animal form as well, but its due to me being labeled King of Hyena's,"

"So why are the gorillas gathering?" Cyndi asks, "Since you are such an expert?"

"Cyn," Casey says, "He was just offering an explanation of whats going on with your body since you were bitten. Calm down. Rigo, what are the possibilities of the Gorillas coming in peace? Gorillas are generally peaceful animals, right? I mean if we believe what Steve Irwin taught us growing up,"

"Normal Gorillas are peaceful creatures. These Were-Gorillas are normal gorillas driven by human greed. There is no telling what their motives are. The only way to know for sure is to go confront them," Rigo says.

"As lead agent here, I'm going," Casey says, "As head Lycan, you have to go too, Rigo. Cyndi, Aidan, stay here and watch the scenario unfold. KIVO, prepare the suppressor if needed,"

"You got it, boss," Aidan smiles, bringing a chair over for Cyndi, "Have a seat,"

"Thank you," Cyndi shyly replies, "Casey, be careful out there,"

“Always. Careful is my middle name,” Casey smiles, giving a thumbs up as Aidan chuckles.

“Just because you stole his heart, doesn’t mean you can steal his catchphrases,” Aidan laughs.

“Who? She stole whose heart?” Cyndi asks as Casey and Rigo walk out of the headquarters.

****

The air in the Lycan National Forest seemed to crackle with tension as Casey and Rigo approached the gathering of Were-Gorillas. The rei manifestation that KIVO had detected was close, the very atmosphere charged with the raw, primal energy of the assembled lycans.

As they stepped into the clearing, the Were-Gorillas turned to face them, their massive frames tensed and their eyes glinting with a fierce intensity. At the center of the group stood Trey Smith, his silver-black fur bristling and his posture radiating a sense of unquestionable authority.

"Agent Casey Elkins," Trey rumbled, his voice a deep, guttural growl. "And Rigo Balderas, the Hyena King. To what do we owe the pleasure of this unexpected visit?"

Casey stepped forward, her expression calm but her senses on high alert. "Trey Smith, I presume? We're here to talk, to understand the reason behind this gathering. Our sensors detected a massive rei manifestation, and we couldn't help but be concerned."

Trey chuckled, a low, menacing sound that sent shivers down Casey's spine. "Concerned? About a simple gathering of lycans in our own territory? I wasn't aware that the RIPD had jurisdiction over the affairs of the Were-Gorillas."

Rigo growled, his posture shifting subtly into a more defensive stance. "It's not about jurisdiction, Trey. It's about maintaining the balance, ensuring that the peace we've worked so hard to achieve isn't threatened by any one group or individual."

Trey's gaze flicked to Rigo, his lips curling into a sneer of disdain. "Ah, yes. The Joker. The self-appointed champion of lycan-human relations. Tell me, do you really think your little experiment in coexistence can last? That the humans will ever truly accept us as equals?"

Casey's brow furrowed, a flicker of unease sparking in her gut. There was something in Trey's tone, a hint of anger and resentment that went beyond mere posturing or bravado.

"Our 'experiment,' as you call it, is founded on the belief that all sentient beings have the right to live in peace and dignity, regardless of their species or origin," she said, her voice firm and unwavering. "And it's an ideal that we're willing to fight for, to protect with everything we have."

Trey's eyes narrowed, his gaze boring into Casey's with a fierce intensity. "Noble words, Agent Elkins. But words alone won't save you, or your precious city, when the time comes."

He stepped closer, his massive frame looming over Casey and Rigo like a gathering storm. "The Were-Gorillas are the future of the lycan world, the only ones with the strength and the vision to lead our kind into a new era of dominance and prosperity. And we will not be denied our rightful place, not by humans, and certainly not by lesser lycans like yourselves."

Casey's heart pounded in her chest, a growing sense of dread settling in the pit of her stomach. There was something in Trey's words, a darkness and a danger that went beyond mere posturing or rhetoric.

"Trey," she said, her voice low and steady, "I don't know what you're planning, but I can assure you that the RIPD will not stand idly by if you threaten the safety and security of Blacksburg or its inhabitants, human or lycan."

Trey's lips twisted into a cold, cruel smile, his eyes glinting with a malevolent purpose. "Oh, Agent Elkins. You have no idea what's coming, do you? The storm that's about to break over your precious city, the chaos and destruction that will be unleashed in the name of lycan supremacy."

He leaned in closer, his breath hot and rancid against Casey's face. "But don't worry. You'll find out soon enough. And when you do, you'll wish you had never crossed paths with the Were-Gorillas, or with me."

With that, Trey turned and strode away, his followers falling into step behind him like a pack of obedient soldiers. Casey and Rigo watched them go, a chill of foreboding settling over them like a shroud.

They didn't know what Trey was planning, or what dark machinations were unfolding in the shadows of Blacksburg. But they knew, with a certainty that went beyond words, that they had just glimpsed the face of a new and terrifying enemy, one that would stop at nothing to achieve its twisted goals.

And as they made their way back through the dense undergrowth of the forest, Casey and Rigo could only wonder what trials and challenges lay ahead, and whether they would be strong enough to face them head-on, for the sake of their city and all those they held dear.

****

Casey and Rigo burst into the command center, their faces etched with a mixture of concern and determination.

Aidan and Cyndi looked up from the screens they had been monitoring, their eyes widening at the sight of their teammates' grim expressions.

"What happened out there?" Aidan asked, his voice tight with worry. "Did you find out what the Were-Gorillas are planning?"

Casey shook her head, frustration evident in the set of her jaw. "Not exactly. But we know it's nothing good. Trey Smith seems hell-bent on establishing lycan supremacy, and he hinted at some kind of impending chaos that's going to hit Blacksburg."

Rigo nodded, his brow furrowed in thought. "We need to get to the bottom of this, and fast. The Idol of Lycoan seems to be at the center of it all, and we still don't fully understand its origins or its true power."

Cyndi leaned forward, her eyes sparkling with curiosity. "So, what's our next move? How do we unravel the secrets of the Idol?"

Casey turned to Aidan, a determined glint in her eye. "Aidan, I need you to dig deeper into the Idol's history. Try to find out which lycan group descends directly from King Lycoan, the ancient Greek ruler who was said to have been cursed by Zeus and transformed into a werewolf."

Aidan's fingers flew across the keyboard, his gaze intense as he searched through the vast database at his disposal. "I'm on it, Casey. KIVO, can you assist with cross-referencing the historical records and lycan genealogies?"

"Affirmative, Aidan," the AI responded, its avatar pulsing with a soft blue light. "Scanning now for any direct descendants of King Lycoan."

For several tense minutes, the only sound in the

command center was the gentle hum of the computers and the soft beeping of KIVO's search algorithms. Then, suddenly, the AI's avatar flickered and expanded, a wealth of information cascading across the screens.

"Match found," KIVO announced, its voice tinged with a hint of excitement. "The most direct descendants of King Lycoan appear to be Jaxson and Emily Pearson, a brother and sister team who lead a small but influential lycan faction known as the Lycoan Legacy."

Casey and Rigo exchanged a glance, a flicker of hope kindling in their eyes. "The Lycoan Legacy? I've never heard of them before. What do we know about Jaxson and Emily?"

Aidan scanned the information on the screens, his brow furrowed in concentration. "Not much, but it seems they hold King Lycoan in high regard, viewing him as a pivotal figure in lycan history and mythology. They may have insights into the Idol that we've been missing."

Rigo nodded, a determined set to his jaw. "We need to reach out to them, see if they're willing to help us understand the Idol's true nature and purpose. If anyone can shed light on this mystery, it's the direct descendants of Lycoan himself."

Casey pulled out her phone, her fingers already dialing the contact number listed in the Lycoan Legacy's file. "I'm on it. Let's hope Jaxson and Emily are open to collaboration, because we're going to need all the allies we can get if we're going to stop Trey and the Were-Gorillas."

As the phone rang, Casey felt a flicker of apprehension mingling with the determination in her gut. She knew that the path ahead was fraught with danger and uncertainty, that the fate of Blacksburg and the entire lycan world hung in the balance.

But she also knew that she had her team by her side, a group of brave and brilliant individuals who would stop at nothing to protect the innocent and unravel the secrets of the Idol.

And with that knowledge, Casey squared her shoulders and prepared to face whatever challenges lay ahead, confident that together, they could overcome any obstacle and emerge victorious in the face of even the darkest of foes.

Casey held her breath as the phone rang, her heart pounding with a mixture of anticipation and apprehension. After what felt like an eternity, the line clicked, and a cheerful, melodic voice filled the air.

"Hello, hello! You've reached Emily Pearson of the Lycoan Legacy. How can I brighten your day?"

Casey blinked, momentarily taken aback by the effervescent greeting. "Uh, hi. This is Special Agent Casey Elkins from the RIPD. I was hoping to speak with you and your brother, Jaxson, about an urgent matter concerning the Idol of Lycoan."

There was a brief pause, followed by a delighted gasp. "Oh, my goodness! The RIPD? How exciting! I've always wanted to work with you guys. It's like a dream come true!"

In the background, Casey could hear a muffled male voice, tinged with exasperation. "Emily, focus. This could be serious."

Emily's voice returned, a hint of sheepishness tempering her enthusiasm. "Oops, sorry about that. My brother, Jaxson, keeps me grounded. He's a bit of a stuffed shirt, but I love him anyway. So, what's this about the Idol of Lycoan?"

Casey glanced at her team, a flicker of amusement passing between them at Emily's bubbly personality. "We've recently come into possession of the Idol, but we're still trying to unravel its secrets and understand its true purpose. As the direct descendants of King Lycoan, we were hoping you and Jaxson might have some insights that could help us."

There was a rustle of movement, and then a deep, commanding voice replaced Emily's on the line. "Agent Elkins, this is Jaxson Pearson. I apologize for my sister's... enthusiasm. She means well, but she can be a bit much at times."

Casey straightened, recognizing the no-nonsense tone of a seasoned leader. "No need to apologize, Jaxson. I appreciate you both taking the time to speak with me. As I mentioned, we're in a bit of a situation here, and we could really use your expertise."

Jaxson's voice was steady, a hint of steel underlying his words. "The Idol of Lycoan is a matter of great importance to our family and our legacy. If it has resurfaced, then the implications could be significant for the entire lycan world."

In the background, Emily piped up, her voice filled with eager curiosity. "Ooh, does this mean we get to go on an adventure? I've always wanted to be part of a secret mission!"

Jaxson sighed, the sound a mixture of fondness and frustration. "Emily, please. This is serious business." He turned his attention back to Casey, his tone brisk and businesslike. "Agent Elkins, my sister and I would be happy to assist you in any way we can. The Lycoan Legacy has extensive records and histories pertaining to the Idol and its origins. We can be in Blacksburg within the day to share what we know and help you unravel this mystery."

Casey felt a surge of relief and gratitude, a glimmer of hope sparking in her chest. "Thank you, Jaxson. That would be incredibly helpful. We'll make sure to have a secure location ready for your arrival, and we'll brief you on the situation as soon as you get here."

As the call ended, Casey turned to her team, a determined glint in her eye. "All right, everyone. We've got some reinforcements on the way. Let's get ready to dive into the history of the Idol and figure out how we can use that knowledge to stop Trey and the Were-Gorillas."

Rigo nodded, a fierce grin spreading across his face. "I've got a feeling that with the Pearson siblings on our side, we just might have a chance of coming out on top of this thing."

Aidan and Cyndi exchanged a look of determination, their own resolve hardening in the face of the challenges ahead.

And as the team set to work, preparing for the arrival of their new allies and the secrets they would bring, Casey couldn't help but feel a flicker of hope amidst the darkness that loomed on the horizon.

With the Lycoan Legacy by their side, they just might have a chance of unraveling the mysteries of the Idol and saving Blacksburg from the chaos that threatened to engulf it.

****

The sleek, black SUV pulled into the parking lot of the Kenta Corp headquarters, followed closely by a second, identical vehicle. Casey and her team stood at the entrance, their eyes fixed on the convoy as it rolled to a stop.

From the first SUV, Jaxson and Emily Pearson emerged, their faces set in expressions of determination and anticipation. Jaxson moved with the confident grace of a trained soldier, his gaze sweeping the area with a practiced eye. Emily, on the other hand, practically bounced with excitement, her vibrant red hair dancing in the warm afternoon breeze.

The second SUV's doors opened, and two older gentlemen stepped out, their postures alert and their eyes sharp. The first, a grizzled man with a jagged scar across his face, scanned the surroundings with a wary intensity. The second, a man with a crew cut and a no-nonsense demeanor, fell into step beside Emily, his presence a silent but formidable guardian.

As the group approached, Casey stepped forward, her hand outstretched in greeting. "Jaxson, Emily, thank you for coming. And I see you've brought some additional members of your pack?"

Jaxson nodded, his hand clasping Casey's in a firm shake. "Yes, this is Roy Moore and Bill Massey, two of our most trusted advisors and guards. Given the sensitive nature of our discussion, I thought it prudent to have them accompany us."

Roy, the man with the scar, grunted in acknowledgment, his gaze never wavering from the potential threats around them. Bill, the man with the crew cut, offered a curt nod, his posture relaxed but ready to spring into action at a moment's notice.

Emily, meanwhile, couldn't contain her excitement. "Oh, my goodness, Agent Elkins! It's so wonderful to finally meet you and your team in person! I can't wait to dive into the mysteries of the Idol and help in any way we can!"

Casey smiled, charmed by Emily's enthusiasm despite the gravity of the situation. "Please, call me Casey. And we're grateful for any assistance you can provide. Come inside, and we'll brief you on the situation."

As the group made their way into the headquarters, Roy and Bill fell into step on either side of Jaxson and Emily, their presence a silent but powerful reminder of the Lycoan Legacy's strength and commitment.

Inside the command center, Aidan and Cyndi looked up from their workstations, their eyes widening at the sight of the new arrivals. Rigo, ever the diplomat, stepped forward to make introductions and ensure that everyone was on the same page.

As they gathered around the central table, the holographic displays casting a soft blue glow over their faces, Casey couldn't help but feel a sense of hope and determination. With the Pearson siblings and their loyal guards by their side, they were one step closer to unraveling the secrets of the Idol and stopping the impending threat to Blacksburg.

And as Jaxson began to speak, his voice low and steady, the weight of history and destiny hanging in the air, Casey knew that this was a turning point in their investigation, a moment that would shape the future of not just Blacksburg, but the entire lycan world.

****

"Excuse me for a moment," she said, stepping away from the table. "I need to take this call. It's my handler from the RIPD."

Casey moved to a quiet corner of the command center, her finger swiping across the screen to accept the call. "Mick, hey. What's up?"

Mick's voice came through the speaker, tinged with a mix of concern and curiosity. "Casey, I wanted to check in on the situation in Blacksburg. How are things going with the Idol and the Panther Prowl?"

Casey sighed, running a hand through her hair. "It's a lot, Mick. I arrested Braydon and pretty much stopped the Panther Prowl from wreaking havoc, but now I've got Trey Smith, the leader of the Were-Gorillas, making some pretty big threats about lycan supremacy and chaos in the city. But I've also got some new allies - Jaxson and Emily Pearson, from the Lycoan Legacy. They're the direct descendants of King Lycoan, and they might have some insights into the Idol that could help me."

Mick hummed thoughtfully, the sound crackling through the connection. "Trey Smith? The Silver Back? He’s in Blacksburg? Since when? And The Lycoan Legacy? That's a name I haven't heard in a while. They're a pretty secretive bunch, but if they're willing to work with you, that's a good sign."

Casey nodded, even though Mick couldn't see her. "Literally came to town just after I arrested Braydon. Yeah, I think so too. We're just about to start going over what they know, see if we can piece together a plan to stop Trey and his followers."

There was a brief pause, and then Mick spoke again, his tone shifting to one of cautious optimism. "Well, I've got some news on my end, too. I've been keeping tabs on the situation with Hawkins and Alex in Polkville."

Casey's heart skipped a beat, her grip tightening on the phone. "And? What's the latest?"

Mick chuckled, the sound warm and reassuring. "It looks like Hawkins is hitting a bit of a wall in his investigation. He's been trying to gather evidence to prove that Alex is a lycan, but so far, he hasn't found anything concrete."

Relief washed over Casey, a small smile tugging at the corners of her mouth. "That's good news, Mick. I know Alex has been worried about what this could mean for his position as Sheriff."

"Exactly," Mick agreed, his voice filled with a hint of satisfaction. "Without hard proof, Hawkins can't force Alex to register as a lycan. From what I’ve been hearing, Alex hasn’t had a single transformation since the investigation began, and he’s only manipulated his rei while showing Hawkins what he can do,"

Casey felt a swell of pride and affection for her friend, her smile growing wider. "That sounds like Alex, all right. He's always been one to face challenges head-on, to find a way to adapt and overcome."

“I think Alex will register as a lycan anyway thought,” Mick says surprisingly.

“What makes you say that?” Casey asks.

“Hawkins threatened Alex if he doesn’t leave you alone. Hawkins knows you and Alex have been seeing each other regularly,” Mick reports.

“This is such bullshit. I’ll go rogue if I have too. Alex will too,” Casey growls, “Why does Hawkins try to control his agents so damned much?”

“I dont know, Ace. But I know that your friend in Polkville is one hard headed individual and he is able to stand his ground against Hawkins and that know it all attitude of his,” Mick chuckles.

“That’s my Tigger. Always gotta have the last word in,” Casey laughs.

Mick's voice softened, a note of understanding creeping into his tone. "Just like you, Casey. You've got a tough road ahead of you, but I know you'll find a way to make it through. And remember, you've got a whole team behind you, both in Blacksburg and over in Polkville. Plus there is little ole me here at RIPD HQ."

Casey's heart warmed, the weight of Mick's support and confidence settling over her like a comforting blanket. "Thanks, Mick. That means a lot. I'd better get back to the others, but I'll keep you posted on any developments."

As she ended the call and slipped the phone back into her pocket, Casey took a moment to let Mick's words sink in. Alex was holding his own against Hawkins, and she had a growing alliance of powerful friends and allies in her corner.

With a renewed sense of determination, Casey rejoined the group at the central table, ready to dive back into the mysteries of the Idol and the battle that lay ahead.

****

In the heart of the Lycan National Forest, Trey Smith paced before his gathered followers, his massive frame casting long shadows in the fading light of dusk. The Were-Gorillas stood at attention, their eyes fixed on their leader as he spoke, his voice a low, rumbling growl.

"My brothers," Trey began, his gaze sweeping over the assembled lycans. "The time of our ascendancy is at hand. For too long, we have lived in the shadows, forced to hide our true nature from the world of men. But no more."

He paused, his hand resting on the hilt of the ceremonial blade at his waist. "With the Idol of Lycoan in our grasp, we will rise up and claim our rightful place as the rulers of this world. The humans, the lesser lycans... they will all bow before the might of the Were-Gorillas."

A chorus of grunts and roars met his words, the Were-Gorillas beating their chests in a primal display of agreement. Zack Burgress and Kenan Holifield, Trey's most trusted lieutenants, stepped forward, their eyes glinting with a fierce loyalty.

"But what of the RIPD?" Roy asked, his voice a rasping snarl. "And these new allies they've found, the Lycoan Legacy? They could pose a threat to our plans."

Trey's lips curled into a sneer, his eyes flashing with a dangerous light. "The RIPD is nothing more than a nuisance, a group of misguided fools who think they can stand against the tide of history. As for the Lycoan Legacy..."

He chuckled, a low, menacing sound that sent shivers down the spines of his followers. "They may be the descendants of the great King Lycoan, but they are weak, corrupted by their ties to the human world. They have forgotten the true power of the lycan race, the strength that flows through our veins."

Zack Burgess nodded, his crew cut bristling in the breeze. "So, what's our next move, boss? How do we flush them out and take what's ours?"

Trey's hand tightened around the hilt of his blade, his eyes narrowing with a predatory intensity. "We strike at the heart of their power. We sow chaos and fear in the streets of Blacksburg, drawing them out into the open. And when they come to face us, we will crush them, one by one, until the Idol is ours and the world trembles at our feet."

Trey Smith stood before his assembled followers, his eyes glinting with a malevolent purpose. He turned to two of his most trusted enforcers, Grayson and Riker, their hulking forms towering over the rest of the Were-Gorillas.

"Grayson, Riker," Trey growled, his voice low and commanding. "I have a special mission for you. One that will strike at the heart of our enemies and pave the way for our victory."

The two lycans stepped forward, their chests puffed with pride at being singled out by their leader. "Whatever you need, boss," Grayson rumbled, his voice like gravel. "We're ready to do what it takes."

Trey smiled, a cold, predatory thing. "I want you to infiltrate Blacksburg's power grid. Shut down every source of electricity, every generator, every backup system. Plunge the city into darkness and chaos."

Riker's brow furrowed, a flicker of confusion crossing his brutish features. "But why, boss? What's the point of cutting the power?"

Trey's eyes narrowed, his patience wearing thin. "The point, you fool, is to level the playing field. To rob our enemies of their precious technology and force them to face us on our terms. We are Panthers, we have night vision. The Hyena doesn't, the human's do not. The Jaguar cannot speak while transformed."

He began to pace, his voice rising with a fevered intensity. "Without power, the RIPD and their allies will be blind and vulnerable. And when the Kenta Corp headquarters goes dark, they'll assume it's just part of the citywide blackout."

Grayson's eyes widened, a glimmer of understanding dawning on his face. "And that's when we strike. When they're confused and disoriented, we'll storm their base and take the Idol for ourselves."

Trey's grin widened, a savage joy spreading across his features. "Exactly. They'll never see us coming. And by the time they realize what's happening, it will be too late."

He turned back to Grayson and Riker, his gaze boring into them with a fierce intensity. "You have your orders. Go now, and do not fail me. The future of our kind depends on your success."

The two lycans beat their chests in salute, their eyes blazing with a fanatical loyalty. They turned and loped off into the darkness, their forms melting into the shadows as they set out to bring Blacksburg to its knees.

As they vanished from sight, Trey addressed the rest of his followers, his voice ringing with a savage triumph. "Prepare yourselves, my brothers. The hour of our victory is at hand. Soon, the streets of Blacksburg will run red with the blood of our enemies, and the Idol of Lycoan will be ours!"

The Were-Gorillas roared their approval, their voices rising in a frenzied chorus that shook the very earth beneath their feet. They began to move, their forms shifting and rippling as they readied themselves for the battle to come.

And in the heart of Blacksburg, Casey and her team remained oblivious to the danger that was fast approaching, their attention focused on unraveling the secrets of the Lycoan Legacy and the Idol that had brought them all together.

Little did they know that the greatest threat they had ever faced was already in motion, a force of primal savagery and unbridled ambition that would stop at nothing to claim the ultimate prize.

****

The command center at Kenta Corp headquarters was a hive of activity, with Casey and her team huddled around the central table, their faces illuminated by the glow of the holographic displays. Jaxson and Emily Pearson, along with their guards, Roy Moore and Bill Massey, stood nearby, their expressions a mix of concentration and concern as they pored over the ancient texts and artifacts related to the Idol of Lycoan.

Suddenly, the room plunged into darkness, the screens and displays blinking out in a heartbeat. For a moment, there was only the sound of startled gasps and the rustle of movement as everyone tried to orient themselves in the sudden gloom.

Then, a soft, pulsing blue light began to emanate from the center of the room, growing brighter and more insistent with each passing second. It was KIVO, the AI's avatar materializing above the table, its face a mask of calm urgency.

"Attention all personnel," KIVO's voice rang out, clear and steady in the darkness. "I have detected a massive power outage affecting the entire city of Blacksburg. All electrical systems and backup generators have been shut down, with the exception of Kenta Corp headquarters."

Casey's eyes widened, her mind racing with the implications of this new development. "KIVO, what's causing the outage? Is it a technical issue, or something more sinister?"

The AI's avatar pulsed, its expression growing grim. "Based on my analysis of the available data, the power outage appears to be the result of a deliberate attack on the city's infrastructure. I have detected unauthorized access to multiple power stations and substations, consistent with an organized effort to sabotage the grid."

Emily Pearson stepped forward, her brow furrowed in confusion. "But wait, why is Kenta Corp headquarters still lit up like a Christmas tree? Shouldn't we be affected by the blackout too?"

Aidan grinned, a hint of pride flickering in his eyes. "Not quite, Emily. You see, Kenta Corp operates on a completely independent power system, one that's not connected to the city grid."

He gestured to the glowing screens and displays, his voice taking on a note of excitement. "We use solar energy to power all of our facilities, with a massive array of panels on the roof that soak up the sun's rays and convert them into electricity. That energy is then stored in a network of high-capacity batteries, which can keep us running for days, even in the event of prolonged cloudy weather or a total grid failure."

Emily's eyes widened, a look of impressed admiration crossing her face. "That's incredible, Aidan. But how do you keep those batteries secure? Surely someone could try to sabotage them, too."

Aidan's grin widened, a mischievous glint in his eye. "Ah, but that's the beauty of the system, Emily. The batteries are housed in a fortified bunker deep beneath the building, accessible only through a heavily encrypted security door. And the code to that door? It's stored solely in my head, never written down or shared with anyone else."

As the team marveled at Aidan's ingenuity and foresight, Casey's mind was already racing ahead, trying to piece together the larger puzzle. "KIVO, based on the timing and the nature of this attack, is it possible that the Were-Gorillas are behind it? Could this be part of some larger plan to weaken the city's defenses and make a play for the Idol?"

The AI's avatar flickered, its processors whirring as it analyzed the available data. "That is a distinct possibility, Agent Elkins. The Were-Gorillas have both the motive and the means to carry out such an attack, and the power outage would certainly create chaos and confusion that they could exploit."

Jaxson Pearson's expression hardened, his hand tightening around the hilt of his blade. "If the Were-Gorillas are behind this, then we need to act fast. They won't be content to simply plunge the city into darkness. They'll use this as an opportunity to strike, to come after the Idol and anyone who stands in their way."

Casey nodded, her jaw set with grim determination. "Jaxson's right. We need to be ready for anything. KIVO, I want you to monitor every inch of the city, every camera and sensor you can access. If the Were-Gorillas make a move, I want to know about it immediately."

"Everyone, I have to admit something to you all. Since The Pearsons have arrived, KIVO has been taking note everyone here, and analyzing your bodies for the development of armor. I'm assuming Jaxon, Rigo, Matt, and Casey are going to go fight these Were-Gorillas?" Aidan interrupts, "Therefore, Emily, KIVO, Mr. Butler, and myself will here, analyzing more data. KIVO's access to the street cameras and everything else is gone, so you will be going in blind. Our drones can't operate in total darkness. I've prepared weapons and armor for the four of you,"

Suddenly a wall rose from the floor in front of Matt, Rigo, Casey, and Jaxon. Each wall contained a specialized kevlar armor set, and two weapons each. Matt received a curved sword and an Indiana Jones inspired chain whip. Rigo received a katana, and a shock baton. Jaxon received dual wrist mounted grappling hooks, and a bo staff. Casey received a larger handgun, and a short sword.

The team hurriedly suited up, with each member thanking Aidan for their new gear. Jaxon smiles and clears his throat.

"I feel like this a moment when someone's uncle named Ben would remind us all that with great power, comes great responsibility. Right now the four of us have the greatest responsibility to protect the Idol of Lycoan and bring peace to to the lycan and human communities," Jaxon says.

"Team, let's Go!" Casey calls out, leading the charge towards the front door of the HQ.

As the team sprang into action, their faces lit by the eerie glow of the emergency lighting, a sense of urgency and purpose filled the air. They knew that the stakes had just been raised, that the battle for Blacksburg and the fate of the Idol had entered a new and dangerous phase.

But they also knew that they were ready, that they had the skills, the knowledge, and the determination to face whatever challenges lay ahead. And with KIVO and Aidan's technological wizardry on their side, they had a fighting chance of staying one step ahead of their enemies, of unraveling the secrets of the Lycoan legacy and stopping the Were-Gorillas' dark designs.

CHAPTER 13

The streets of Blacksburg were eerily silent, the usual bustle of city life replaced by an unsettling stillness. The only light came from the moon overhead, casting long shadows across the pavement and lending an otherworldly quality to the scene.

Casey and her team moved swiftly through the darkened streets, their heightened senses on high alert for any sign of the Were-Gorillas. The custom-made armor and weapons provided by Aidan felt reassuring against their skin, a tangible reminder of the support and ingenuity of their friends back at Kenta Corp.

Suddenly, a low growl echoed through the night, followed by the sound of heavy footsteps and the scrape of claws against concrete. The team froze, their bodies tensing as they scanned the shadows for the source of the noise.

And then, they saw them. A group of massive, hulking figures emerged from the darkness, their eyes glinting with a feral intensity in the moonlight. At their head stood Trey Smith, his silver-black fur bristling and his lips pulled back in a snarl of challenge.

"Well, well, well," Trey growled, his voice dripping with menace. "If it isn't the RIPD's pet humans and their lycan lapdogs. I see you've come to play, even without your precious technology to back you up."

Casey stepped forward, her hand resting on the hilt of her short sword. "We're not here to play, Trey. We're here to stop you from terrorizing this city and stealing the Idol of Lycoan."

Trey laughed, a harsh, grating sound that sent shivers down the spines of the team. "Stop me? You really think you stand a chance against the might of the Were-Gorillas, against the true heirs of King Lycoan's legacy?"

Jaxon Pearson moved to stand beside Casey, his eyes narrowed and his jaw set with determination. "The Lycoan Legacy belongs to all lycans, Trey, not just those who would use it for their own selfish gain. We won't let you twist our history and our heritage to suit your own twisted ends."

Trey's eyes flashed with anger, his claws flexing at his sides. "Enough talk," he snarled. "Let's see how well you fight, when the odds are stacked against you and the darkness is your only ally."

With a roar of fury, he lunged forward, his followers close behind. Casey and her team met them head-on, their weapons flashing in the moonlight as they clashed with the Were-Gorillas in a brutal, no-holds-barred battle for the fate of Blacksburg and the Idol that had brought them all together.

****

Matt stood his ground, his curved sword glinting in the moonlight as he faced off against two hulking Were-Gorillas. The creatures snarled, their eyes glinting with a feral intensity as they circled him, their claws flexing in anticipation of the kill.

Suddenly, one of the Were-Gorillas lunged forward, its massive fist swinging towards Matt's head with devastating force. But Matt was ready, his reflexes honed by years of training and combat. He ducked beneath the blow, his sword flashing out in a lightning-fast strike that sliced across the creature's chest, drawing a howl of pain and rage.

The second Were-Gorilla attacked from the side, its claws raking towards Matt's face with blinding speed. Matt spun, his sword meeting the creature's claws in a shower of sparks, the impact sending shockwaves up his arm.

For a moment, the three combatants were locked in a deadly dance, their movements a blur of slashing claws and flashing steel. Matt's heart pounded in his chest, his breath coming in ragged gasps as he fought to keep the Were-Gorillas at bay.

Suddenly, he saw an opening, a momentary weakness in the creatures' defenses. With a roar of determination, he leaped forward, his sword a blur of motion as he unleashed a devastating combo.

His blade sliced across the first Were-Gorilla's throat, sending a spray of blood arcing through the air. Before the creature could even fall, Matt was spinning, his sword flashing out in a wide arc that caught the second Were-Gorilla across the chest, cutting deep into the flesh and bone.

But even as the creatures staggered back, their eyes wide with shock and pain, Matt knew that the fight was far from over. With a snarl of rage, the first Were-Gorilla lunged forward, its claws slashing towards his heart with a speed and ferocity that seemed impossible.

In that moment, Matt felt a surge of power rising up from deep within him, a primal energy that had lain dormant for so long. With a roar that shook the very ground beneath his feet, he let the transformation take hold, his body rippling and changing as he shifted into his jaguar form.

The Were-Gorillas hesitated, their eyes wide with fear

and confusion as they faced this new, terrifying threat. But Matt didn't give them a chance to react. With a snarl of fury, he leaped forward, his claws and fangs flashing in the moonlight as he tore into the creatures with a savagery that was both beautiful and terrible to behold.

In a matter of moments, it was over. The Were-Gorillas lay broken and bleeding on the ground, their lifeless eyes staring up at the night sky. Matt stood over them, his chest heaving with exertion, his jaguar form sleek and powerful in the darkness.

Slowly, he shifted back into his human form, his curved sword once again clasped in his hand. He turned to face his teammates, his eyes filled with a fierce determination.

"Let's finish this," he growled, his voice low and deadly. "Trey and his followers won't know what hit them."

As he strode forward, ready to rejoin the battle, Matt couldn't help but feel a sense of pride and purpose rising up within him. He had faced his fears, embraced his true nature, and emerged victorious against impossible odds.

And with his friends by his side, he knew that there was nothing they couldn't achieve, no foe they couldn't vanquish. The battle for Blacksburg was far from over, but with each passing moment, the tide was turning in their favor.

The Were-Gorillas had underestimated them, had thought them weak and helpless without their technology to aid them. But they had forgotten one crucial thing - that the greatest strength of all lay not in gadgets and gizmos, but in the unbreakable bonds of friendship and the indomitable power of the human and lycan spirit.

****

Rigo Balderas stood his ground, his katana and shock

baton at the ready as he faced off against Trey's two best fighters. The Were-Gorillas were massive, their muscles rippling beneath their dark fur, their eyes glinting with a malevolent intelligence as they circled him, looking for an opening.

Suddenly, one of the fighters lunged forward, its fists swinging towards Rigo's head with devastating force. But Rigo was ready, his katana flashing out in a lightning-fast strike that sliced across the creature's knuckles, drawing a howl of pain and rage.

The second fighter attacked from the side, its claws raking towards Rigo's face with blinding speed. Rigo ducked, his shock baton crackling with electricity as he jammed it into the creature's ribs, sending it staggering back with a grunt of pain.

For a moment, Rigo seemed to have the upper hand, his weapons a blur of motion as he danced and wove around the Were-Gorillas, always one step ahead of their attacks. But then, a familiar figure stepped out from the shadows, a figure that made Rigo's blood run cold.

John Crawford, his former classmate and the only person to ever best him on the football field, stood before him, his eyes glinting with a cruel amusement. "Well, well, well," he drawled, his voice dripping with disdain. "If it isn't Rigo Balderas, the so-called Hyena King. I always knew you were a freak, but I never thought you'd stoop so low as to fight alongside humans."

Rigo gritted his teeth, his grip tightening on his weapons. "Crawford," he growled, his voice low and deadly. "I should have known you'd be working with Trey. You always were a coward, hiding behind your size and your strength."

Crawford laughed, a harsh, grating sound that sent shivers down Rigo's spine. "And you always were a self-righteous prick, Balderas. But now, we'll see who's the real king of the jungle."

With a roar of fury, Crawford charged forward, his fists

pummeling towards Rigo's chest with a force that would have shattered a lesser man's ribs. But Rigo was ready, his katana flashing out in a wide arc that caught Crawford across the face, drawing a spray of blood and a howl of pain.

But Crawford was relentless, his attacks coming faster and harder with each passing moment. Rigo felt his strength beginning to wane, his arms burning with fatigue as he fought to keep the massive Were-Gorilla at bay.

And then, in a moment of terrible clarity, Rigo realized that he couldn't win this fight as a human. Crawford was too strong, too fast, his lycan form a perfect fusion of raw power and lightning-quick reflexes.

With a snarl of determination, Rigo let the transformation take hold, his body rippling and changing as he shifted into his hyena form. His skin melted away, replaced by a coat of sandy fur, his muscles bulging and his senses sharpening to an almost unbearable intensity.

Crawford hesitated, his eyes wide with fear and confusion as he faced this new, terrifying threat. But Rigo didn't give him a chance to react. With a snarl of fury, he leaped forward, his claws and fangs flashing in the moonlight as he tore into the massive Were-Gorilla with a savagery that was both beautiful and terrible to behold.

Crawford fought back with all his strength and speed, his fists and claws a blur of motion as he tried to overpower the mighty hyena. But Rigo was too strong, too fast, his lycan form a perfect fusion of raw power and lightning-quick reflexes.

In a matter of moments, it was over. Crawford lay broken and bleeding on the ground, his eyes filled with a mixture of fear and grudging respect. Rigo stood over him, his chest heaving with exertion, his hyena form sleek and powerful in the darkness.

"Hyenas live in the savanna, jackass. And the Lion is king there. The Tiger rules the jungle," Rigo snarls as he walks away from Crawford's dying form.

Slowly, Rigo shifted back into his human form, his katana and shock baton once again clasped in his hands. He turned to face his teammates, his eyes filled with a fierce determination.

"Let's finish this," he growled, his voice low and deadly. "Trey and his followers won't know what hit them."

As he strode forward, ready to rejoin the battle, Rigo couldn't help but feel a sense of pride and purpose rising up within him. He had faced his past, embraced his true nature, and emerged victorious against impossible odds.

And with his friends by his side, he knew that there was nothing they couldn't achieve, no foe they couldn't vanquish. The battle for Blacksburg was far from over, but with each passing moment, the tide was turning in their favor.

The Were-Gorillas had underestimated them, had thought them weak and helpless without their technology to aid them. But they had forgotten one crucial thing - that the greatest strength of all lay not in gadgets and gizmos, but in the unbreakable bonds of friendship and the indomitable power of the lycan spirit.

****

Casey Elkins stood tall and defiant, her eyes locked on the imposing figure of Trey Smith as he loomed before her, his silver-black fur bristling with barely contained rage. The Were-Gorilla leader exuded an aura of raw power and menace, his every movement a testament to the primal strength that coursed through his veins.

"Agent Elkins," Trey growled, his voice dripping with

disdain. "I must admit, I'm surprised to see you here, facing me alone. I thought you'd be cowering behind your lycan allies, letting them fight your battles for you."

Casey gritted her teeth, her grip tightening on her handgun. "I'm not afraid of you, Trey. I've faced worse than you and come out on top. And I'm not going to let you terrorize this city any longer."

Trey laughed, a harsh, grating sound that sent shivers down Casey's spine. "You think you can stop me, human? You think your little toys and your pitiful bravado can match the might of a true lycan?"

With a roar of fury, Trey charged forward, his fists pummeling towards Casey's chest with a force that would have shattered a lesser person's ribs. But Casey was ready, her body twisting to the side as she fired off a shot from her handgun, the bullet ricocheting off Trey's dense musculature with a metallic ping.

Trey laughed again, his eyes glinting with a cruel amusement. "Is that the best you can do, Agent Elkins? Your puny bullets are like mosquito bites to me."

Casey gritted her teeth, her mind racing as she tried to come up with a plan. She had hoped that the special bullet KIVO had designed would be enough to take Trey down, but even that had barely fazed him.

As Trey pressed his attack, his claws and fists a blur of motion, Casey felt herself being pushed back, her body bruised and battered by the relentless onslaught. She knew she couldn't keep this up for long, that she needed to find a way to turn the tables before it was too late.

And then, in a moment of desperate inspiration, Casey remembered her training with Jeet Kundo in Polkville. She remembered the ways in which she had learned to harness her own rei, to channel it into her attacks and imbue them with a power beyond the physical.

With a deep breath, Casey reached deep within herself, tapping into the wellspring of energy that flowed through her veins. She could feel the rei crackling at her fingertips, a tingling sensation that spread up her arm and into her chest.

As Trey lunged forward again, his claws slashing towards her throat, Casey raised her handgun, her eyes narrowing with a fierce determination. She focused all of her rei into the bullet, pouring every ounce of her strength and will into the tiny piece of metal.

“Sensei Jeet Kundo sends her regards,” Casey says through gritted teeth.

And then, with a deafening crack, she fired.

The bullet struck Trey square in the chest, a blinding flash of blue light erupting from the point of impact. The Were-Gorilla leader staggered back, his eyes wide with shock and pain as the rei-infused projectile tore through his flesh, knocking the wind from his lungs and sending him crashing to the ground.

For a moment, Trey lay there, his body twitching and convulsing as the rei energy coursed through his system. But then, with a snarl of rage, he pushed himself back to his feet, his eyes blazing with an inhuman fury.

"You'll pay for that, human," he growled, his voice low and deadly. "I'll tear you apart, piece by piece, until there's nothing left but a bloody smear on the ground."

But Casey didn't flinch, her gaze steady and unwavering as she stared down the enraged lycan. She knew that the battle was far from over, that Trey's strength and resilience were not to be underestimated.

But she also knew that she had something he didn't, something that could never be taken away or broken. She had the power of her own spirit, the unbreakable will and determination that had carried her through countless challenges and trials.

Casey noticed that Trey's strikes were becoming more sluggish. She realized that her Rei Bullet had inflicted more damage than she realized. Casey was able to use her brief training with Jeet Kundo to maximum effect, as she effortlessly deflect Trey's strikes.

"For an all powerful lycan, you sure aren't fighting at full strength," Casey taunts, pain coursing through her body from the blows she had endured early in the fight, "Whats the matter? Did the tiny human harm the big powerful gorilla?"

Trey's eyes filled with rage as he attempted to launch an attack, but he fell to one knee. He flinched in pain, as his body convulsed. Looking up at Casey, he speaks.

"Agent Elkins, you think because I am an all powerful leader that my pride will stop me from calling reinforcements to take you down?" Trey growls.

"The human in me wants to believe that you will give up peacefully but the Special Agent in me knows you won't, Trey. I will hit you with another Rei Bullet if I must, but give up. Join Braydon in the cell beneath our HQ and put this to rest," Casey begs.

"Pinskrogele! Oapofairo or ubldralobeir! Shyro or phgra akoisu or acro kouro!" Trey called in a language that Casey didn't understand.

"Agent Elkins, I believe he just ordered his troops to attack you in the name of The Silver Back," KIVO says in Casey's ear.

Casey quickly turns to see six were-gorillas approaching her from all sides. She felt her breath catch in her throat. She quickly reloaded her gun, ensuring a full magazine was in it and drew her short sword, wielding it like a dagger.

"Awww, Trey, you shouldn't have," Casey says seductively, "I always wanted to hang mounted gorilla heads on my office,"

"pinskrogele! Tiwieskboro oapofairo onusolo!" Trey bellows as KIVO translates in Casey's ear. "Gorillas! Standard Attack Formation!"

Before anyone could move, a loud roar filled the night sky. Three hulking lycans landed between Casey and her six would-be attackers.

"Trey, allow me to introduce my trusted team!" Casey smiles, "The Hyena King, Rigo. The Lycoan Legacy, Jaxon Pearson. And The Jaguar Reaper, Matt Mauney,"

Trey laughs, coughing up blood.

"Perhaps its your Blacksburg Education, perhaps its pure ignorance. But either way, i will break this to you. You are still out numbered," Trey laughs.

CHAPTER 14

As Trey's words hung in the air, a tense silence fell over the battlefield. Casey, Rigo, Jaxon, and Matt stood their ground, their eyes locked on the six Were-Gorillas that surrounded them, ready to attack at any moment.

But just as the tension reached its breaking point, a new voice cut through the night, strong and confident.

"Panther Queen, Kari Byars. And my Panthers outnumber your Gorillas, three to one."

All eyes turned to the source of the voice, and there, perched atop a nearby building, stood Kari, her sleek black form silhouetted against the moonlit sky. Behind her, a sea of glinting eyes and gleaming fangs revealed the presence of her loyal Were-Panther subjects, their numbers far exceeding those of Trey's forces.

Trey's eyes widened, a flicker of fear and disbelief crossing his face as he took in the sight of Kari and her army. He had never expected the Panther Queen to intervene, had never thought that she would choose to side with the humans and their lycan allies.

Casey felt a surge of relief and gratitude wash over her, a small smile tugging at the corners of her mouth. She had always known that Kari was a force to be reckoned with, but seeing her here, ready to stand with them against Trey and his minions, was a testament to the strength of the bonds they had forged.

Rigo, Jaxon, and Matt exchanged glances, their own expressions mirroring Casey's. They knew that with Kari and her Panthers on their side, the odds had just shifted dramatically in their favor.

Trey, however, was not ready to admit defeat. With a snarl of rage, he pushed himself to his feet, his body trembling with the effort. "You think this changes anything?" he growled, his voice dripping with venom. "You think a few mangy cats can stop the might of the Were-Gorillas?"

Kari leaped down from her perch, landing gracefully beside Casey. Her eyes flashed with a fierce determination, her claws flexing at her sides. "We're not just a few mangy cats, Trey. We're the protectors of Blacksburg, the guardians of the innocent. And we will not stand by and let you terrorize our city any longer."

She turned to Casey and the others, her expression softening with a mix of affection and respect. "We stand with you, Agent Elkins. With all of you. Together, we will put an end to Trey's reign of terror and restore peace to Blacksburg."

Casey nodded, her heart swelling with a newfound sense of hope and determination. She knew that the battle ahead would not be easy, that Trey and his followers would fight tooth and nail to maintain their grip on power.

But she also knew that with her team by her side, with the strength and courage of the lycans and humans who had come together to defend their home, there was nothing they couldn't achieve.

As the two sides faced off, the tension crackling in the air like electricity, Casey raised her handgun, her eyes locked on Trey's.

"Last chance, Trey," she said, her voice steady and unwavering. "Surrender now, and we can end this without any more bloodshed. Refuse, and we will not hesitate to use every ounce of our strength to stop you."

For a moment, Trey seemed to hesitate, his eyes darting between Casey and the assembled forces arrayed against him. But then, with a roar of defiance, he lifted his head, his gaze filled with a savage, unyielding fury.

"Never," he snarled, his voice echoing through the night. "The Were-Gorillas will never submit to the likes of you. We will fight to the last breath, to the last drop of blood, before we bow to your will."

As the battle raged on, Casey found herself at the center of a whirlwind of claws and fangs, her handgun and short sword flashing in the moonlight as she fought to keep the Were-Gorillas at bay. Beside her, Rigo, Jaxon, and Matt were a blur of motion, their own weapons and lycan abilities put to the test as they fought to protect their friend and leader.

Kari and her Panthers were a force of nature, their sleek black forms darting in and out of the fray with a speed and agility that left the Were-Gorillas reeling. They worked in perfect harmony, their movements synchronized and their attacks precise, as they sought to drive back the invading force and secure victory for their allies.

Trey, despite his weakened state, was a formidable opponent, his strength and ferocity undiminished by the wounds he had suffered at Casey's hands. He lashed out with his claws and fists, his eyes blazing with a madness born of desperation and rage, as he sought to break through the line of defenders and claim the Idol for himself.

But Casey and her team were unyielding, their resolve

and determination a match for even the most savage of foes. They fought with a unity and a purpose that transcended the boundaries of species and allegiance, their hearts bound by a common cause and an unbreakable bond of friendship.

As the battle reached its fever pitch, Casey caught a glimpse of Trey through the chaos, his form looming large and menacing as he pushed his way towards her. She braced herself, ready to meet his charge head-on, when suddenly, a flash of white fur caught her eye.

It was Jaxon, his lycan form a blur of speed and power as he leaped into Trey's path, his teeth bared in a snarl of challenge. The two lycans collided with a force that shook the ground beneath their feet, their claws and fangs tearing at each other in a deadly embrace.

For a moment, it seemed as though Jaxon would be overwhelmed, his smaller form no match for Trey's brute strength. But then, with a burst of speed and agility, he twisted out of the larger lycan's grasp, his jaws clamping down on Trey's throat in a vice-like grip.

Trey let out a howl of pain and rage, his body thrashing and convulsing as he fought to break free. But Jaxon held fast, his eyes blazing with a fierce determination as he sought to put an end to the Were-Gorilla leader's reign of terror.

And then, with a sickening crack, it was over. Trey's body went limp, his eyes glazing over as the life drained from his form. Jaxon released his grip, his own chest heaving with exertion as he turned to face his teammates.

Around them, the battle was winding down, the Were-Gorillas falling back in disarray as they realized that their leader had fallen. Kari and her Panthers pressed the advantage, their claws and fangs flashing in the moonlight as they drove the invaders back, their victory all but assured.

Casey lowered her weapons, her heart pounding with a mix of relief and exhaustion. She turned to Jaxon, her eyes shining with gratitude and respect. "Thank you," she said, her voice hoarse with emotion. "You saved my life."

Jaxon shifted back to his human form, a small smile playing at the corners of his mouth. "We're a team, Casey. We look out for each other, no matter what."

As the dust settled and the adrenaline began to fade, Casey looked around at the faces of her friends and allies, her heart swelling with a sense of pride and accomplishment. They had faced the darkness and the chaos, the threats and the challenges, and they had emerged victorious, their bond stronger than ever.

And as they gathered together, their wounds tended and their spirits high, Casey knew that this was only the beginning. The battle for Blacksburg was far from over, and there would be many more trials and tribulations to come.

“Trey Smith! You are under arrest,” Casey says applying a pair of surpressor cuffs to Trey, “Book’Em Rigo!”

“I bet she’s always wanted to say that,” Rigo says under his breath to Jaxon and Matt, before joining Casey.

“I still wonder where Dustin Blackwell is. As Police Chief of Blacksburg, he is supposed to oversee all RIPD arrests,” Casey scans the area, “He is nowhere to be seen,” Casey pressed a finger to her ear, “Aidan, do you read me?”

Within Kenta Corp Headquarters, Aidan spun around on his chair to bring himself to the computer in front of him.

“Loud and Clear, Case. What’s up?” Aidan asks.

“Can you and KIVO do a scan on Dustin Blackwell?” Casey

asks, her eyes still scanning for Blackwell.

“Affirmative,” Aidan chuckles cracking his fingers and beginning to type, “Looks like Blackwell’s cellphone is pinging on Shelby Street, near the train tracks,”

“Aidan, can you and KIVO get a visual?” Casey asks, “Rigo, Matt, Jackson, Kari, I’ve got to handle other business. Can you finish up here?”

“Sure thing, boss,” was her reply from the team and Aidan.

****

Casey nodded to her team and turned her attention back to her communications link. "Aidan, I'm heading over to Shelby Street now. Keep me updated on Blackwell's location and any other details you can gather."

"Will do, Case. KIVO and I are on it," Aidan's voice crackled through the earpiece.

With a final glance at her teammates, Casey set off at a brisk pace, her mind already racing with possibilities. It was highly unusual for the Chief of Police to be unaccounted for during such a critical operation, and a knot of unease twisted in her gut.

As she made her way through the winding streets of Blacksburg, Casey couldn't shake the feeling that something wasn't right. Dustin Blackwell was a dedicated law enforcement officer, known for his unwavering commitment to Braydon Mitchell. If Blackwell wasn’t here, that meant someone or something was hindering him. Dustin was normally here looking for ways to pin this on someone else.

Casey's footsteps echoed off the pavement as she approached the deserted train tracks on Shelby Street. The area was eerily quiet, the only sound the distant rumble of a passing freight train.

"Aidan, anything new?" she murmured into her comm, her senses on high alert.

"Blackwell's signal is still pinging in that general vicinity, but I'm not getting any visuals on him yet. KIVO is enhancing the imagery now."

Casey nodded, her hand resting on the grip of her sidearm as she scanned the shadows for any sign of movement. Suddenly, a faint whimpering sound caught her attention, the unmistakable noise of someone trying to stifle their cries.

With her heart pounding in her ears, Casey followed the sound, her steps cautious and measured. Rounding the corner of an abandoned warehouse, she froze, her breath catching in her throat.

There, huddled in the shadows, was Dustin Blackwell. His uniform was disheveled, and his face was pale, his eyes wide with terror. He was alive, but clearly in a state of shock, rocking back and forth as he mumbled incoherently to himself.

"Blackwell!" Casey hissed, rushing to his side. "What happened? Are you hurt?"

The police chief's head snapped up, his eyes wild and unfocused. His lips moved, forming garbled words that made no sense. "C'thulhu... R'lyeh... Azrael... coming..."

Casey's brow furrowed in confusion and concern. Azrael? The name sent a chill down her spine. She had heard whispers of this figure, a powerful and terrifying being that struck fear into the hearts of even the bravest warriors.

"Blackwell, listen to me," she said, her voice low and urgent. "You need to tell me what's going on. Who is Azrael, and why are they coming to Blacksburg?"

Blackwell's eyes finally focused on her, and he reached out, grasping her arm with a strength that belied his fragile state. "Pissed off... the wrong one..." he rasped, his voice thick with terror. "Azrael... converging... on Blacksburg... unstoppable..."

Casey's mind raced, putting the pieces together. Whoever – or whatever – Azrael was, they were a force to be reckoned with, and Blackwell had somehow incurred their wrath. And now, this terrifying being was setting their sights on Blacksburg, a prospect that filled her with a sense of dread she had never known.

"Aidan..." Casey's voice was barely above a whisper. "Tell the team to regroup at headquarters. We may have just stumbled onto something bigger than we ever imagined. Azrael is coming, and we need to be ready."

****

The team quickly regrouped at RIPD headquarters, a sense of urgency and apprehension hanging thick in the air. They gathered in the main chamber, a cavernous space lined with high-tech monitors and command consoles.

Casey strode into the room, her expression grave. Rigo, Jaxon, Matt, and Kari turned to face her, their faces etched with concern.

"What's going on, Casey?" Rigo asked, his voice low. "You look like you've seen a ghost."

Casey took a deep breath, steeling herself for the weight of the news she was about to deliver. "I found Blackwell," she began, her gaze sweeping over her team. "He was in a state of complete terror, mumbling incoherently about some being called Azrael."

A collective gasp rippled through the group, and Kari's eyes widened in recognition. "Azrael? The Angel of Death?"

Casey nodded grimly. "According to Blackwell, this Azrael is converging on Blacksburg, and it seems Blackwell did something to incur their wrath."

A heavy silence fell over the chamber as the gravity of the situation sank in. They had faced formidable foes before, but this was something entirely different – a being of immense power and terrifying legend.

"What do we know about this Azrael?" Matt asked, his brow furrowed in concentration.

"Not much, unfortunately," Casey admitted. "But if the tales are true, we're dealing with an entity of unimaginable strength and destructive capabilities."

Jaxon let out a low growl, his lycan instincts heightened by the sense of impending danger. "So, what's the plan? We can't just sit idly by and wait for this thing to show up."

Casey turned to him, her expression hardening with resolve. "We need to gather as much information as we can, and that means questioning anyone who might know something about Azrael and their motivations."

Her gaze shifted to the entrance of the chamber, where two figures stood, their wrists bound by suppressor cuffs. "Braydon and Trey. Bring them in."

The two were roughly escorted into the room, their eyes darting nervously as they took in the assembled group. Braydon's face was a mask of defiance, while Trey's expression was one of barely concealed fear.

"What's the meaning of this?" Braydon snarled, his eyes locking onto Casey's. "You can't just haul us in here like common criminals!"

Casey stepped forward, her gaze unwavering. "We have reason to believe you might have information about a being called Azrael – information that could be vital to the safety of Blacksburg."

At the mention of the name, Trey visibly flinched, his face paling. Braydon, however, remained steadfast in his defiance.

"Azrael?" he scoffed. "You're chasing fairy tales and ghost stories now?"

Casey's jaw tightened. "This is no fairy tale, Braydon. Azrael is real, and they're coming for Blacksburg. Now, you can either cooperate and tell us what you know, or face the consequences of obstructing a RIPD investigation."

The two captives exchanged a tense glance, and for a moment, it seemed as though they might remain silent. But then, Trey's resolve crumbled, and he spoke up, his voice trembling.

"I... I don't know much," he admitted, his eyes downcast. "But I've heard the legends, the whispers of a being so powerful, so merciless, that even the strongest of us cower in fear."

Casey listened intently as Trey began to recount what he knew about the fearsome Azrael. With each passing word, the knot of dread in her stomach tightened.

"They say Azrael is the embodiment of death itself," Trey continued, his voice hushed as if afraid the mere mention of the name would summon the entity. "An unstoppable force of destruction, capable of laying waste to entire realms with a single thought."

A heavy silence hung in the air as the others absorbed this chilling information. Finally, Casey turned to the figure standing in the corner of the chamber.

"KIVO, I need you to cross-reference everything we have on Azrael – any legends, myths, or historical accounts. We need to know what we're up against."

The AI's metallic form whirred to life, its optics glowing brilliantly as it began its search. "Compiling data on Azrael now, Agent Elkins."

Moments later, a holographic display flickered to life in the center of the chamber, projecting a vast array of information culled from ancient texts and obscure lore.

"According to these records," KIVO's synthesized voice echoed through the room, "Azrael is a primordial being, older than time itself. They are said to be the embodiment of the void, the eternal darkness that exists between the stars."

Images flashed across the display – shadowy illustrations of a towering, winged figure shrouded in darkness, its very presence radiating a sense of overwhelming dread.

"Legends speak of Azrael as the harbinger of the End Times, the force that will one day consume all of existence," KIVO continued. "It is said that they can manifest in any form, from a terrifying monstrosity to a being of pure, seductive beauty."

Rigo let out a low whistle, his eyes glued to the holographic display. "Sounds like we're in for one hell of a fight."

Casey nodded grimly, her mind racing as she processed the information. "KIVO, what do we know about Azrael's motivations? Why would they target Blacksburg?"

The AI's optics flickered as it continued its analysis. "There is little concrete information on Azrael's specific goals or desires. However, several accounts suggest that they are drawn to places where the veil between realms is thin, where the boundaries between worlds are weakened."

Kari's eyes widened in realization. "Like the dimensional rifts we've been dealing with lately."

"Precisely," KIVO affirmed. "It is possible that the recent increase in interdimensional activity in Blacksburg has attracted Azrael's attention, and that they seek to exploit these rifts for their own purposes."

A heavy silence settled over the chamber as the weight of the situation fully sank in. They were facing an entity of unimaginable power, a being that had existed since the dawn of creation itself. And yet, Casey knew they had no choice but to stand and fight.

"Whatever Azrael's motivations," she said, her voice ringing with determination, "we cannot allow them to succeed. Blacksburg is our home, and we will defend it with everything we have."

Her gaze swept over the assembled team, her expression hardening with resolve. "Prepare yourselves, because the battle to come will be like nothing we've ever faced before. But together, we are stronger than any force, even one as ancient and terrifying as Azrael."

Around the chamber, nods of grim affirmation met her words. They were a team, a family bound by more than just blood or duty. And in the face of this ultimate darkness, they would stand united, ready to defend their world against the endless night.

"According to these records," KIVO's synthesized voice echoed through the room, "Azrael is an ancient demonic entity, older than most civilizations. However, he is not the harbinger of the End Times as previously thought."

The holographic display flickered, replacing the ominous illustrations with arcane texts and shadowy runes.

"Instead, legends suggest that Azrael is driven by an insatiable hunger – a desire to absorb the rei, or life force, of all living beings."

Rigo's brow furrowed in confusion. "Rei? You mean like souls or something?"

"Not quite," KIVO clarified. "Rei is a deeper, more fundamental essence that exists within all sentient creatures. It is the spark of life itself, the energy that animates our physical forms."

A collective shudder ran through the group as the implications sank in. An entity capable of devouring the very essence of life itself was a terrifying prospect.

"So, this Azrael wants to absorb our rei? Why?" Matt asked, his voice tinged with apprehension.

"The texts are unclear on his ultimate goal," KIVO admitted. "But it is believed that by consuming the rei of others, Azrael grows in strength and power, becoming an increasingly formidable force."

Casey's jaw tightened as she processed this new information. "And you're certain the recent interdimensional activity in Blacksburg has drawn his attention?"

"It is highly likely," KIVO affirmed. "The dimensional rifts we've been dealing with have likely created fluctuations in the fabric of reality, making it easier for Azrael to sense and locate sources of rei."

A heavy silence fell over the chamber as the severity of the situation sank in. They were no longer facing a harbinger of the apocalypse, but a ravenous, immortal predator driven by an endless hunger for the very essence of life itself.

"Regardless of his motivations," Casey said, her voice steely with determination, "we cannot allow Azrael to feed on the rei of Blacksburg's inhabitants. We must find a way to stop him, whatever it takes."

Kari nodded, her eyes glinting with a fierce resolve. "The Panthers stand ready to defend our home and our people. We will not let this demon consume us."

One by one, the others echoed Kari's sentiment, a united front against the looming threat. Casey felt a swell of pride and gratitude for her team, her family. Together, they would face this ancient evil and emerge victorious, no matter the cost.

"Then it's settled," she declared, her gaze sweeping over the assembled group. "We prepare for battle, and we do not rest until Azrael is defeated and Blacksburg is safe once more."

As the team dispersed to make their preparations, Casey couldn't help but feel a sense of trepidation gnawing at her. They had faced overwhelming odds before, but this was different – a foe older than time itself, driven by an insatiable hunger that could consume them all.

But she pushed those doubts aside, her resolve hardening like steel. They were the defenders of Blacksburg, the guardians of life itself. And they would not falter, no matter how dark or ancient the evil they faced.

The battle lines had been drawn, and the fate of their world hung in the balance. It was time to stand and fight, with every ounce of strength and courage they possessed.

CHAPTER 15

The streets of Blacksburg were bathed in the warm glow of the setting sun as Casey said her farewells to her team. After the harrowing ordeal they had endured, a well-deserved respite was in order.

"Take some time, all of you," she said, her voice tinged with equal parts pride and affection. "You've more than earned it."

Rigo, Jaxon, Matt, and Kari exchanged weary but satisfied looks, the bonds of friendship and camaraderie forged in the fires of battle shining bright in their eyes.

"We'll hold down the fort here in Blacksburg," Rigo assured her, clapping a hand on Jaxon's shoulder. "Jax and Matt have decided to stick around, keep an eye on things without the official RIPD badges."

Casey nodded, a small smile playing at the corners of her mouth. "I wouldn't have it any other way. Just don't have too much fun without me."

With a final round of hugs and well-wishes, Casey turned, stepping through the portal and heading towards the RIPD headquarters, as snow blows around her. The Idol of Lycoan was safely secured in a reinforced case, its ancient power now contained and protected.

As she stepped through the doors of the imposing building, she was greeted by the familiar sight of Mick Parker, her field support agent and former partner, and Sargent Leon Hawkins, her superior officer and leader.

"Welcome back, Casey," Hawkins said, his gruff exterior belied by the warmth in his eyes. "I take it the mission was a success?"

Casey held up the case containing the Idol, a triumphant grin spreading across her face. "You know it. The Idol is secure, and Blacksburg is safe once more."

Mick let out a low whistle, admiring the intricately carved artifact through the reinforced glass. "Nicely done, kid. Now let's get that thing locked up tight before any more trouble comes knocking."

They made their way to the RIPD's secure vault, a veritable fortress designed to safeguard the world's most dangerous and powerful artifacts. With a series of complex security protocols and biometric scans, the vault's heavy doors swung open, revealing a cavernous chamber lined with state-of-the-art containment units.

Casey carefully placed the Idol in one of the vacant units, feeling a sense of finality and relief as the reinforced doors sealed shut, encasing the ancient relic in an impenetrable cocoon.

"That's one ancient evil safely contained," she said, turning to face Mick and Hawkins. "Now, if you'll excuse me, I have a few questions for the chief."

Hawkins raised an eyebrow, his expression a mix of curiosity and amusement. "Fire away, Agent Elkins."

Casey took a deep breath, steeling herself for the request she was about to make. "Sir, with everything we've been through in Blacksburg, I've come to rely heavily on the skills and expertise of some remarkable individuals – people who have proven themselves time and again in the face of overwhelming adversity."

She thought of Rigo, whose unwavering loyalty and quick thinking had saved her life on more than one occasion. Of Aidan, the brilliant tech genius whose innovative solutions had been instrumental in their success. And of Jaxon and Matt, the lycans whose courage and strength had been an invaluable asset.

"I want to officially deputize them as RIPD agents," she continued, her voice ringing with conviction. "Rigo Balderas and Aidan Kenta, They've more than earned the right to wear the badge and be a part of our team."

Hawkins regarded her for a long moment, his expression unreadable. Finally, a hint of a smile tugged at the corners of his weathered mouth.

"You know, when I first started this outfit, I never could have imagined the caliber of agents we'd one day have under our roof," he mused. "But if your crew is anything like you, I'd be foolish to say no."

He extended a calloused hand, his eyes shining with a mixture of pride and approval. "You are officially, Senior Agent Elkins. You and your team have more than proven your worth."

As Casey clasped Hawkins' hand, she felt a surge of gratitude and determination course through her veins. The road ahead was sure to be fraught with new challenges, new threats to face and overcome. But with her newly expanded team by her side, she knew they were more than ready to face whatever the world – or the universe – threw their way.

“Sarge, one more question. About Sheriff Alex Ruler? What did you find?”

Hawkins entire body seemed to sigh in disbelief. He pinched the bridge of his nose and turned to Casey.

“Elkins. Ruler has some series abilities that need to be observed. We have to measure his ability to maintain those abilities,” Hawkins explained.

“So what does that mean?” Casey asks.

“I am agreeing to allow you and Ruler to work together whenever needed. But Casey, I wish you wouldn’t get involved with him until we finish our full investigation,” Hawkins says.

"You can't control who I'm involved with, Sarge," Casey chuckles, "I can guarantee Ruler isn't a threat to the preternatural order of the world,"

With that Casey turned to leave the HQ, her mind filling with ways Aidan and Rigo could begin helping her patrol her region.

As she turned to leave the vault, Casey couldn't help but feel a sense of excitement and anticipation for the adventures that lay ahead. With her team at her side and the world as their playground, there was no limit to the good they could achieve, the lives they could save, and the ancient evils they could vanquish.

The RIPD's ranks had grown, their power solidified, and their purpose reaffirmed. They were the lights in the darkness, the beacons of hope and justice that shone through even the blackest of nights.

And as Casey strode forth, ready to embrace the future, she knew that their legacy was only just beginning.

****
*

Casey exited RIPD headquarters, the weight of her new responsibilities as Senior Agent settling comfortably on her shoulders. With Rigo and Aidan officially deputized, and Jaxon and Matt affiliating themselves with the organization, her team was stronger than ever before.

She made her way across the snowy courtyard, her boots crunching against the fresh powder, and approached the shimmering portal that would transport her back to Blacksburg. Taking a deep breath, she stepped through, the world around her dissolving into a kaleidoscope of colors and energy.

In the blink of an eye, she found herself back in the familiar streets of her hometown, the warm glow of the setting sun casting long shadows across the pavement. Casey allowed herself a moment to bask in the comforting familiarity of her surroundings before setting off towards her next destination – Kenta Corp Headquarters.

As she approached the towering edifice, its sleek lines and modern architecture cutting an imposing figure against the skyline, Casey couldn't help but feel a sense of pride and excitement. This was Aidan's domain, the hub of innovation and technological prowess that had played such a pivotal role in their recent victories.

The security systems recognized her biometric signatures, and the reinforced doors slid open with a soft hiss, granting her entry into the cutting-edge facility. The interior was a marvel of cutting-edge design, with gleaming surfaces and holographic displays lining the walls, humming with the constant buzz of activity.

"Welcome back, Agent Elkins," a familiar voice called out, and Casey turned to see Aidan striding towards her, a broad grin etched across his features. "I take it everything went well with the Idol's secure storage?"

Casey nodded, returning his smile. "Like a charm. And I have some news – you're officially a deputized RIPD agent now, along with Rigo."

Aidan's eyes widened, and for a moment, he seemed genuinely taken aback. "Seriously? That's... wow, I don't know what to say."

"Say you'll accept," Casey replied, her expression turning serious. "We're going to need all hands on deck, Aidan. With the interdimensional rifts continuing to destabilize, and who knows what other threats lurking out there, the RIPD needs your brilliance more than ever."

Aidan didn't hesitate, his jaw setting in a determined

line. "You know I'm in, Casey. Kenta Corp's resources are at your disposal, and I'll be right by your side, helping however I can."

Casey felt a surge of gratitude and affection for her friend and newfound colleague. With Aidan's technological genius and unwavering support, she knew they could overcome any challenge that lay ahead.

"Speaking of resources," she said, gesturing to the state-of-the-art facility around them, "what do you have cooking up in those labs of yours? Anything that could give us an edge against the interdimensional incursions?"

Aidan's eyes lit up with an almost manic gleam, and he motioned for her to follow him deeper into the labyrinthine complex. "You have no idea, Casey. No idea at all..."

As they made their way through the winding corridors, passing by teams of scientists and engineers hard at work on cutting-edge projects, Casey couldn't help but feel a sense of excitement and anticipation bubbling within her. With her team solidified, her resources bolstered, and her determination unwavering, she knew that whatever challenges lay ahead, they were more than ready to face them head-on.

The battle to safeguard Blacksburg – and the world – was far from over. But with the RIPD's ranks swelling, and allies like Aidan and Kenta Corp by their side, Casey knew that they were poised to emerge victorious, no matter what ancient evils or interdimensional threats dared to cross their path.

As they delved deeper into the heart of Kenta Corp's research and development wing, Casey felt a sense of purpose and resolve settling over her like a mantle. She was a guardian, a protector, and a beacon of hope in the darkness.

And with her team at her side, their light would never be extinguished.

EPILOGUE

In the depths of the void between realms, a presence stirred – ancient, malevolent, and utterly insatiable. Azrael, the devourer of rei, had sensed the ripples cast by the events in Blacksburg, the ebb and flow of life essences that called to it like a siren's song.

Though Casey and her team had succeeded in securing the Idol of Lycoan, their victory was fleeting, a mere hiccup in Azrael's grand design. For the demon had set its sights on a much grander prize – the very souls that inhabited the mortal plane.

With a mere exertion of will, Azrael reached out across the dimensional boundaries, its consciousness slithering through the cracks and fissures that permeated reality. It could taste the fear, the uncertainty that still lingered in the hearts of the mortals, a tantalizing prelude to the feast that awaited.

In the heart of Kenta Corp's research and development wing, Casey felt a sudden chill run down her spine, as if an icy finger had traced its way along the nape of her neck. She turned, her senses on high alert, scanning the state-of-the-art facility for any sign of danger.

"Everything okay?" Aidan asked, his brow furrowed with concern.

Casey opened her mouth to respond, but the words caught in her throat as a disembodied voice seemed to reverberate through her very being, its timbre laced with malice and an insatiable hunger.

"So, you are the one who dares to defy me, mortal," the voice hissed, its otherworldly tones sending tremors of dread rippling through Casey's core. "You have won a minor skirmish, but the war for your realm's very essence has only just begun."

Aidan's eyes widened, his face paling as he, too, became aware of the sinister presence that had infiltrated the sanctity of his laboratory.

"Who... what are you?" Casey demanded, her hand instinctively reaching for her sidearm, even as she knew deep down that conventional weapons would be useless against such a foe.

A cruel, mirthless chuckle echoed through the chamber, sending a chill down their spines. "I am Azrael, the devourer of rei, the consumer of souls. And your world, your pathetic existence, will soon be nothing more than a fleeting memory, a mere morsel to sate my endless hunger."

Casey felt her resolve harden, her fear transmuting into a burning determination. "We've faced your kind before, demon," she spat, her voice ringing with defiance. "And we've always emerged victorious. Whatever twisted game you're playing, it ends here and now."

The voice laughed again, a sound that grated against their very souls. "Brave words, little mortal. But you have no inkling of the forces you are trifling with. I will strip the rei from your bones, devour your essence until nothing remains but a hollow husk."

And then, as suddenly as it had appeared, the presence vanished, leaving only a lingering chill and a sense of dread in its wake.

Casey and Aidan stood in stunned silence, their minds reeling from the ominous encounter. It was clear that they had drawn the attention of a being far more ancient and powerful than anything they had faced before – a primordial force that sought to consume not just their world, but the very fabric of existence itself.

But as Casey looked around at the determined faces of Kenta Corp's scientists and engineers, she knew that they would not face this threat alone. They were the guardians of Blacksburg, the sentinels of reality itself, and they would muster every ounce of their strength, their courage, and their ingenuity to face the coming storm.

"You heard the demon," she said, her voice steady and resolute. "We don't have a choice – we have to stop Azrael, whatever the cost."

Aidan nodded grimly, his eyes hardening with resolve. "Then we'd better get to work. Because that sick bastard just declared war on all of existence, and we're the only ones standing in his way."

As they delved into the heart of Kenta Corp's research and development efforts, Casey couldn't help but feel a sense of determination and purpose burning within her like a wildfire. The road ahead would be fraught with peril, with challenges and adversaries the likes of which they could scarcely comprehend.

But she was Casey Elkins, Senior Agent of the RIPD, guardian of the veil between realms, and protector of all that was good and true in the world. And with her team – her family – by her side, she knew that they would emerge victorious, no matter how formidable the foe.

For they were the lights in the darkness, the beacons of hope that shone through even the blackest of nights. And their light would never be extinguished, not as long as a single ember of their determination still burned.

Azrael had issued his challenge, had thrown down the gauntlet in his quest for cosmic annihilation. But Casey and her allies would answer that challenge with every fiber of their being, with the full force of their unwavering courage and unbreakable bonds.

The battle for existence itself was about to begin. And they would be ready, no matter what eldritch horrors or ancient evils dared to cross their path.

For they were the RIPD, guardians of reality, sentinels of the rei that flowed through all living things.

And their legacy was only just beginning.

BOOKS BY THIS AUTHOR

Hometown Justice: Homecoming

Hometown Justice: Rebellion

Hometown Justice: Aftermath

Spartan: Blood And Sand (Kindle Only)

Tigapagon: Enter The Tiger

Made in the USA
Columbia, SC
24 February 2025

54297490R00148